Jack London on Adventure

Also by Terry Mort

Nonfiction (available from The Lyons Press)

The Reasonable Art of Fly Fishing

Zane Grey on Fishing

Fiction

Showdown at Verity

The Lawless Breed

JACK LONDON ON ADVENTURE

JACK LONDON

Edited and with an Introduction by
TERRY MORT

THE LYONS PRESS

Guilford, Connecticut

An imprint of The Globe Pequot Press

10 9 8 7 6 5 4 3 2 1

Printed in the United States of America.

Library of Congress Cataloging-in-Publication Data
London, Jack, 1876-1916.
Jack London on Adventure / Jack London ; edited and with an introduction by Terry Mort.
p. cm.
ISBN 1-59228-609-7 (trade cloth)
1. Adventure stories, American. I. Mort, T. A. (Terry A.) II. Title.
PS3523.O46A6 2005
813´.52—dc22

2005040772

Contents

Contents

Introduction

In 1907, thirty-one-year-old Jack London sailed his brand new, custom built ketch, *Snark*, out of the Golden Gate and headed for Hawaii. It was the first leg of a planned voyage around the world. He was on what he called "the adventure path," again. On board were his wife, Charmian, his wife's Uncle Roscoe, and a crew of three young amateur sailors. They had been planning this trip for months, but despite all their preparations, they ran into difficulty almost immediately. For one thing, there were problems with the boat—lots of them. For another, although London didn't quite realize it until they were out of sight of land, no one on board knew how to navigate.

That's not to say London was an inexperienced sailor. On the contrary. As a teenager he had spent many dark nights sailing his sloop *Razzle Dazzle* around San Francisco Bay raiding private oyster beds and selling the take on the Oakland waterfront. He was called an oyster pirate, a more romantic and colorful term than thief—which is what the owners of the oyster beds called him. Later he went over to the other side and worked for the California Fish Patrol chasing other oyster pirates. So he knew how to sail. And he was no stranger to ocean voyaging, for at age seventeen he had spent seven months as a common seaman on a seal hunting vessel, following the migrating herds from the Bonin Islands off Japan to their rookeries in the Bering Sea.

But neither seal hunting nor oyster pirating prepared him for blue water navigation, an art in those days before satellites that involved plotting your position in relation to the stars. He could not do that. He had intended to rely on Uncle Roscoe for navigation but soon learned that his confidence in Roscoe was misplaced. If they were going to get anywhere, Jack would have to teach himself celestial navigation. So he settled down to do it, somewhere out in the Pacific. And they did make it to Hawaii, albeit after a few course corrections.

That sort of challenge was nothing new for Jack London. Just about everything he knew he had taught himself. His brushes with formal education were limited to grammar school, a year of high school and a few weeks at University of California, Berkeley. His real schools were the waterfronts and bars of Oakland, canneries and factories, the Pacific sealing grounds, the Klondike gold fields, the hobo road and railroad lines, the Erie County (New York) Penitentiary, the slums of London, England and the Oakland Public Library. Along the way he met radical union organizers, railroad bulls, penitentiary guards, waterfront toughs, hard bitten sailors, Klondike sourdoughs, fellow hobos and assorted down and outers, loose women and an occasional middle class lady—and, as important as the others, a friendly librarian who took him under her wing. He taught himself what he needed to know by reading, watching, and doing, and he did all those things the way he drank—eclectically, copiously, and wholeheartedly.

Jack London was born poor and illegitimate in 1876 in San Francisco. His father was an itinerant astrologer who disappeared soon after Jack's birth, and his mother was an odd, unstable spiritualist who tried to make ends meet by conducting seances during which she communed with an Indian chief named "Plume." More conventionally she also gave music lessons. When Jack was still an infant she married John London, a kind, well meaning older man, a Civil War veteran whose disabilities from wounds made it difficult for him to earn a living. Jack had to help out from the earliest possible days. At age fourteen he got a job working in a cannery twelve hours a day. He also swept up in saloons, delivered newspapers and set up pins in bowling alleys. Later he would toil in a jute mill for ten cents an hour and then graduate to a steam laundry. It was an early and thorough education in brute labor, and those experiences planted the seeds that grew into his intuitive and lifelong attachment to socialism.

The attachment only grew stronger during his hobo-ing days—days that started out as a youthful lark, he was just eighteen—but ended in the Erie County (New York) Penitentiary, a place where he said his strong sense of individualism was "hammered out" of him and replaced by something else. He called that something else "socialism," but it was less a coherent political doctrine and more a feeling that the underclass (which included himself) deserved a better chance.

". . . I have opened many books, but no economic argument, no lucid demonstration of the logic and inevitableness of socialism affects me as profoundly and convincingly as I was affected on the day when I first saw the Social Pit rise around me and felt myself slipping down, down, into the shambles at the bottom." He had been jailed for vagrancy, and it was in the Erie County Pen that he was gripped by the clammy fear of falling even further into "the submerged tenth," the bottom from which no one seemed able to rise. It was a fear that stayed with him throughout his short life. After doing his thirty days he went home to Oakland determined to find a way out of poverty. But not through the drudgery of manual labor: "I shall climb out of the Pit, but not by the muscles of my body shall I climb out. I shall do no more hard work, and may God strike me dead if I do another day's hard work with my body more than I absolutely have to."

He decided the only way out was to educate himself. "I ran back to California and opened the books." Now and then he came across middle class people who took an interest in his informal education. They saw something in him, even though he was awkward, uncouth, and painfully eager. Part of him was attracted to these people who were from a different, more genteel world, and he was grateful to them for letting him in, if only as a visitor. But another part was repelled by their cramped and sterile conventionality, though he could never seem to get over his longing to be accepted by them. His semi-autobiographical novel *Martin Eden* ends with Martin committing suicide because he is in a despairing social limbo: "Up above nobody had wanted Martin Eden for his own sake, and he could not go back to those of his own class who had wanted him in the past. He did not want them. He could not stand them. . ." This is not the sentiment of a politically doctrinaire socialist like London's contemporary, Eugene V. Debs, who once said: "There is no good capitalist and no bad working-man. Every capitalist is your enemy and every workingman is your friend." Rather, it is the statement of someone who wants acceptance but who, through some odd combination of ego-tism and neediness, despises the people who offer it to him—the statement of an individual with a strong sense of class consciousness who can't decide whether he's a Superman, a comrade, or just a lonely outcast. On another level, London's attitude reminds us of Groucho Marx's old joke that he would not want to be a member of any club that would accept him.

But unlike Martin Eden, Jack London did not commit suicide. Not all at once anyway, although there is a grim sort of irony about the way Martin and Jack both died—Martin dying young from drowning, Jack dying at forty from kidney failure, a condition at least partially resulting from years of heavy drinking.

His reading led him in a number of intellectual directions, many of them divergent. He was like the college freshman taking his first philosophy course and working through the rationalists and the empiricists and finding he agrees with both. Though he never lost his intuitive attachment to socialism, the individualism that he said was lost was not lost for long, and that led to his interest in the ideas of Herbert Spencer, a Darwinian who believed that society is best served if the strongest and most capable are left free to produce. The logical conclusion of these ideas is laissez faire capitalism, pure and simple. Socialists view this sort of thing with horror, saying it turns society into a Roman Coliseum in which the strongest and most rapacious gather up the lion's share of wealth at the expense of their victims. The opposing position is that wealth is not a zero sum game in which the winners win at the expense of the losers; wealth is an elastic result of a free person's energy, talent, and productivity, and society as a whole benefits when people are free to compete. These debates go on endlessly even today, of course. But the point here is that London had these debates with himself—embodied them, in fact. Socialists are supposed to be suspicious of private property. But the last decade of his life London lived on his 1,100-acre ranch in Sonoma. And then there was the yacht. He even invested in stocks and new inventions, disastrously as it turned out, but he did not intend to lose money; he intended to make it. And what is a capitalist but someone who invests capital for profit? These are inconsistencies by any standard, but these inconsistencies—in his thought and his personality—make London's writing more complex and interesting than it would have been had he simply churned out doctrinaire political stuff in the "boy meets tractor" genre. As George Orwell writes of London: ". . . if he had been a politically reliable person,"—in other words, an orthodox socialist—"he would probably have left behind nothing of interest."

Orwell also says that London "was a socialist with the instincts of a buccaneer." Some of that shows up in his stories. One of London's fictional heroes, David Grief, would have been at home with Robert Louis Stevenson's collection of pirates and adventurers. Grief is "a youth questing romance and adventure along the sun washed path of the tropics," a South

Seas trader, handsome, wealthy, daring, resolute. But he's also a man who plays the game "for the joy of the playing." Most likely London thought of himself this way, at least part of the time, and it is hardly the image of a proletarian hero.

London also had the instincts of an entrepreneur, though he probably would not have described himself that way. After all, the purest example of entrepreneurship is the prospector—someone who hears of a gold strike in far off Yukon Territory and gets the itch to go, gets a little grubstake together, gathers up the tools of the trade and heads out into the unknown, filled with hope and the intention of applying energy and skill to the pursuit of wealth—as much wealth as he can dig out and keep from squandering in saloons. And although the gold fields seem like an odd place for a socialist, that's where London went in 1897—to the Klondike, like thousands of others, hoping to get rich. He landed in Juneau, struggled on foot over the awesome, seemingly vertical Chilkoot Pass, built a boat and then followed the Yukon River system north to Dawson City, got trapped by winter some seventy miles short of Dawson, found an abandoned cabin and settled in to wait for spring in minus sixty degree weather.

His prospecting was not successful. In fact, he found nothing, nothing in the way of yellow metal, at least. (He did find some fool's gold that gave him a temporary thrill.) He suffered through the long winter of 1897–1898, got scurvy and then, destitute, floated out of the Yukon territory the following summer in a leaky boat that he bought with the last of his grubstake after a few weeks of carousing in Dawson. Floating down the Yukon River across the breadth of Alaska to the Bering Sea was the cheapest way out—a journey of nearly 2,000 miles. From there he worked his way south on a steamer to Vancouver and then rode the rails home, in a reprise of his hobo days. On the surface it would seem that his Klondike prospecting days were failures. But of course that's where he gathered the raw material for stories that would make him famous and help him buy his ranch, build his yacht, and set off for the South Seas.

When he came home from the Klondike, still only twenty-two, he decided to make his living by writing. It wasn't much of a change, really. A writer is not very different from a prospector, as Jack found out. Both start with nothing; many end up that way, too. The ones who succeed usually do so the way London did—by doggedly weathering blizzards of rejection slips and keeping at it until something good happens. In London's case it came a year after he got back from the Klondike. That year was filled with manic bouts of writing, submitting, and waiting, followed by disappointment and visits to the pawn shop, sometimes to raise money for postage for his manuscripts, sometimes to pay the rent on his typewriter. The first acceptance wasn't much—a sale for five dollars—but it was progress. He continued to work at a furious pace, and gradually the editors who had seen nothing in his work began to appreciate its merits. He sold a few more stories, including one to the prestigious *Atlantic Monthly*. It was a time when there was an appetite for adventure tales, and Jack had plenty to tell. And then in 1900 his first book, a collection of his Yukon stories, was published, and it finally seemed that he might be able to make a living at this business after all.

That was the same year he married his first wife, Bess Maddern. He did not love Bess. He told her as much. But it seemed the right thing to do at the time. It would settle him, he reasoned. Despite his travels and experience, he was still only twenty-four and just getting started in the writing game. Besides, Bess admired his work, and that was a kind of aphrodisiac to the aspiring writer. And she came from that group of middle class people who had encouraged him. But after they were married Jack began to feel a predictable sense of imprisonment, even though he was pleased when his two daughters came along. By this time Jack was becoming famous, and he began to think that Bess was a bit too cold, too disapproving of his high spirits, too confining, too unfashionable, too bourgeois—and so in 1903 the couple separated. By then Jack was already involved with Charmian Kittredge, the woman who would become his second wife. Charmian was outgoing, adventuresome, physically responsive, passionate, sexually uninhibited. She even liked to box; she and Jack would put on the gloves now and then and spar a few rounds. In every way, it seemed, Charmian was a better match for Jack's personality and needs.

Through all the turmoil of domestic problems, growing success, and increasing demands on his time, he kept working, kept moving. He was disciplined in that way, at least. Like a man pursued by a wolf pack in *White Fang*, he did not dare stop. It was not hard to remember the days of poverty and failure. They were not that long ago.

This idea of movement, of continued effort of will, appears repeatedly in London's stories. Movement is life to a man caught outside in the dead of a Yukon winter; a man on the trail must keep going or die. A ship at sea must keep moving forward to maintain steerageway or risk being broached, battered by waves, capsized or driven on the rocks. Movement means survival. The image is at least partially a reflection of Spencer's evolutionary ideas. Many of London's stories deal with people who cannot adapt to the new environment, because they are weak or incompetent or prisoners of the wrong set of habits, ideas. They cannot keep going, and so, like the man in "To Build a Fire," they stop, and that is the end of them.

If life is movement, powered by dogged and determined effort of will, the hostile environment, by contrast, is often portrayed as something utterly still. One of the starkest images in London's Klondike stories is a wind vane that never changes direction, because there is no movement in the winter air. The men cooped up in their makeshift cabins watch this wind vane in hopes of seeing something that reminds them of life. But it never stirs. It represents the utter indifference of nature, what London called the "white silence."

Of course the natural world is not always frozen and still in London's stories. Whether in the form of storms at sea or a pack of wolves on the trail of men who are slowly running out of cartridges, there is plenty of deadly motion to alternate with the white silence.

London was an omnivorous reader, but his ideas did not just come from books. They also came from his experience, his observations of unalterable facts. As he says when describing the way the *Snark* handled in a rough sea, "I am not telling you what I believe; I am telling you what I saw." That line helps explain the inconsistencies that show up in London's writing. He *believed* in socialism; he was called a "passionate gospel"; but he *saw* that nature required strength, that its essence was the struggle to survive. Those who could not adapt, those who were weak or inept or unlucky were defeated by the strong or by the pitiless elements—the cold, the sea, the wild animals, the natives of the country in which you were a stranger. It was not a pretty picture, but it was real. Maybe it was not the way it should be, but it was the way it was. In this kind of desperate environment it was impossible for London not to admire and respect the strong and the capable and to feel some contempt for the weak or inept, even though it was the weak and powerless who attracted his political sympathies. No amount of political theorizing or action could do anything about Nature's inherent dangers; you might as well try to stop a wolf pack with a speech. Life was a struggle. It was naïve to think otherwise. Interestingly, toward the end of his life London resigned from the Socialist Party, not because he had become wealthy and successful, but because he thought the party had lost its "fire and fight" and had grown too soft, too accommodating, too reluctant to struggle.

This theme of constant struggle may be the key to reconciling some of the contradictions in London's thinking, may be the common denominator that rationalizes all of his inconsistencies and makes cohesive sense out of his work. There's the evolutionary struggle to adapt and survive, regardless of whether the animal is human or otherwise; there's a class struggle over the levers of power and wealth creation; there's the artist's personal struggle against the usual pantheon of literary demons—alcohol, rejection, temptation, loneliness, middle class conventions, debt. You could depend on that at least—the essential fact of life in all its forms was struggle.

It sounds pretty grim. But it wasn't always. Not many people think of Jack London as a humorous writer, but his stories about the seemingly endless problems with the building of the *Snark* are remarkable for his wry self-deprecation and for the good natured stoicism with which he greeted each new frustration. Even the name *"Snark"* suggests a playful lack of self-importance. For all his passionate devotion to his politics, London was anything but a gloomy theorist. By all accounts he was charming and good humored and fun to be with.

What's more, London enjoyed parts of the struggle—grim or otherwise. He admired physical strength. He took pride in his own body, referred frequently to his muscles, power, skill in fighting. There is a tinge of Narcissism in all of this; he was a handsome man, attractive to women across a wide moral and social spectrum. And references to physical prowess and sensuality are common in his writing and indeed in his life and adventures. He referred to Charmian as his "mate woman," a term that conjures up Lady Chatterley's gamekeeper or, perhaps, more risibly, Tarzan. But his writing was circumscribed by the moral conventions of his time, so that in *The Sea Wolf* he presents us with the improbable spectacle of two marooned lovers living in separate huts and only exchanging a glance here and there. Given his own exuberant adventures, London must have chaffed at that sort of conventional tether.

Not surprisingly, he was attracted to the writings of Nietzsche, especially to Nietzsche's concept of the Superman, someone who rises above the pack through force of will and the application of power and creates for himself a position beyond conventional morality. "The sick are the greatest danger for the healthy; it is not from the strongest that harm comes to the strong, but from the weakest," so said Nietzsche. Such sentiments are hardly compatible with London's socialist concern for the downtrodden. Nevertheless, he found them appealing, for they fit easily in that side of his personality that admired strength and achievement.

It's easy to say that this is an example of London's essentially muddled worldview. After all how do you reconcile the notion of a super individual—someone who answers only to himself—with the collectivist ideals of socialism? They seem to be inherently incompatible. But in the context of London's ideas about life as a struggle, it makes a certain amount of sense. Will and power are necessary elements if you expect your struggles to be successful, whether the struggle is between individuals or classes. The impulses and necessary energy are the same in either case.

Then, too, London was well aware of the incompatibility of what he wanted to believe and what he saw around him, between what was and what he thought should be. And perhaps the greatest appeal of the Superman was his ability to look reality in the face and not flinch from what he saw there, even though despair might be the result. As London's most famous Nietzschean character, Wolf Larsen, says in *The Sea Wolf:* "I sometimes catch myself wishing that I, too, were blind to the facts of life and only knew its fancies and illusions. They're wrong, of course, and contrary to reason; but in the face of them my reason tells me, wrong and most wrong, that to dream and live illusions gives greater delight—your dreams and unrealities are less disturbing to you and more gratifying than are my facts to me."

Critics might say that Nietzsche's ideas appeal most powerfully to someone with a strong sense of individualism and a corresponding sense of social inferiority—the resentful underdog with an "I'll show them" agenda, the flawed but formidable primitive. Certainly many of the Nazi thugs who co-opted Nietzsche's ideas fit that description. And it seems fair to say that there was a trace of that in London's attitudes and personality. As Orwell points out, had London lived into the thirties and forties it would be hard to say which side of the political debates he would have chosen—far left, far right or some "quixotic" place beyond the two.

Because of his writing success, his political outspokenness and his physical attractions, Jack London became one of America's first literary celebrities. In 1901 he ran for mayor of Oakland on the Socialist ticket and received 245 votes. He ran again in 1905 and improved to 981 votes. But despite the lack of political success, he was in the public eye. He became a sought after speaker and delivered stem-winding political speeches on college campuses and in lecture halls across the country. His books became best sellers.

And he was an innovator in what we know today as investigative journalism. In 1902 he went to England where he lived incognito for six weeks in the slums of London's East End. It was in a sense a repeat of his hobo days—a dip into the submerged tenth from which would come a book filled with passionate criticism of the social system that allowed the shocking poverty of London to exist. The book, *The People of the Abyss*, was well received and successful in this country, less so in England, for obvious reasons. Then four years later he published *The Road*, the story of his hobo days. It was a model for all the subsequent road books—Kerouac, Steinbeck, William Least Heat Moon, Tom Wolfe, and for legions of young men who just feel like getting up and going.

But the most conspicuous of London's literary offspring was Hemingway. Adventurous, successful, world famous, well traveled, envied, controversial, self-destructive, London and Hemingway both regarded themselves as the heroes of their own lives. They thrust themselves into events and then turned the results into stories that have the ring of authenticity, because they were grounded in personal experience. Interestingly, both men seemed to falter when it came to portraying women as romantic interests. They had plenty of personal experience but never seemed to figure out what made women tick. Or if they did, they weren't able to get it down on paper very well. *The Sea Wolf*, for example, goes along quite well until the female poet, Maud Brewster, enters the story. Maud is, to put it mildly, unlikely.

London was not a very careful craftsman, though, unlike Hemingway. He was disciplined and dedicated, and he turned out a thousand words a day regardless of where he was or what else he was doing. But he did not revise. He considered it a waste of time, and so the quality of his work is uneven. Or maybe the better word is inconsistent.

Like Hemingway, Jack London spent some time as a war correspondent. In 1904 he covered the Russo-Japanese war for the Hearst organization. He had other offers, but Hearst paid best. He managed to get arrested three times by the Japanese, the first time as a suspected spy, the second for pushing too far into the Korean frontlines and the third for punching a Japanese who had been stealing from him. But his reporting and his photographs from the front lines were printed throughout the U.S. and helped to make the famous writer that much more famous.

His problems with the Japanese served to increase his contempt for them, an attitude that was surely reinforced by Jack's ideas on race—he was quite certain that the white race and the Anglo-Saxons, especially, were the highest form of humanity. Not only is this incompatible with his socialist ideals, it is ironic because the person who lent him the $300 he needed to buy the *Razzle Dazzle* when he was an aspiring young oyster pirate was Virginia Prentiss, the black woman who had wet nursed him and given him the maternal affection he never got from his own mother. But in those days few people had difficulty with that sort of irony. And London often surprises us with another kind of inconsistency, for in many of his stories there is an obvious sympathy for native people who have been victimized by white men. Here again, he wrote what he saw, not what he believed.

In 1914 he went to Mexico to cover their latest revolution. Originally he had been sympathetic to the goals of the revolution. But over time he changed his mind and attacked the aims and leaders in print. Predictably he was pilloried by the left for selling out to international capitalism, this time in the form of the oil companies with interests in Mexico. But Jack shrugged off the criticism. As far as he was concerned, he had reported what he had seen.

Jack London was a product of his times, of course. And they were difficult times in which the harshest elements of industrial capitalism were obvious to anyone who cared to look— child labor, wild swings in the economic cycles, widespread unemployment and a growing belief that the social classes were walled cities that allowed no passage between them. In one sense it was a time of simple and binary "us versus them" attitudes with little or no allowance for nuances. It was also a time of the naturalist novel in which characters are buffeted by forces completely beyond their control—economics, social brutality, simple biology. Characters did not act so much as they were acted upon and usually defeated. And a lot of Jack London's work reflects these same beliefs: art as sociology, or perhaps the other way around. But it was also a time in which people believed in the possibilities of a poor young man rising in the world through a combination of hard work and personal virtue, the sort of philosophy that would make Horatio Alger novels popular. It was a time of Teddy Roosevelt's virile individualism and optimism. A time when immigrants came here in their millions because it was the land of opportunity. Socialist and self-made man, hobo and literary entrepreneur, mill worker and yachtsman, Jack London embodied both strains in the contemporary culture.

The animal imagery in his most famous work reflects that dualism. In *The Call of the Wild* the main character, Buck, is taken from a comfortable California ranch life and transformed, through circumstance and effort of will, into a wolf, a leader of the pack. In *White Fang,* the story is reversed—a Yukon wolf cub ends up in a California ranch, domesticated, more or less, but still harboring the instincts of the wild. It is a progression—to the wild and back again—that reflects London's personality: ambivalence mixed with energy and hunger. His thinking mirrors the action of a wild animal stealthily approaching a possible prey while being alert, always, to the possibility of becoming prey. Jack London was repelled by the terrible harshness of nature but drawn to confront it and to enjoy the freedom that came with the willingness to leave civilization behind. He was drawn to the upper classes but repelled by their conventions. He was nursed by a black woman but thought the white man superior in all respects. He was drawn to socialism but admired Nietzsche's Superman. He seemed to accept socialism's inherent belief that upward mobility among the classes is either impossible or so restricted as to be virtually so. But he consciously decided to educate himself out of the submerged tenth—specifically in order to rise, specifically in order to escape the working class. If he didn't believe it was possible, why did he struggle so hard? What he believed and what he saw, what he said and what he did, were so often at odds that his life and work seems a mass of interesting contradictions and inconsistencies.

Perhaps that's why his most enduring work has little to do with politics; political writing requires at least some coherent principles and a consistent point of view. He was happiest and most productive when he cut loose and hit the road leaving behind all the squabbles over doctrine and theory. On the road or in the wild he could feel the invigorating rush of individual freedom, even though survival sometimes meant a fierce struggle against a hostile environment. And by surviving, he gathered the material that allowed him to break away from the orthodoxies of his time and create something unique.

The stories and excerpts in this book are divided into two parts, the first having to do with the Klondike, the second with the sea. Those two places—the wilderness and the sea—are the settings of London's best work. There are many

Introduction

Jack London anthologies, and some of the stories in this book will be familiar. "To Build a Fire," for example, appears often, but it is too good and too representative of London's art and thought to leave out. Others are less well known, but all, I think, reflect Jack London's qualities.

A complex man and artist is hard to capture in a single image. But one of the most apposite and appealing is the picture of Jack London sitting in the cockpit of the *Snark*, scudding along at a good six knots somewhere in the Pacific, miles from land. At that moment he does not know his round-the-world voyage will be called off in Australia because of illness and endless difficulties. He does not know, of course, how short his life will be; his body has not yet given him any clues about that. No, the cruise is just beginning. He has finished his thousand words for the day, and the *Snark* is practically sailing herself, and he is hunched over a book, studying celestial navigation so that he can find his place in relation to the stars. There are struggles behind and many more struggles ahead, but at this moment he is undoubtedly happy— happy to be teaching himself something new, happy to be leaving civilization behind, happy to be on the "adventure path" again.

—Terry Mort
July 2004

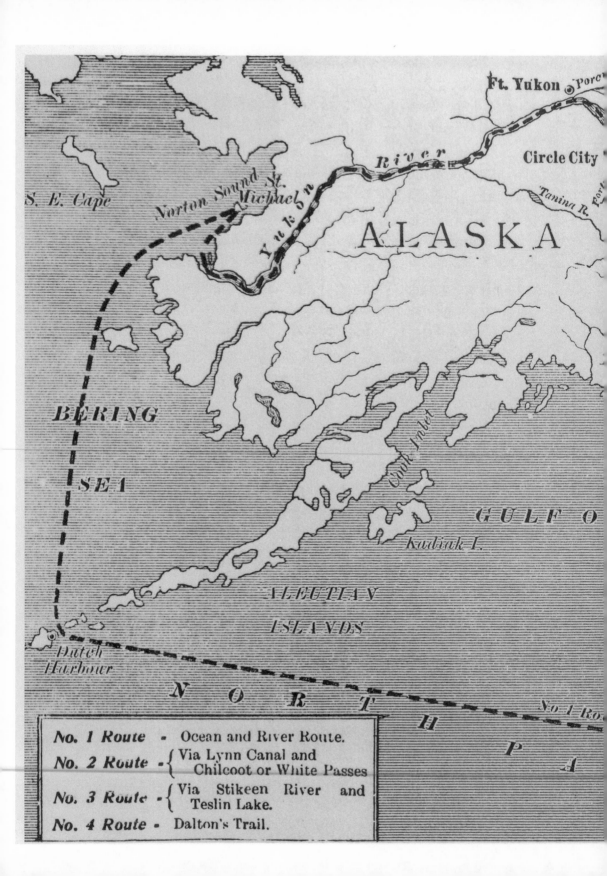

Ft. Yukon · Porc

Circle City

River

S. E. Cape   Norton Sound St. Michael

Tanina R.

ALASKA

Yukon

BERING

SEA

Cook Inlet

GULF O

Kadiak I.

ALEUTIAN

ISLANDS

Dutch
Harbour

N   O   R   T   H

No. 1 Ro

P   A

No. 1 Route	-	Ocean and River Route.
No. 2 Route	- {	Via Lynn Canal and Chilcoot or White Passes
No. 3 Route	- {	Via Stikeen River and Teslin Lake.
No. 4 Route	-	Dalton's Trail.

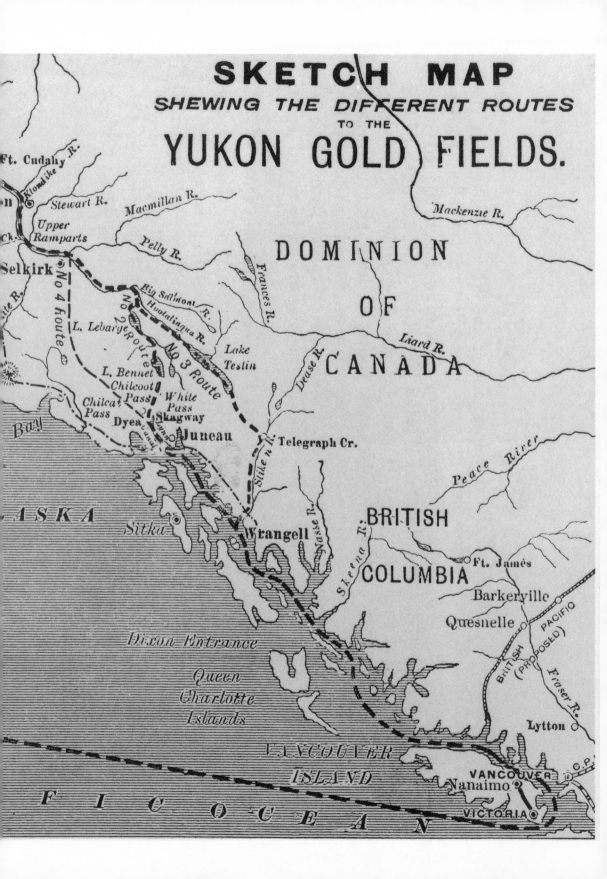

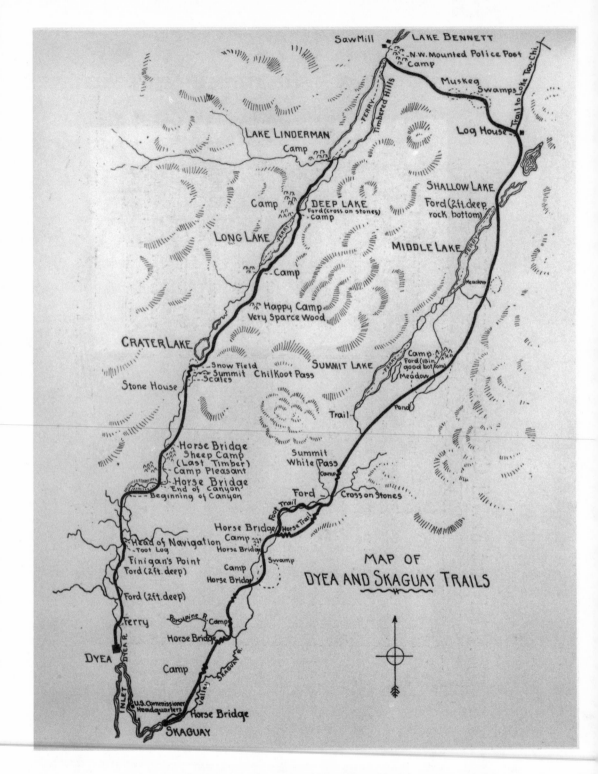

The trails north, en route to the Klondike. Sheep camp and the
Chilkoot Pass are on the Dyea Trail.

I

The White Silence of the North

The afternoon wore on, and with awe, born of the White Silence, the voiceless travelers bent to their work. Nature has many tricks wherewith she convinces man of his finity— the ceaseless flow of the tides, the fury of the storm, the shock of earthquake, the long roll of heaven's artillery—but the most tremendous, the most stupefying of all is the passive phase of the White Silence. All movement ceases, the sky clears, the heavens are as brass; the slightest whisper seems sacrilege, and man becomes timid, affrighted at the sound of his own voice. Sole speck of life journeying across the ghostly wastes of a dead world, he trembles at his audacity, realizes that his is a maggot's life, nothing more. Strange thoughts arise unsummoned, and the mystery of all things strives for utterance. And the fear of death, of God, of the universe, comes over him—the hope of the Resurrection and the Life, the yearning for immortality, the vain striving of the imprisoned essence—it is then, if ever, man walks alone with God.

from: *White Fang*

I. The Trail of the Meat

Dark spruce forest frowned on either side the frozen water-way. The trees had been stripped by a recent wind of each other, black and ominous, in the fading light. A vast silence reigned over the land. The land itself was a desolation, life-less, without movement, so lone and cold that the spirit of it was not even that of sadness. There was a hint in it of laugh-ter, but of a laughter more terrible than any sadness—a laugh-ter that was mirthless as the smile of the Sphinx, a laughter cold as the frost and partaking of the grimness of infallibility. It was the masterful and incommunicable wisdom of eternity laughing at the futility of life and the effort of life. It was the Wild, the savage, frozen-hearted Northland Wild.

But there *was* life, abroad in the land and defiant. Down the frozen waterway toiled a string of wolfish dogs. Their bristly fur was rimed with frost. Their breath froze in the air as it left their mouths, spouting forth in spumes of vapor that settled upon the hair of their bodies and formed into crystals of frost. Leather harness was on the dogs, and leather traces attached them to a sled which dragged along behind. The sled was within runners. It was made of stout birch-bark, and its full surface rested on the snow. The front end of the sled was turned up, like a scroll, in order to force down and under the bore of soft snow that surged like a wave before it. On the sled, securely lashed, was a long and narrow oblong box. There were other things on the sled—blankets, an axe, and a coffee-pot and frying-pan; but prominent; occupying most of the space, was the long and narrow oblong box.

In advance of the dogs, on wide snowshoes, toiled a man. At the rear of the sled toiled a second man. On the sled, in the box, lay a third man whose toil was over—a man whom the Wild had conquered and beaten down until he would never move nor struggle again. It is not the way of the Wild to like movement. Life is an offence to it, for life is movement; and the Wild aims always to destroy movement. It freezes the water to prevent it running to the sea; it drives the sap out of the trees till they are frozen to their mighty hearts; and most ferociously and terribly of all does the Wild harry and crush into submission man—man, who is the most restless of life, ever in revolt against the dictum that all movement must in the end come to the cessation of movement.

But at front and rear, unawed and indomitable, toiled the two men who were not yet dead. Their bodies were covered with fur and soft-tanned leather. Eyelashes and cheeks and lips were so coated with crystals from their frozen breath that their faces were not discernible. This gave them the seeming of ghostly masques, undertakers in a spectral world at the funeral of some ghost. But under it all they were men, penetrating the land of desolation and mockery and silence, puny adventurers bent on colossal adventure, pitting themselves against the might of a world as remote and alien and pulseless as the abysses of space.

They traveled on without speech, saving their breath for the work of their bodies. On every side was the silence, pressing upon them with a tangible presence. It affected their minds as the many atmospheres of deep water affect the body of the diver. It crushed them with the weight of unending vastness and unalterable decree. It crushed them into the remotest recesses of their own minds, pressing out of them, like juices from the grape, all the false ardors and exaltations and undue self-values of the human soul, until they perceived themselves finite and small, specks and motes, moving with weak cunning and little wisdom amidst the play and interplay of the great blind elements and forces.

An hour went by, and a second hour. The pale light of the short sunless day was beginning to fade, when a faint far cry arose on the still air. It soared upward with a swift rush, till it reached its topmost note, where it persisted, palpitant and tense, and then slowly died away. It might have been a lost soul wailing, had it not been invested with a certain sad fierceness and hungry eagerness. The front man turned his head until his eyes met the eyes of the man behind. And then, across the narrow oblong box, each nodded to the other.

A second cry arose, piercing the silence with needlelike shrillness. Both men located the sound. It was to the rear, somewhere in the snow expanse they had just traversed. A third and answering cry arose, also to the rear and to the left of the second cry.

"They're after us, Bill," said the man at the front.

His voice sounded hoarse and unreal, and he had spoken with apparent effort.

"Meat is scarce," answered his comrade. "I ain't seen a rabbit sign for days."

Thereafter they spoke no more, though their ears were keen for the hunting-cries that continued to rise behind them.

At the fall of darkness they swung the dogs into a cluster of spruce trees on the edge of the waterway and made a camp. The coffin, at the side of the fire, served for seat and table. The wolfdogs, clustered on the far side of the fire, snarled and bickered among themselves, but evinced no inclination to stray off into the darkness.

"Seems to me, Henry, they're stayin' remarkable close to camp," Bill commented.

Henry, squatting over the fire and settling the pot of coffee with a piece of ice, nodded. Nor did he speak till he had taken his seat on the coffin and begun to eat.

"They know where their hides is safe," he said. "They'd sooner eat grub than be grub. They're pretty wise, them dogs."

Bill shook his head. "Oh, I don't know."

His comrade looked at him curiously. "First time I ever heard you say anythin' about their not bein' wise."

"Henry," said the other, munching with deliberation the beans he was eating, "did you happen to notice the way them dogs kicked up when I was a-feedin' 'em?"

"They did cut up more'n usual," Henry acknowledged.

"How many dogs've we got, Henry?"

"Six."

"Well, Henry . . ." Bill stopped for a moment in order that his words might gain greater significance. "As I was sayin', Henry, we've got six dogs. I took six fish out of the bag. I gave one fish to each dog, an', Henry, I was one fish short."

"You counted wrong."

"We've got six dogs," the other reiterated dispassionately. "I took out six fish. One Ear didn't get no fish. I come back to the bag afterward an' got'm his fish."

"We've only got six dogs," Henry said.

"Henry," Bill went on, "I won't say they was all dogs, but there was seven of 'm that got fish."

Henry stopped eating to glance across the fire and count the dogs.

"There's only six now," he said.

"I saw the other one run off across the snow," Bill announced with cool positiveness. "I saw seven."

His comrade looked at him commiseratingly, and said, "I'll be almighty glad with this trip's over."

"What d'ye mean by that?" Bill demanded.

"I mean that this load of ourn is getting' on your nerves, an' that you're beginnin' to see things."

"I thought of that," Bill answered gravely. "An' so, when I saw it run off across the snow, I looked in the snow an' saw its tracks. Then I counted the dogs an' there was still six of 'em. The tracks is there in the snow now. D'ye want to look at 'em? I'll show 'm to you."

Henry did not reply, but munched on in silence, until, the meal finished, he topped it with a final cup of coffee. He wiped his mouth with the back of his hand and said:

"Then you're thinkin' as it was—"

A long wailing cry, fiercely sad, from somewhere in the darkness, had interrupted him. He stopped to listen to it, then he finished his sentence with a wave of his hand toward the sound of the cry, "—one of them?"

Bill nodded. "I'd a blame sight sooner think that than anything else. You noticed yourself the row the dogs made."

Cry after cry, and answering cries, were turning the silence into a bedlam. From every side the cries arose, and the dogs betrayed their fear by huddling together and so close to the fire that their hair was scorched by the heat. Bill threw on more wood, before lighting his pipe.

"I'm thinkin' you're down in the mouth some," Henry said.

"Henry . . ." He sucked meditatively at his pipe for some time before he went on. "Henry, I was a-thinkin' what a blame sight luckier he is than you an' me'll ever be."

He indicated the third person by the downward thrust of the thumb to the box on which they sat.

"You an' me, Henry, when we die, we'll be lucky if we get enough stones over our carcasses to keep the dogs off of us."

"But we ain't got people an' money an' all the rest, like him," Henry rejoined. "Long-distance funerals is somethin' you an' me can't exactly afford."

"What gets me, Henry, is what a chap like this, that's a lord or something in his own country, and that's never had to bother about grub nor blankets, why he comes a-buttin' round the God-forsaken ends of the earth—that's what I can't exactly see."

"He might have lived to a ripe old age if he'd stayed to home," Henry agreed.

Bill opened his mouth to speak, but changed his mind. Instead, he pointed toward the wall of darkness that pressed about them from every side. There was no suggestion of form in the utter blackness; only could be seen a pair of eyes gleaming like live coals. Henry indicated with his head a second pair, and a third. A circle of the gleaming eyes had drawn about their camp. Now and again a pair of eyes moved, or disappeared to appear again a moment later.

The unrest of the dogs had been increasing, and they stampeded, in a surge of sudden fear, to the near side of the fire, cringing and crawling about the legs of the men. In the scramble one of the dogs had been overturned on the edge of the fire, and it had yelped with pain and fright as the smell of its singed coat possessed the air. The commotion caused the circle of eyes to shift restlessly for a moment and even to withdraw a bit, but it settled down again as the dogs became quiet.

"Henry, it's a blame misfortune to be out of ammunition."

Bill had finished his pipe and was helping his companion spread the bed of fur and blanket upon the spruce boughs which he had laid over the snow before supper. Henry grunted, and began unlacing his moccasins.

"How many cartridges did you say you had left?" he asked.

"Three," came the answer. "An' I wisht 'twas three hundred. Then I'd show 'em what for, damn 'em!"

He shook his fist angrily at the gleaming eyes, and began securely to prop his moccasins before the fire.

"An' I wisht this cold snap'd break," he went on. "It's been fifty below for two weeks now. An' I wisht I'd never started on this trip, Henry. I don't like the looks of it. It don't feel right, somehow. An' while I'm wishin', I wisht the trip was over an' done with, an' you an' me a-sittin' by the fire in Fort McGurry just about now an' playin' cribbage—that's what I wisht."

Henry grunted and crawled into bed. As he dozed off he was aroused by his comrade's voice.

"Say, Henry, that other one that come in an' got a fish— why didn't the dogs pitch into it? That's what's botherin' me."

"You're botherin' too much, Bill," came the sleepy response. "You was never like this before. You jes' shut up now, an' go to sleep, an' you'll be all hunkydory in the mornin'. Your stomach's sour, that's what's botherin' you."

The men slept, breathing heavily, side to side, under the one covering. The fire died down, and the gleaming eyes drew closer the circle they had flung about the camp. The dogs clustered together in fear, now and again snarling menacingly as a pair of eyes drew close. Once their uproar became so loud that Bill woke up. He got out of bed carefully, so as not to disturb the sleep of his comrade, and threw more wood on the fire. As it began to flame up, the circle of eyes drew farther back. He glanced casually at the huddling dogs. He rubbed his eyes and looked at them more sharply. Then he crawled back into the blankets.

"Henry," he said. "Oh, Henry."

Henry groaned as he passed from sleep to waking, and demanded, "What's wrong now?"

"Nothin'," came the answer; "only there's seven of 'em again. I just counted."

Henry acknowledged receipt of the information with a grunt that slid into a snore as he drifted back into sleep.

In the morning it was Henry who awoke first and routed his companion out of bed. Daylight was yet three hours away, though it was already six o'clock; and in the darkness Henry went about preparing breakfast, while Bill rolled the blankets and made the sled ready for lashing.

"Say, Henry," he asked suddenly, "how many dogs did you say we had?"

"Six."

"Wrong," Bill proclaimed triumphantly.

"Seven again?" Henry queried.

"No, five; one's gone."

"The hell!" Henry cried in wrath, leaving the cooking to come and count the dogs.

"You're right, Bill," he concluded. "Fatty's gone."

"An' he went like greased lightnin' once he got started. Couldn't 've seen 'm for smoke."

"No chance at all," Henry concluded. "they jes' swallowed 'm alive. I bet he was yelpin' as he went down their throats, damn 'em!"

"He always was a fool dog," said Bill.

"But no fool dog ought to be fool enough to go off an' commit suicide that way." He looked over the remainder of the team with a speculative eye that summed up instantly the salient traits of each animal. "I bet none of the others would do it."

"Couldn't drive 'em away from the fire with a club," Bill agreed. "Always did think there was somethin' wrong with Fatty, anyway."

And this was the epitaph of a dead dog on the Northland trail—less scant than the epitaph of many another dog, of many a man.

II. The She-Wolf

Breakfast eaten and the slim camp-outfit lashed to the sled, the men turned their backs on the cheery fire and launched out into the darkness. At once began to rise the cries that were fiercely sad—cries that called through the darkness and cold to one another and answered back. Conversation ceased. Daylight came at nine o'clock. At midday the sky to the south warmed to rose-color, and marked where the bulge of the earth intervened between the meridian sun and the northern world. But the rose-color swiftly faded. The gray light of day that remained lasted until three o'clock, when it, too, faded, and the pall of the Arctic night descended upon the lone and silent land.

As darkness came on, the hunting-cries to right and left and rear drew closer—so close that more than once they sent surges of fear through the toiling dogs, throwing them into short-lived panics.

At the conclusion of one such panic, when he and Henry had got the dogs back in the traces, Bill said:

"I wisht they'd strike game somewheres, an' go away an' leave us alone."

"They do get on the nerves horrible," Henry sympathized.

They spoke no more until camp was made.

Henry was bending over and adding ice to the bubbling pot of beans when he was startled by the sound of a blow, an exclamation from Bill, and a sharp snarling cry of pain from among the dogs. He straightened up in time to see a dim form disappearing across the snow into the shelter of the dark. Then he saw Bill, standing amid the dogs, half triumphant, half crest-fallen, in one hand a stout club, in the other the tail and part of the body of a sun-cured salmon.

"It got half of it," he announced, "but I got a whack at it jes' the same. D'ye hear it squeal?"

"What'd it look like?" Henry asked.

"Couldn't see. But it had four legs an' a mouth an' hair an' looked like any dog."

"Must be a tame wolf, I reckon."

"It's damned tame, whatever it is, comin' in here at feedin' time an' gettin' its whack of fish."

That night, when supper was finished and they sat on the oblong box and pulled at their pipes, the circle of gleaming eyes drew in even closer than before.

"I wisht they'd spring up a bunch of moose or somethin', an' go away an' leave us alone," Bill said.

Henry grunted with an intonation that was not all sympathy, and for a quarter of an hour they sat on in silence, Henry staring at the fire, and Bill at the circle of eyes that burned in the darkness just beyond the firelight.

"I wisht we was pullin' into McGurry right now," he began again.

"Shut up your wishin' an' your croakin'," Henry burst out angrily. "Your stomach's sour. That's what's ailin' you. Swallow a spoonful of sody, an' you'll sweeten up wonderful an' be more pleasant company."

In the morning, Henry was aroused by fervid blasphemy that proceeded from the mouth of Bill. Henry propped himself up on an elbow and looked to see his comrade standing among the dogs beside the replenished fire, his arms raised in objurgation, his face distorted with passion.

"Hello!" Henry called. "What's up now?"

"Frog's gone," came the answer.

"No."

"I tell you yes."

Henry leaped out of the blankets and to the dogs. He counted them with care, and then joined his partner in cursing the powers of the Wild that had robbed them of another dog.

"Frog was the strongest dog of the bunch," Bill pronounced finally.

"An' he was no fool dog neither," Henry added.

And so was recorded the second epitaph in two days.

A gloomy breakfast was eaten, and the four remaining dogs were harnessed to the sled. The day was a repetition of the days that had gone before. The men toiled without speech across the face of the frozen world. The silence was unbroken save by the cries of their pursuers, that, unseen, hung upon their rear. With the coming of night in the mid-afternoon, the cries sounded closer as the pursuers drew in according to their custom; and the dogs grew excited and frightened, and were guilty of panics that tangled the traces and further depressed the two men.

"There, that'll fix you fool critters," Bill said with satisfaction that night, standing erect at completion of his task.

Henry left his cooking to come and see. Not only had his partner tied the dogs up, but he had tied them, after the Indian fashion, with sticks. About the neck of each dog he had fastened a leather thong. To this, and so close to the neck that the dog could not get his teeth to it, he had tied a stout stick four or five feet in length. The other end of the stick, in turn, was made fast to a stake in the ground by means of a leather thong. The dog was unable to gnaw through the leather at his own end of the stick. The stick prevented him from getting at the leather that fastened the other end.

Henry nodded his head approvingly.

"It's the only contraption that'll ever hold One Ear," he said. "He can gnaw through leather as clean as a knife an' jes' about half as quick. They all 'll be here in the morning' hunkydory."

"You jes' bet they will," Bill affirmed. "If one of 'em turns up missin', I'll go without my coffee."

"They jes' know we ain't loaded to kill," Henry remarked at bed-time, indicating the gleaming circle that hemmed them in. "If we could put a couple of shots into 'm, they'd be more respectful. They come closer every night. Get the firelight out of your eyes an' look hard—there! Did you see that one?"

For some time the two men amused themselves with watching the movement of vague forms on the edge of the firelight. By looking closely and steadily at where a pair of eyes burned in the darkness, the form of the animal would slowly take shape. They could even see these forms move at times.

A sound among the dogs attracted the men's attention. One Ear was uttering quick, eager whines, lunging at the length of his stick toward the darkness, and desisting now and again in order to make frantic attacks on the stick with his teeth.

"Look at that, Bill," Henry whispered.

Full into the firelight, with a stealthy, sidelong movement, glided a doglike animal. It moved with commingled mistrust and daring, cautiously observing the men, its attention fixed on the dogs. One Ear strained the full length of the stick toward the intruder and whined with eagerness.

"That fool One Ear don't seem scairt much," Bill said in a low tone.

"It's a she-wolf," Henry whispered back, "an' that accounts for Fatty an' Frog. She's the decoy for the pack. She draws out the dog an' then all the rest pitches in an' eats 'm up."

The fire crackled. A log fell apart with a loud spluttering noise. At the sound of it the strange animal leaped back into the darkness.

"Henry, I'm a-thinkin'," Bill announced.

"Thinkin' what?"

"I'm a-thinkin' that was the one I lambasted with the club."

"Ain't the slightest doubt in the world," was Henry's response.

"An' right here I want to remark," Bill went on, "that that animal's familyarity with campfires is suspicious an' immoral."

"It knows for certain more'n a self-respectin' wolf ought to know," Henry agreed. "A wolf that knows enough to come in with the dogs at feedin' time has had experiences."

"Ol' Villan had a dog once that run away with the wolves," Bill cogitated aloud. "I ought to know. I shot it out of the pack in a moose pasture over on Little Stick. An' Ol' Villan cried like a baby. Hadn't seen it for three years, he said. Ben with the wolves all that time."

"I reckon you've called the turn, Bill. That wolf's a dog, an' it's eaten fish many's the time from the hand of man."

"An' if I get a chance at it, that wolf that's a dog'll be jes' meat," Bill declared. "We can't afford to lose no more animals."

"But you've only got three cartridges," Henry objected.

"I'll wait for a dead sure shot," was the reply.

In the morning Henry renewed the fire and cooked breakfast to the accompaniment of his partner's snoring.

"You was sleepin' jes' too comfortable for anythin'," Henry told him, as he routed him out for breakfast. "I hadn't the heart to rouse you."

Bill began to eat sleepily. He noticed that his cup was empty and started to reach for the pot. But the pot was beyond arm's length and beside Henry.

"Say, Henry," he chided gently, "ain't you forgot somethin'?"

Henry looked about with great carefulness and shook his head. Bill held up the empty cup.

"You don't get no coffee," Henry announced.

"Ain't run out?" Bill asked anxiously.

"Nope."

"Ain't thinkin' it'll hurt my digestion?"

"Nope."

A flush of angry blood pervaded Bill's face.

"Then it's jes' warm an' anxious I am to be hearin' you explain yourself," he said.

"Spanker's gone," Henry answered.

Without haste, with the air of one resigned to misfortune, Bill turned his head, and from where he sat counted the dogs.

"How'd it happen?" he asked apathetically.

Henry shrugged his shoulders. "Don't know. Unless One Ear gnawed 'm loose. He couldn't a-done it himself, that's sure."

"The darned cuss." Bill spoke gravely and slowly, with no hint of the anger that was raging within. "Jes' because he couldn't chew himself loose, he chews Spanker loose."

"Well, Spanker's troubles is over, anyway; I guess he's digested by this time an' cavortin' over the landscape in the bellies of twenty different wolves," was Henry's epitaph on this, the latest lost dog. "Have some coffee, Bill."

But Bill shook his head.

"Go on," Henry pleaded, elevating the pot.

Bill shoved his cup aside. "I'll be ding-dong-danged if I do. I said I wouldn't if any dog turned up missin', an' I won't."

"It's darn good coffee," Henry said enticingly.

But Bill was stubborn, and he ate a dry breakfast, washed down with mumbled curses at One Ear for the trick he had played.

"I'll tie 'em up out of reach of each other to-night," Bill said, as they took the trail.

They had traveled little more than a hundred yards, when Henry, who was in front, bent down and picked up something with which his snowshoe had collided. It was dark, and he could not see it, but he recognized it by the touch. He flung it back, so that it struck the sled and bounded along until it fetched up on Bill's snowshoes.

"Mebbe you'll need that in your business," Henry said.

Bill uttered an exclamation. It was all that was left of Spanker—the stick with which he had been tied.

"They ate 'm hide an' all," Bill announced. "The stick's as clean as a whistle. They've ate the leather offen both ends. They're dam hungry, Henry, an' they'll have you an' me guessin' before this trip's over."

Henry laughed defiantly. "I ain't been trailed this way by wolves before, but I've gone through a whole lot worse an' kept my health. Takes more 'n a handful of them pesky critters to do for yours truly, Bill, my son."

"I don't know, I don't know," Bill muttered ominously.

"Well, you'll know all right when we pull into McGurry."

"I ain't feelin' special enthusiastic," Bill persisted.

"You're off color, that's what's the matter with you," Henry dogmatized. "What you need is quinine, an' I'm goin' to dose you up stiff as soon as we make McGurry."

Bill grunted his disagreement with the diagnosis, and lapsed into silence. The day was like all the days. Light came at nine o'clock. At twelve o'clock the southern horizon was warmed by the unseen sun; and then began the cold gray of afternoon that would merge, three hours later, into night.

It was just after the sun's futile effort to appear, that Bill slipped the rifle from under the sled-lashings and said:

"You keep right on, Henry, I'm goin' to see what I can see."

"You'd better stick by the sled," his partner protested. "You've only got three cartridges, an' there's no tellin' what might happen."

"Who's croakin' now?" Bill demanded triumphantly.

Henry made no reply, and plodded on alone, though often he cast anxious glances back into the gray solitude where his partner had disappeared. An hour later, taking advantage of the cut-offs around which the sled had to go, Bill arrived.

"They're scattered an' rangin' along wide," he said; "keepin' up with us an' lookin' for game at the same time. You see, they're sure of us, only they know they've got to wait to get us. In the meantime they're willin' to pick up anythin' eatable that comes handy."

"You mean they *think* they're sure of us," Henry objected pointedly.

But Bill ignored him. "I seen some of them. They're pretty thin. They ain't had a bite in weeks, I reckon, outside of Fatty an' Frog an' Spanker; an' there's so many of 'em that that didn't go far. They're remarkable thin. Their ribs is like washboards, an' their stomachs is right up against their backbones. They're pretty desperate, I can tell you. They'll be goin' mad, yet, an' then watch out."

A few minutes later, Henry, who was now traveling behind the sled, emitted a low, warning whistle. Bill turned and looked, then quietly stopped the dogs. To the rear, from around the last bend and plainly into view, on the very trail they had just covered, trotted a furry, slinking form. Its nose was to the trail, and it trotted with a peculiar, sliding, effortless gait. When they halted, it halted, throwing up its head and regarding them steadily with nostrils that twitched as it caught and studied the scent of them.

"It's the she-wolf," Bill whispered.

The dogs had lain down in the snow, and he walked past them to join his partner at the sled. Together they watched the strange animal that had pursued them for days and that had already accomplished the destruction of half their dog-team.

After a searching scrutiny, the animal trotted forward a few steps. This it repeated several times, till it was a short hundred yards away. It paused, head up, close by a clump of spruce trees, and with sight and scent studied the outfit of the watching men. It looked at them in a strangely wistful way, after the manner of a dog; but in its wistfulness there was none of the dog affection. It was a wistfulness bred of hunger, as cruel as its own fangs, as merciless as the frost itself.

It was large for a wolf, its gaunt frame advertising the lines of an animal that was among the largest of its kind.

"Stands pretty close to two feet an' a half at the shoulders," Henry commented. "An' I'll bet it ain't far from five feet long."

"Kind of strange color for a wolf," was Bill's criticism. "I never seen a red wolf before. Looks almost cinnamon to me."

The animal was certainly not cinnamon-colored. Its coat was the true wolf-coat. The dominant color was gray, and yet there was to it a faint reddish hue—a hue that was baffling, that appeared and disappeared, that was more like an illusion of the vision, now gray, distinctly gray, and again giving hints and glints of a vague redness of color not classifiable in terms of ordinary experience.

"Looks for all the world like a big husky sled-dog," Bill said. "I wouldn't be s'prised to see it wag its tail.

"Hello, you husky!" he called. "Come here, you, whatever-your-name-is."

"Ain't a bit scairt of you," Henry laughed.

Bill waved his hand at it threateningly and shouted loudly; but the animal betrayed no fear. The only change in it that they could notice was an accession of alertness. It still regarded them with the merciless wistfulness of hunger. They were meat, and it was hungry; and it would like to go in and eat them if it dared.

"Look here, Henry," Bill said, unconsciously lowering his voice to a whisper because of what he meditated. "We've got three cartridges. But it's a dead shot. Couldn't miss it. It's got away with three of our dogs, an' we oughter put a stop to it. What d'ye say?"

Henry nodded his consent. Bill cautiously slipped the gun from under the sled-lashing. The gun was on the way to his shoulder, but it never got there. For in that instant the she-wolf leaped sidewise from the trail into the clump of spruce trees and disappeared.

The two men looked at each other. Henry whistled long and comprehendingly.

"I might have knowed it," Bill chided himself aloud, as he replaced the gun. "Of course a wolf that knows enough to come in with the dogs at feedin' time, 'd know all bout shootin-irons.

I tell you right now, Henry, that critter's the cause of all our trouble. We'd have six dogs at the present time, 'stead of three, if it wasn't for her. An' I tell you right now, Henry, I'm goin' to get her. She's too smart to be shot in the open. But I'm goin' to lay for her. I'll bushwhack her as sure as my name is Bill."

"You needn't stray off too far in doin' it," his partner admonished. "If that pack ever starts to jump you, them three cartridges 'd be wuth no more 'n three whoops in hell. Them animals is damn hungry, an' once they start in, they'll sure get you, Bill."

They camped early that night. Three dogs could not drag the sled so fast nor for so long hours as could six, and they were showing unmistakable signs of playing out. And the men went early to bed, Bill first seeing to it that the dogs were tied out of gnawing-reach of one another.

But the wolves were growing bolder, and the men were aroused more than once from their sleep. So near did the wolves approach, that the dogs became frantic with terror, and it was necessary to replenish the fire from time to time in order to deep the adventurous marauders at safe distance.

"I've hearn sailors talk of sharks followin' a ship," Bill remarked, as he crawled back into the blankets after one such replenishing of the fire. "Well, them wolves is land sharks. They know their business better 'n we do, an' they ain't a-holdin' our trail this way for their health. They're goin' to get us. They're sure goin' to get us, Henry."

"They've half got you a'ready, a-talkin' like that," Henry retorted sharply. "A man's half licked when he says he is. An' you're half eaten from the way you're goin' on about it."

"They've got away with better men than you an' me," Bill answered.

"Oh, shet up your croakin'. You make me all-fired tired."

Henry rolled over angrily on his side, but was surprised that Bill made no similar display of temper. This was not Bill's way, for he was easily angered by sharp words. Henry thought long over it before he went to sleep, and as his eyelids fluttered down and he dozed off, the thought in his mind was: "There's no mistakin' it, Bill's almighty blue. I'll have to cheer him up to-morrow."

III. The Hunger Cry

The day began auspiciously. They had lost no dogs during the night, and they swung out upon the trail and into the silence, the darkness, and the cold with spirits that were fairly light. Bill seemed to have forgotten his forebodings of the previous night, and even waxed facetious with the dogs when, at mid-day, they overturned the sled on a bad piece of trail.

It was an awkward mix-up. The sled was upside down and jammed between a tree-trunk and a huge rock, and they were forced to unharness the dogs in order to straighten out the tangle. The two men were bent over the sled and trying to right it, when Henry observed One Ear sidling away.

"Here, you, One Ear!" he cried, straightening up and turning around on the dog.

But One Ear broke into a run across the snow, his traces trailing behind him. And there, out in the snow of their backtrack, was the she-wolf waiting for him. As he neared her, he became suddenly cautious. He slowed down to an alert and mincing walk and then stopped. He regarded her carefully and dubiously, yet desirefully. She seemed to smile at him, showing her teeth in an ingratiating rather than a menacing way. She moved toward him a few steps, playfully, and then halted. One Ear drew near to her, still alert and cautious, his tail and ears in the air, his head held high.

He tried to sniff noses with her, but she retreated playfully and coyly. Every advance on his part was accompanied by a corresponding retreat on her part. Step by step she was luring him away from the security of his human companionship. Once, as though a warning had in vague ways flitted through his intelligence, he turned his head and looked back at the overturned sled, at his team-mates, and at the two men who were calling to him.

But whatever idea was forming in his mind was dissipated by the she-wolf, who advanced upon him, sniffed noses with him for a fleeting instant, and then resumed her coy retreat before his renewed advances.

In the meantime, Bill had bethought himself of the rifle. But it was jammed beneath the overturned sled, and by the time Henry had helped him to right the load, One Ear and the she-wolf were too close together and the distance too great to risk a shot.

Too late, One Ear learned his mistake. Before they saw the cause, the two men saw him turn and start to run back toward them. Then, approaching at right angles to the trail and cutting off his retreat, they saw a dozen wolves, lean and gray, bounding across the snow. On the instant, the she-wolf's coyness and playfulness disappeared. With a snarl she sprang upon One Ear. He thrust her off with his shoulder, and, his retreat cut off and still intent on regaining the sled, he altered his course in an attempt to circle around to it. More wolves were appearing every moment and joining in the chase. The she-wolf was one leap behind One Ear and holding her own.

"Where are you goin'?" Henry suddenly demanded, laying his hand on his partner's arm.

Bill shook it off. "I won't stand it," he said. "They ain't a-goin' to get any more of our dogs if I can help it."

Gun in hand, he plunged into the underbrush that lined the side of the trail. His intention was apparent enough. Taking the sled as the center of the circle that One Ear was making, Bill planned to tap that circle at a point in advance of the pursuit. With his rifle, in the broad daylight, it might be possible for him to awe the wolves and save the dog.

"Say, Bill!" Henry called after him. "Be careful! Don't take no chances!"

Henry sat down on the sled and watched. There was nothing else for him to do. Bill had already gone from sight; but now and again, appearing and disappearing amongst the underbrush and the scattered clumps of spruce, could be seen One Ear. Henry judged his case to be hopeless. The dog was thoroughly alive to its danger, but it was running on the outer circle while the wolf-pack was running on the inner and shorter circle. It was vain to think of One Ear so outdistancing his pursuers as to be able to cut across their circle in advance of them and to regain the sled.

The different lines were rapidly approaching a point. Somewhere out there in the snow, screened from his sight by trees and thickets, Henry knew that the wolf-pack, One Ear, and Bill were coming together. All too quickly, far more quickly than he had expected, it happened. He heard a shot, then two shots in rapid succession, and he knew that Bill's ammunition was gone. Then he heard a great outcry of snarls and yelps. He recognized One Ear's yell of pain and terror, and he heard a wolf-cry that bespoke a stricken animal. And that was all. The snarls ceased. The yelping died away. Silence settled down again over the lonely land.

He sat for a long while upon the sled. There was no need for him to go and see what had happened. He knew it as though it had taken place before his eyes. Once, he roused with a start and hastily got the axe out from underneath the lashings. But for some time longer he sat and brooded, the two remaining dogs crouching and trembling at his feet.

At last he arose in a weary manner, as though all the resilience had gone out of his body, and proceeded to fasten the dogs to the sled. He passed a rope over his shoulder, a man-trace, and pulled with the dogs. He did not go far. At the first hint of darkness he hastened to make a camp, and he saw to it that he had a generous supply of firewood. He fed the dogs, cooked and ate his supper, and made his bed close to the fire.

But he was not destined to enjoy that bed. Before his eyes closed the wolves had drawn too near for safety. It no longer required an effort of the vision to see them. They were all about him and the fire, in a narrow circle, and he could see them plainly in the firelight, lying down, sitting up, crawling forward on their bellies, or slinking back and forth. They even slept. Here and there he could see one curled up in the snow like a dog, taking the sleep that was now denied himself.

He kept the fire brightly blazing, for he knew that it alone intervened between the flesh of his body and their hungry fangs. His two dogs stayed close by him, one on either side, leaning against him for protection, crying and whimpering, and at times snarling desperately when a wolf approached a little closer than usual. At such moments, when his dogs snarled, the whole circle would be agitated, the wolves coming to their feet and pressing tentatively forward, a chorus of snarls and eager yelps rising about him. Then the circle would lie down again, and here and there a wolf would resume its broken nap.

But this circle had a continuous tendency to draw in upon him. Bit by bit, an inch at a time, with here a wolf bellying forward, and there a wolf bellying forward, the circle would narrow until the brutes were almost within springing distance. Then he would seize brands from the fire and hurl them into the pack. A hasty drawing back always resulted, accompanied by angry yelps and frightened snarls when a well-aimed brand struck and scorched a too daring animal.

Morning found the man haggard and worn, wide-eyed from want of sleep. He cooked breakfast in the darkness, and at nine o'clock, when, with the coming of daylight, the wolf-pack drew back, he set about the task he had planned through the long hours of the night. Chopping down young saplings he made them cross-bars of a scaffold by lashing them high up to the trunks of standing trees. Using the sled-lashing for a heaving rope, and with the aid of the dogs, he hoisted the coffin to the top of the scaffold.

"They got Bill, an' they may get me, but they'll sure never get you, young man," he said, addressing the dead body in its tree-sepulcher.

Then he took the trail, the lightened sled bounding along behind the willing dogs; for they, too, knew that safety lay only in the gaining of Fort McGurry. The wolves were now more open in their pursuit, trotting sedately behind and ranging along on either side, their red tongues lolling out, their lean sides showing the undulating ribs with every movement. They were very lean, mere skin-bags stretched over bony frames, with strings for muscles—so lean that Henry found it in is mind to marvel that they still kept their feet and did not collapse forthright in the snow.

He did not dare travel until dark. At midday, not only did the sun warm the southern horizon, but it even thrust its upper rim, pale and golden, above the sky-line. He received it as a sign. The days were growing longer. The sun was returning. But scarcely had the cheer of its light departed, then he went into camp. There were still several hours of gray daylight and somber twilight, and he utilized them in chopping an enormous supply of firewood.

With night came horror. Not only were the starving wolves growing bolder, but lack of sleep was telling upon Henry. He dozed despite himself, crouching by the fire, the blankets about his shoulders, the axe between his knees, and on either side a dog pressing close against him. He awoke once and saw in front of him, not a dozen feet away, a big gray wolf, one of the largest of the pack. And even as he looked, the brute deliberately stretched himself after the manner of a lazy dog, yawning full in his face and looking upon him with a possessive eye, as if, in truth, he were merely a delayed meal that was soon to be eaten.

This certitude was shown by the whole pack. Fully a score he could count, staring hungrily at him or calmly sleeping in the snow. They reminded him of children gathered about a spread table and awaiting permission to begin to eat. And he was the food they were to eat! He wondered how and when the meal would begin.

As he piled wood on the fire he discovered an appreciation of his own body which he had never felt before. He watched his moving muscles and was interested in the cunning mechanism of his fingers. By the light of the fire he crooked his fingers slowly and repeatedly, now one at a time, now all together, spreading them wide or making quick gripping movements. He studied the nail-formation, and prodded the finger-tips, now sharply, and again softly, gauging the while the nerve-sensations produced. It fascinated him, and he grew suddenly fond of this subtle flesh of his that worked so beautifully and smoothly and delicately. Then he would cast a glance of fear at the wolf-circle drawn expectantly about him, and like a blow the realization would strike him that this wonderful body of his, this living flesh, was no more than so much meat, a quest of ravenous animals, to be torn and slashed by their hungry fangs, to be sustenance to them as the moose and the rabbit had often been sustenance to him.

He came out of a doze that was half nightmare, to see the red-hued she-wolf before him. She was not more than half a dozen feet away, sitting in the snow and wistfully regarding him. The two dogs were whimpering and snarling at his feet, but she took no notice of them. She was looking at the man, and for some time he returned her look. There was

31

nothing threatening about her. She looked at him merely with a great wistfulness, but he knew it to be the wistfulness of an equally great hunger. He was the food, and the sight of him excited in her the gustatory sensations. Her mouth opened, the saliva drooled forth, and she licked her chops with pleasure of anticipation.

A spasm of fear went through him. He reached hastily for a brand to throw at her. But even as he reached, and before his fingers had closed on the missile, she sprang back into safety; and he knew that she was used to having things thrown at her. She had snarled as she sprang away, baring her white fangs to their roots, all her wistfulness vanishing, being replaced by a carnivorous malignity that made him shudder. He glanced at the hand that held the brand, noticing the cunning delicacy of the fingers that gripped it, how they adjusted themselves to all the inequalities of the surface, curling over and under and about the rough wood, and one little finger, too close to the burning portion of the brand, sensitively and automatically writhing back from the hurtful heat to a cooler gripping-place; and in the same instant he seemed to see a vision of those same sensitive and delicate fingers being crushed and torn by the white teeth of the she-wolf. Never had he been so fond of this body of his as now when his tenure of it was so precarious.

All night, with burning brands, he fought off the hungry pack. When he dozed despite himself, the whimpering and snarling of the dogs aroused him. Morning came but for the first time the light of day failed to scatter the wolves. The man waited in vain for them to go. They remained in a circle about him and his fire, displaying an arrogance of possession that shook his courage born of the morning light.

He made one desperate attempt to pull out on the trail. But the moment he left the protection of the fire, the boldest wolf leaped for him, but leaped short. He saved himself by springing back, the jaws snapping together a scant six inches from his thigh. The rest of the pack was now up and surging upon him, and a throwing of firebrands right and left was necessary to drive them back to a respectful distance.

Even in the daylight he did not dare leave the fire to chop fresh wood. Twenty feet away towered a huge dead spruce. He spent half the day extending his campfire to the tree, at any moment a half dozen burning fagots ready at hand to fling at his enemies. Once at the tree, he studied the surrounding forest in order to fell the tree in the direction of the most firewood.

The night was a repetition of the night before, save that the need for sleep was becoming overpowering. The snarling of his dogs was losing its efficacy. Besides, they were snarling all the time, and his benumbed and drowsy senses no longer took note of changing pitch and intensity. He awoke with a start. The she-wolf was less than a yard from him. Mechanically, at short range, without letting go of it, he thrust a brand full into her open and snarling mouth. She sprang away, yelling with pain, and while he took delight in the smell of burning flesh and hair, he watched her shaking her head and growling wrathfully a score of feet away.

But this time, before he dozed again, he tied a burning pine-knot to his right hand. His eyes were closed but a few minutes when the burn of the flame on his flesh awakened him. For several hours he adhered to this program. Every time he was thus awakened he drove back the wolves with flying brands, replenished the fire, and rearranged the pine-knot on his hand. All worked well, but there came a time when he fastened the pine knot insecurely. As his eyes closed it fell away from his hand.

He dreamed. It seemed to him that he was in Fort McGurry. It was warm and comfortable, and he was playing cribbage with the Factor. Also, it seemed to him that the fort was besieged by wolves. They were howling at the very gates, and sometimes he and the Factor paused from the game to listen and laugh at the futile efforts of the wolves to get in. And then, so strange was the dream, there was a crash. The door was burst open. He could see the wolves flooding into the big living room of the fort. They were leaping straight for him and the Factor. With the bursting open of the door, the noise of their howling had increased tremendously. This howling now bothered him. His dream was merging into something else—he knew not what; but through it all, following him, persisted the howling.

And then he awoke to find the howling real. There was a great snarling and yelping. The wolves were rushing him. They were all about him and upon him. The teeth of one had closed upon his arm. Instinctively he leaped into the fire, and as he leaped, he felt the sharp slash of teeth that tore through the flesh of his leg. Then began a fire fight. His stout mittens temporarily protected his hands, and he scooped live coals into the air in all directions, until the campfire took on the semblance of a volcano.

But it could not last long. His face was blistering in the heat, his eyebrows and lashes were singed off, and the heat was becoming unbearable to his feet. With a flaming brand in each hand, he sprang to the edge of the fire. The wolves had been driven back. On every side, wherever the live coals had fallen, the snow was sizzling, and every little while a retiring wolf, with wild leap and snort and snarl, announced that one such live coal had been stepped upon.

Flinging his brands at the nearest of his enemies, the man thrust his smoldering mittens into the snow and stamped about to cool his feet. His two dogs were missing, and he well knew that they had served as a course in the protracted meal which had begun days before with Fatty, the last course of which would likely be himself in the days to follow.

"You ain't got me yet!" he cried, savagely shaking his fist at the hungry beasts; and at the sound of his voice the whole circle was agitated, there was a general snarl, and the she-wolf slid up close to him across the snow and watched him with hungry wistfulness.

He set to work to carry out a new idea that had come to him. He extended the fire into a large circle. Inside this circle he crouched, his sleeping outfit under him as a protection against the melting snow. When he had thus disappeared within his shelter of flame, the whole pack came curiously to the rim of the fire to see what had become of him. Hitherto they had been denied access to the fire, and they now settled down in a close-drawn circle, like so many dogs, blinking and yawning and stretching their lean bodies in the unaccus-tomed warmth. Then the she-wolf sat down, pointed her nose at a star, and began to howl. One by one the wolves joined her, till the whole pack, on haunches, with noses pointed skyward, was howling its hunger cry.

Dawn came, and daylight. The fire was burning low. The fuel had run out, and there was need to get more. The man attempted to step out of his circle of flame, but the wolves surged to meet him. Burning brands made them spring aside, but they no longer sprang back. In vain he strove to drive them back. As he gave up and stumbled inside his circle, a wolf leaped for him, missed, and landed with all four feet in the coals. It cried out with terror, at the same time snarling, and scrambled back to cool its paws in the snow.

The man sat down on his blankets in a crouching position. His body leaned forward from the hips. His shoulders, relaxed and dropping, and his head on his knees advertised that he had given up the struggle. Now and again he raised his head to note the dying down of the fire. The circle of flame and coals was breaking into segments with openings in between. These openings grew in size, the segments diminished.

"I guess you can come an' get me any time," he mumbled. "Anyway, I'm goin' to sleep."

Once he wakened, and in an opening in the circle, directly in front of him, he saw the she-wolf gazing at him.

Again he awakened, a little later, though it seemed hours to him. A mysterious change had taken place—so mysterious a change that he was shocked wider awake. Something had happened. He could not understand at first. Then he discovered it. The wolves were gone. Remained only the trampled snow to show how closely they had pressed him. Sleep was welling up and gripping him again, his head was sinking down upon his knees, when he roused with a sudden start.

There were cries of men, the churn of sleds, the creaking of harnesses, the eager whimpering of straining dogs. Four sleds pulled in from the river bed to the camp among the trees. Half a dozen men were about the man who crouched in the center of the dying fire. They were shaking and prodding him into consciousness. He looked at them like a drunken man and maundered in strange, sleepy speech:

"Red she-wolf. . . . Come in with the dogs at feedin' time. . . . First she ate the dog-food. . . . Then she ate the dogs. . . . An' after that she ate Bill. . . ."

"Where's Lord Alfred?" one of the men bellowed in his ear, shaking him roughly.

He shook his head slowly. "No, she didn't eat him. . . . He's roostin' in a tree at the last camp."

"Dead?" the man shouted.

"An' in a box," Henry answered. He jerked his shoulder petulantly away from the grip of his questioner. "Say, you lemme alone. . . . I'm jes' plumb tuckered out. . . . Goo' night, everybody."

His eyes fluttered and went shut. His chin fell forward on his chest. And even as they eased him down upon the blankets his snores were rising on the frosty air.

But there was another sound. Far and faint it was, in the remote distance, the cry of the hungry wolf-pack as it took the trail of other meat than the man it had just missed.

from: *The Son of the Wolf*

In a Far Country

When a man journeys into a far country, he must be prepared to forget many of the things he has learned, and to acquire such customs as are inherent with existence in the new land; he must abandon the old ideals and the old gods, and oftentimes he must reverse the very codes by which his conduct has hitherto been shaped. To those who have the protean faculty of adaptability, the novelty of such change may even be a source of pleasure; but to those who happen to be hardened to the ruts in which they were created, the pressure of the altered environment is unbearable, and they chafe in body and in spirit under the new restrictions which they do not understand. This chafing is bound to act and react, producing diverse evils and leading to various misfortunes. It were better for the man who cannot fit himself to the new groove to return to his own country; if he delay too long, he will surely die.

The man who turns his back upon the comforts of an elder civilization, to face the savage youth, the primordial simplicity of the North, may estimate success at an inverse ratio to the quantity and quality of his hopelessly fixed habits. He will soon discover, if he be a fit candidate, that the material habits are the less important. The exchange of such things as a dainty menu for rough fare, of the stiff leather shoe for the soft, shapeless moccasin, of the feather bed for a couch in the snow, is after all a very easy matter. But his pinch will come in learning properly to shape his mind's attitude toward all things, and especially toward his fellow man. For the courtesies of ordinary life, he must substitute unselfishness, forbearance, and tolerance. Thus, and thus only, can he gain that pearl of great price—true comradeship. He must not say "Thank you"; he must mean it without opening his mouth, and prove it by responding in kind. In short, he must substitute the deed for the word, the spirit for the letter.

When the world rang with the tale of Artic gold, and the lure of the North gripped the heartstrings of men, Carter Weatherbee threw up his snug clerkship, turned the half of his savings over to his wife, and with the remainder bought an outfit. There was no romance in his nature—the bondage of commerce had crushed all that; he was simply tired of the ceaseless grind, and wished to risk great hazards in view of corresponding returns. Like many another fool, disdaining the old trails used by the Northland pioneers for a score of years, he hurried to Edmonton in the spring of the year; and there, unluckily for his soul's welfare, he allied himself with a party of men.

There was nothing unusual about this party, except its plans. Even its goal, like that of all other parties, was the

Klondike. But the route it had mapped out to attain that goal took away the breath of the hardiest native, born and bred to the vicissitudes of the Northwest. Even Jacques Baptiste, born of a Chippewa woman and a renegade *voyageur* (having raised his first whimpers in a deerskin lodge north of the sixty-fifth parallel, and had the same hushed by blissful sucks of raw tallow), was surprised. Though he sold his services to them and agreed to travel even to the never-opening ice, he shook his head ominously whenever his advice was asked.

Percy Cuthfert's evil star must have been in the ascendant, for he, too, joined this company of argonauts. He was an ordinary man, with a bank account as deep as his culture, which is saying a good deal. He had no reason to embark on such a venture—no reason in the world, save that he suffered from an abnormal development of sentimentality. He mistook this for the true spirit of romance and adventure. Many another man has done the like, and made as fatal a mistake.

The first break-up of spring found the party following the ice-run of Elk River. It was an imposing fleet, for the outfit was large, and they were accompanied by a disreputable contingent of half-breed *voyageurs* with their women and children. Day in and day out, they labored with the *bateaux* and canoes, fought mosquitoes and other kindred pests, or sweated and swore at the portage. Severe toil like this lays a man naked to the very roots of his soul, and ere Lake Athabasca was lost in the south, each member of the party had hoisted his true colors.

The two shirks and chronic grumblers were Carter Weatherbee and Percy Cuthfert. The whole party complained less of its aches and pains than did either of them.

Not once did they volunteer for the thousand and one petty duties of the camp. A bucket of water to be brought, an extra armful of wood to be chopped, the dishes to be washed and wiped, a search to be made through the outfit for some suddenly indispensable article—and these two effete scions of civilization discovered sprains or blisters requiring instant attention. They were the first to turn in at night, with a score of tasks yet undone; the last to turn out in the morning, when the start should be in readiness before the breakfast was begun. They were the first to fall to at meal-time, the last to have a hand in the cooking; the first to dive for a slim delicacy, the last to discover they had added to their own another man's share. If they toiled at the oars, they slyly cut the water at each stroke and allowed the boat's momentum to float up the blade. They thought nobody noticed; but their comrades swore under their breaths and grew to hate them, while Jacques Baptiste sneered openly and damned them from morning till night. But Jacques Baptiste was no gentleman.

At the Great Slave, Hudson Bay dogs were purchased, and the fleet sank to the guards with its added burden of dried fish and pemmican. Then canoe and *bateau* answered to the swift current of the Mackenzie, and they plunged into the Great Barren Ground. Every likely-looking "feeder" was prospected, but the elusive "pay-dirt" danced ever to the north. At the Great Bear, overcome by the common dread of the Unknown Lands, their *voyageurs* began to desert, and Fort of Good Hope saw the last and bravest bending to the tow-lines as they bucked the current down which they had so treacherously glided. Jacques Baptiste alone remained. Had he not sworn to travel even to the never-opening ice?

The lying charts, compiled in main from hearsay, were now constantly consulted. And they felt the need of hurry, for the sun had already passed its northern solstice and was leading the winter south again. Skirting the shores of the bay, where the Mackenzie disembogues into the Arctic Ocean, they entered the mouth of the Little Peel River. Then began the arduous up-stream toil, and the two Incapables fared worse than ever. Tow-line and pole, paddle and tump-line, rapids and portages—such tortures served to give the one a deep disgust for great hazards, and printed for the other a fiery text on the true romance of adventure. One day they waxed mutinous and being vilely cursed by Jacques Baptiste, turned, as worms sometimes will. But the half-breed thrashed the twain, and sent them, bruised and bleeding, about their work. It was the first time either had been man-handled.

Abandoning their river craft at the headwaters of the Little Peel, they consumed the rest of the summer in the great portage over the Mackenzie watershed to the West Rat. This little stream fed the Porcupine, which in turn joined the Yukon where that mighty highway of the North counter-marches on the Arctic Circle. But they had lost in the race with winter, and one day they tied their rafts to the thick eddy-ice and hurried their goods ashore. That night the river jammed and broke several times; the following morning it had fallen asleep for good.

*   *   *

"We can't be more 'n four hundred miles from the Yukon," concluded Sloper, multiplying his thumbnails by the scale of the map. The council, in which the two Incapables had whined to excellent disadvantage, was drawing to a close.

"Hudson Bay Post, long time ago. No use um now." Jacques Baptiste's father had made the trip for the Fur Company in the old days, incidentally marking the trail with a couple of frozen toes.

"Sufferin' cracky!" cried another of the party. "No whites?"

"Nary white," Sloper sententiously affirmed; "but it's only five hundred more up the Yukon to Dawson. Call it a rough thousand from here."

Weatherbee and Cuthfert groaned in chorus.

"How long 'll that take, Baptiste?"

The half-breed figured for a moment. "Work 'um like hell, no man play out, ten—twenty—forty—fifty days. Um babies come" (designating the Incapables), "no can tell. Mebbe when hell freeze over; mebbe not then."

The manufacture of snowshoes and moccasins ceased. Somebody called the name of an absent member, who came out of an ancient cabin at the edge of the campfire and joined them. The cabin was one of the many mysteries which lurk in the vast recesses of the North. Built when and by whom, no man could tell. Two graves in the open, piled high with stones, perhaps contained the secret of those early wanderers. But whose hand had piled the stones?

The moment had come. Jacques Baptiste paused in the fitting of a harness and pinned the struggling dog in the snow. The cook made mute protest for delay, threw a handful of bacon into a noisy pot of beans, then came to attention. Sloper rose to his feet. His body was a ludicrous contrast to the healthy physiques of the Incapables. Yellow and weak, fleeing from a South American fever-hole, he had not broken his flight across the zones, and was still able to toil with men. His weight was probably ninety pounds, with the heavy hunting-knife thrown in, and his grizzled hair told of a prime which had ceased to be. The fresh young muscles of either Weatherbee or Cuthfert were equal to ten times the endeavor of his; yet he could walk them into the earth in a day's journey. And all this day he had whipped his stronger comrades into venturing a thousand miles of the stiffest hardship man can conceive. He was the incarnation of the unrest of his race, and the old Teutonic stubbornness, dashed with the quick grasp and action of the Yankee, held the flesh in the bondage of the spirit.

"All those in favor of going on with the dogs as soon as the ice sets, say ay."

"Ay!" rang out eight voices—voices destined to string a trail of oaths along many a hundred miles of pain.

"Contrary minded?"

"No!" For the first time the Incapables were united without some compromise of personal interests.

"And what are you going to do about it?" Weatherbee added belligerently.

"Majority rule! Majority rule!" clamored the rest of the party.

"I know the expedition is liable to fall through if you don't come," Sloper replied sweetly; "but I guess, if we try real hard, we can manage to do without you. What do you say, boys?"

The sentiment was cheered to the echo.

"But I say, you know," Cuthfert ventured apprehensively; "what's a chap like me to do?"

"Ain't you coming with us?"

"No-o."

"Then do as you damn well please. We won't have nothing to say."

"Kind o' calkilate yuh might settle it with that canoodlin' pardner of yourn," suggested a heavy-going Westerner from the Dakotas, at the same time pointing out Weatherbee. "He 'll be shore to ask yuh what yur a-goin' to do when it comes to cookin' an' gatherin' the wood."

"Then we'll consider it all arranged," concluded Sloper. "We 'll pull out to-morrow, if we camp within five miles—just to get everything in running order and remember if we've forgotten anything."

* * *

The sleds groaned by on their steel-shod runners, and the dogs strained low in the harnesses in which they were born to die. Jacques Baptiste paused by the side of Sloper to get a last glimpse of the cabin. The smoke curled up pathetically from the Yukon stove-pipe. The two Incapables were watching them from the doorway.

Sloper laid his hand on the other's shoulder.

"Jacques Baptiste, did you ever hear of the Kilkenny cats?"

The half-breed shook his head.

"Well, my friend and good comrade, the Kilkenny cats fought till neither hide, nor hair, nor yowl, was left. You understand?—till nothing was left. Very good. Now, these two men don't like work. They won't work. We know that. They'll be all alone in the cabin all winter—a mighty long, dark winter. Kilkenny cats—well?"

The Frenchman in Baptiste shrugged his shoulders, but the Indian in him was silent. Nevertheless, it was an eloquent shrug, pregnant with prophecy.

* * *

Things prospered in the little cabin at first. The rough badinage of their comrades had made Weatherbee and Cuthfert conscious of the mutual responsibility which had devolved upon them; besides, there was not so much work after all for two healthy men. And the removal of the cruel whip-hand, or in other words the bulldozing half-breed, had brought with it a joyous reaction. At first, each strove to outdo the other, and they performed petty tasks with an unction which would have opened the eyes of their comrades who were now wearing out bodies and souls on the Long Trail.

All care was banished. The forest, which shouldered in upon them from three sides, was an inexhaustible woodyard. A few yards from their door slept the Porcupine, and a hole through its winter robe formed a bubbling spring of water, crystal clear and painfully cold. But they soon grew to find fault with even that. The hole would persist in freezing up, and thus gave them many a miserable hour of ice-chopping. The unknown builders of the cabin had extended the side-logs so as to support a cache at the rear. In this was stored the bulk of the party's provisions. Food there was, without stint, for three times the men who were fated to live upon it. But the most of it was the kind which built up brawn and sinew, but did not tickle the palate. True, there was sugar in plenty for two ordinary men; but these two were little else than children.

They early discovered the virtues of hot water judiciously saturated with sugar, and they prodigally swam their flapjacks and
soaked their crusts in the rich, white syrup. Then coffee and
tea, and especially the dried fruits, made disastrous inroads
upon it. The first words they had were over the sugar question.
And it is a really serous thing when two men, wholly dependent upon each other for company, begin to quarrel.

Weatherbee loved to discourse blatantly on politics, while
Cuthfert, who had been prone to clip his coupons and let the
commonwealth jog on as best it might, either ignored the subject or delivered himself of startling epigrams. But the clerk
was too obtuse to appreciate the clever shaping of thought,
and this waste of ammunition irritated Cuthfert. He had been
used to blinding people by his brilliancy, and it worked him
quite a hardship, this loss of an audience. He felt person-
ally aggrieved and unconsciously held his mutton-head
companion responsible for it.

Save existence, they had nothing in common—came in
touch on no single point. Weatherbee was a clerk who had
known naught but clerking all his life; Cuthfert was a master
of arts, a dabbler in oils, and had written not a little. The one
was a lower-class man who considered himself a gentleman,
and the other was a gentleman who knew himself to be such.
From this it may be remarked that a man can be a gentleman
without possessing the first instinct of true comradeship. The
clerk was as sensuous as the other was aesthetic, and his love
adventures, told at great length and chiefly coined from his
imagination, affected the supersensitive master of arts in the
same way as so many whiffs of sewer gas. He deemed the
clerk a filthy, uncultured brute, whose place was in the muck

with the swine, and told him so; and he was reciprocally informed that he was a milk-and-water sissy and a cad. Weatherbee could not have defined "cad" for his life; but it satisfied its purpose, which after all seems the main point in life.

Weatherbee flatted every third note and sang such songs as "The Boston Burglar" and "The Handsome Cabin Boy," for hours at a time, while Cuthfert wept with rage, till he could stand it no longer and fled into the outer cold. But there was no escape. The intense frost could not be endured for long at a time, and the little cabin crowded them—beds, stove, table, and all—into a space of ten by twelve. The very presence of either became a personal affront to the other, and they lapsed into sullen silences which increased in length and strength as the days went by. Occasionally, the flash of an eye or the curl of a lip got the better of them, though they strove to wholly ignore each other during these mute periods. And a great wonder sprang up in the breast of each, as to how God had ever come to create the other.

With little to do, time became an intolerable burden to them. This naturally made them still lazier. They sank into a physical lethargy which there was no escaping, and which made them rebel at the performance of the smallest chore. One morning when it was his turn to cook the common breakfast, Weatherbee rolled out of his blankets, and to the snoring of his companion, lighted first the slush-lamp and then the fire. The kettles were frozen hard, and there was no water in the cabin with which to wash. But he did not mind that. Waiting for it to thaw, he sliced the bacon and plunged into the hateful task of bread-making. Cuthfert had been slyly watching through his half-closed lids. Consequently there was a scene, in which they fervently blessed each other, and agreed, thenceforth, that each do his own cooking. A week later, Cuthfert neglected his morning ablutions, but none the less complacently ate the meal which he had cooked. Weatherbee grinned. After that the foolish custom of washing passed out of their lives.

As the sugar-pile and other little luxuries dwindled, they began to be afraid they were not getting their proper shares, and in order that they might not be robbed, they fell to gorging themselves. The luxuries suffered in this gluttonous contest, as did also the men. In the absence of fresh vegetables and exercise, their blood became impoverished, and a loathsome, purplish rash crept over their bodies. Yet they refused to heed the warning. Next, their muscles and joints began to swell, the flesh turning black, while their mouths, gums, and lips took on the color of rich cream. Instead of being drawn together by their misery, each gloated over the other's symptoms as the scurvy took its course.

They lost all regard for personal appearance, and for that matter, common decency. The cabin became a pigpen, and never once were the beds made or fresh pine boughs laid underneath. Yet they could not keep to their blankets, as they would have wished; for the frost was inexorable, and the fire box consumed much fuel. The hair of their heads and faces grew long and shaggy, while their garments would have disgusted a rag picker. But they did not care. They were sick, and there was no one to see; besides, it was very painful to move about.

To all this was added a new trouble—the Fear of the North. This Fear was the joint child of the Great Cold and the Great Silence, and was born in the darkness of December, when the sun dipped below the southern horizon for good. It affected them according to their natures. Weatherbee fell prey to the grosser superstitions, and did his best to resurrect the spirits which slept in the forgotten graves. It was a fascinating thing, and in his dreams they came to him from out of the cold, and snuggled into his blankets, and told him of their toils and troubles ere they died. He shrank away from the clammy contact as they drew closer and twined their frozen limbs about him, and when they whispered in his ear of things to come, the cabin rang with his frightened shrieks. Cuthfert did not understand—for they no longer spoke—and when thus awakened he invariably grabbed for his revolver. Then he would sit up in bed, shivering nervously, with the weapon trained on the unconscious dreamer. Cuthfert deemed the man going mad, and so came to fear for his life.

His own malady assumed a less concrete form. The mysterious artisan who had laid the cabin, log by log, had pegged a wind-vane to the ridge-pole. Cuthfert noticed it always pointed south, and one day, irritated by its steadfastness of purpose, he turned it toward the east. He watched eagerly, but never a breath came by to disturb it. Then he turned the vane to the north, swearing never again to touch it till the wind did blow. But the air frightened him with its unearthly calm, and he often rose in the middle of the night to see if the vane had veered— ten degrees would have satisfied him. But no, it poised above him as unchangeable as fate. His imagination ran riot, till it became to him a fetish. Sometimes he followed the path it pointed across the dismal dominions, and allowed his soul to become saturated with the Fear. He dwelt upon the unseen and the unknown till the burden of eternity appeared to be crushing him. Everything in the Northland had that crushing effect—the absence of life and motion; the darkness; the infinite peace of the brooding land; the ghastly silence, which made the echo of each heart-beat a sacrilege; the solemn forest which seemed to guard an awful, inexpressible something, which neither word nor thought could compass.

The world he had so recently left, with its busy nations and great enterprises, seemed very far away. Recollections occasionally obtruded—recollections of marts and galleries and crowded thoroughfares, of evening dress and social functions, of good men and dear women he had known—but they were dim memories of a life he had lived long centuries agone, on some other planet. The phantasm was the Reality. Standing beneath the wind-vane, his eyes fixed on the polar skies, he could not bring himself to realize that the Southland really existed, that at that very moment it was a-roar with life and action. There was no Southland, no men being born of women, no giving and taking in marriage. Beyond his bleak sky-line there stretched vast solitudes, and beyond these still vaster solitudes. There were no lands of sunshine, heavy with the perfume of flowers. Such things were only old dreams of paradise. The sunlands of the West and the spicelands of the East, the smiling Arcadias and blissful Islands of the Blest—ha! Ha! His laughter split the void and shocked him with its unwonted sound. There was no sun. This was the Universe, dead and cold and dark, and he its only citizen. Weatherbee? At such moments Weatherbee did not count. He was a Caliban, a monstrous phantom, fettered to him for untold ages, the penalty of some forgotten crime.

He lived with Death among the dead, emasculated by the sense of his own insignificance, crushed by the passive mastery of the slumbering ages. The magnitude of all things appalled him. Everything partook of the superlative save himself—the perfect cessation of wind and motion, the immensity of the snow-covered wilderness, the height of the sky and the depth of the silence. That wind-vane—if it would only move. If a thunderbolt would fall, or the forest flare up in flame. The rolling up of the heavens as a scroll, the crash of Doom—anything, anything! But no, nothing moved; the Silence crowded in, and the Fear of the North laid icy fingers on his heart.

Once, like another Crusoe, by the edge of the river he came upon a track—the faint tracery of a snowshoe rabbit on the delicate snow-crust. It was a revelation. There was life in the Northland. He would follow it, look upon it, gloat over it. He forgot his swollen muscles, plunging through the deep snow in an ecstasy of anticipation. The forest swallowed him up, and the brief midday twilight vanished; but he pursued his quest till exhausted nature asserted itself and laid him helpless in the snow. There he groaned and cursed his folly, and knew the track to be the fancy of his brain; and late that night he dragged himself into the cabin on hands and knees, his cheeks frozen and a strange numbness about his feet. Weatherbee grinned malevolently, but made no offer to help him. He thrust needles into his toes and thawed them out by the stove. A week later mortification set in.

But the clerk had his own troubles. The dead men came out of their graves more frequently now, and rarely left him, waking or sleeping. He grew to wait and dread their coming, never passing the twin cairns without a shudder. One night they came to him in his sleep and led him forth to an appointed task. Frightened into inarticulate horror, he awoke between the heaps of stones and fled wildly to the cabin. But he had lain there for some time, for his feet and cheeks were also frozen.

Sometimes he became frantic at their insistent presence, and danced about the cabin, cutting the empty air with an axe, and smashing everything within reach. During these ghostly encounters, Cuthfert huddled into his blankets and followed the madman about with a cocked revolver, ready to shoot him if he came too near. But, recovering from one of these spells, the clerk noticed the weapon trained upon him. His suspicions were aroused, and thenceforth he, too, lived in fear of his life. They watched each other closely after that, and faced about in startled fright whenever either passed behind the other's back. This apprehensiveness became a mania which controlled them even in their sleep. Through mutual fear they tacitly let the slush-lamp burn all night, and saw to a plentiful supply of bacon-grease before retiring. The slightest movement on the part of one was sufficient to arouse the other, and many a still watch their gazes countered as they shook beneath their blankets with fingers on the trigger-guards.

What with the Fear of the North, the mental strain, and the ravages of the disease, they lost all semblance of humanity, taking on the appearance of wild beasts, hunted and desperate. Their cheeks and noses, as an aftermath of the freezing, had turned black. Their frozen toes had begun to drop away at the first and second joints. Every movement brought pain, but the fire box was insatiable, wringing a ransom of torture from their miserable bodies. Day in, day out, it demanded its food—a veritable pound of flesh—and they dragged themselves into the forest to chop wood on their knees. Once, crawling thus in search of dry sticks, unknown to each other they entered a thicket from opposite sides. Suddenly, without warning, two peering death's-heads confronted each other. Suffering had so transformed them that recognition was impossible. They sprang to their feet, shrieking with terror, and dashed away on their mangled stumps; and falling at the cabin door, they clawed and scratched like demons till they discovered their mistake.

*   *   *

Occasionally they lapsed normal, and during one of these sane intervals, the chief bone of contention, the sugar, had been divided equally between them. They guarded their separate sacks, stored up in the cache, with jealous eyes; for there were but a few cupfuls left, and they were totally devoid of faith in each other. But one day, Cuthfert made a mistake. Hardly able to move, sick with pain, with his head swimming and eyes blinded, he crept into the cache, sugar canister in hand, and mistook Weatherbee's sack for his own.

January had been born but a few days when this occurred. The sun had some time since passed its lowest southern declination, and at meridian now threw flaunting streaks of yellow light upon the northern sky. On the day following his mistake with the sugar-bag, Cuthfert found himself feeling better, both in body and in spirit. As noontime drew near and the day brightened, he dragged himself outside to feast on the evanescent glow, which was to him an earnest of the sun's future intentions. Weatherbee was also feeling somewhat better, and crawled out beside him. They propped themselves in the snow beneath the moveless wind-vane, and waited.

The stillness of death was about them. In other climes, when nature falls into such moods, there is a subdued air of expectancy, a waiting for some small voice to take up the broken strain. Not so in the North. The two men had lived seeming aeons in this ghostly peace. They could remember no song of the past; they could conjure no song of the future. This unearthly calm had always been—the tranquil silence of eternity.

Their eyes were fixed upon the north. Unseen, behind their backs, behind the towering mountains to the south, the sun swept toward the zenith of another sky than theirs. Sole spectators of the mighty canvas, they watched the false dawn slowly grow. A faint flame began to glow and smolder. It deepened in intensity, ringing the changes of reddish-yellow, purple, and saffron. So bright did it become that Cuthfert thought the sun must surely be behind it—a miracle, the sun rising in the north! Suddenly, without warning and without fading, the canvas was swept clean. There was no color in the sky. The light had gone out of the day. They caught their breaths in half-sobs. But lo! The air was a-glint with particles of scintillating frost, and there, to the north, the wind-vane lay in vague outline on the snow. A shadow! A shadow! It was exactly midday. They jerked their heads hurriedly to the south. A golden rim peeped over the mountain's snowy shoulder, smiled upon them an instant, then dipped from sight again.

There were tears in their eyes as they sought each other. A strange softening came over them. They felt irresistibly drawn toward each other. The sun was coming back again. It would be with them to-morrow, and the next day, and the next. And it would stay longer every visit, and a time would come when it would ride their heaven day and night, never once dropping below the sky-line. There would be no night. The ice-locked winter would be broken; the winds would blow and the forest answer; the land would bathe in the blessed sunshine, and life renew. Hand in hand, they would quit this horrid dream and journey back to the Southland. They lurched blindly forward, and their hands met—their poor maimed hands, swollen and distorted beneath their mittens.

But the promise was destined to remain unfulfilled. The Northland is the Northland, and men work out their souls by strange rules, which other men, who have not journeyed into far countries, cannot come to understand.

* * *

An hour later, Cuthfert put a pan of bread into the oven, and fell to speculating on what the surgeons could do with his feet when he got back. Home did not seem so very far away now. Weatherbee was rummaging in the cache. Of a sudden, he raised a whirlwind of blasphemy, which in turn ceased with startling abruptness. The other man had robbed his sugar-sack. Still, things might have happened differently, had not the two dead men come out from under the stones and hushed the hot words in this throat. They led him quite gently from the cache, which he forgot to close. That consummation was reached; that something they had whispered to him in his dreams was about to happen. They guided him gently, very gently to the woodpile, where they put the axe in his hands. Then they helped him shove open the cabin door, and he felt sure they shut it after him—at least he heard it slam and the latch fall sharply into place. And he knew they were waiting just without, waiting for him to do his task.

"Carter! I say, Carter!"

Percy Cuthfert was frightened at the look on the clerk's face, and he made haste to put the table between them.

Carter Weatherbee followed, without haste and without enthusiasm. There was neither pity nor passion in his face, but rather the patient, stolid look of one who has certain work to do and goes about it methodically.

"I say, what's the matter?"

The clerk dodged back, cutting off his retreat to the door, but never opening his mouth.

"I say, Carter, I say; let's talk. There's a good chap."

The master of arts was thinking rapidly, now, shaping a skillful flank movement on the bed where his Smith & Wesson lay. Keeping his eyes on the madman, he rolled backward on the bunk, at the same time clutching the pistol.

"Carter!"

The powder flashed full in Weatherbee's face, but he swung his weapon and leaped forward. The axe bit deeply at the base of the spine, and Percy Cuthfert felt all consciousness of his lower limbs leave him. Then the clerk fell heavily upon him, clutching him by the throat with feeble fingers. The sharp bite of the axe had caused Cuthfert to drop the pistol, and as his lungs panted for release, he fumbled aimlessly for it among the blankets. Then he remembered. He slid a hand up the clerk's belt to the sheath-knife; and they drew very close to each other in that last clinch.

Percy Cuthfert felt his strength leave him. The lower portion of his body was useless. The inert weight of Weatherbee crushed him—crushed him and pinned him there like a bear under a trap. The cabin became filled with a familiar odor, and he knew the bread to be burning. Yet what did it matter? He would never need it. And there were all of six cupfuls of sugar in the cache—if he had foreseen this he would not have been so saving the last several days. Would the wind-vane ever move? It might even be veering now. Why not? Had he not seen the sun to-day? He would go and see. No; it was impossible to move. He had not thought the clerk so heavy a man.

How quickly the cabin cooled! The fire must be out. The cold was forcing in. It must be below zero already, and the ice creeping up the inside of the door. He could not see it, but his past experience enabled him to gauge its progress by the cabin's temperature. The lower hinge must be white ere now. Would the tale of this ever reach the world? How would his friends take it? They would read it over their coffee, most likely, and talk it over at the clubs. He could see them very clearly. "Poor Old Cuthfert," they murmured; "not such a bad sort of a chap, after all." He smiled at their eulogies, and passed on in search of a Turkish bath. It was the same old crowd upon the streets. Strange, they did not notice his moosehide moccasins and tattered German socks! He would take a cab. And after the bath a shave would not be bad. No; he would eat first. Steak, and potatoes, and green things— how fresh it all was! And what was that? Squares of honey, streaming liquid amber! But why did they bring so much? Ha! Ha! He could never eat it all. Shine! Why certainly. He put his foot on the box. The bootblack looked curiously up at him, and he remembered his moosehide moccasins and went away hastily.

Hark! The wind-vane must be surely spinning. No; a mere singing in his ears. That was all—a mere singing. The ice must have passed the latch by now. More likely the upper hinge was covered. Between the moss-chinked roof-poles, little points of frost began to appear. How slowly they grew! No; not so slowly. There was a new one, and there another. Two—three—four; they were coming too fast to count. There were two growing together. And there, a third had joined them. Why, there were no more spots. They had run together and formed a sheet.

Well, he would have company. If Gabriel ever broke the silence of the North, they would stand together, hand in hand, before the great White Throne. And God would judge them, God would judge them!

Then Percy Cuthfert closed his eyes and dropped off to sleep.

from: *The Son of the Wolf*

The White Silence

"Carmen won't last more than a couple of days," Mason spat out a chunk of ice and surveyed the poor animal ruefully, then put her foot in his mouth and proceeded to bite out the ice which clustered cruelly between the toes.

"I never saw a dog with a highfalutin' name that ever was worth a rap," he said, as he concluded his task and shoved her aside. "They just fade away and die under the responsibility. Did ye ever see one go wrong with a sensible name like Cassiar, Siwash, or Husky? No, sir! Take a look at Shookum here, he's—"

Snap! The lean brute flashed up, the white teeth just missing Mason's throat.

"Ye will, will ye?" A shrewd clout behind the ear with the butt of the dogwhip stretched the animal in the snow, quivering softly, a yellow slaver dripping from its fangs.

"As I was saying, just look at Shookum, here—he's got the spirit. Bet ye he eats Carmen before the week's out."

"I'll bank another proposition against that," replied Malemute Kid, reversing the frozen bread placed before the fire to thaw. "We'll eat Shookum before the trip is over. What d' ye say, Ruth?"

The Indian woman settled the coffee with a piece of ice, glanced from Malemute Kid to her husband, then at the dogs, but vouchsafed no reply. It was such a palpable truism that none was necessary. Two hundred miles of unbroken trail in prospect, with a scant six days' grub for themselves and none for the dogs, could admit no other alternative. The two men and the woman grouped about the fire and began their meager meal. The dogs lay in their harnesses, for it was a midday halt, and watched each mouthful enviously.

"No more lunches after to-day," said Malemute Kid. "And we've got to keep a close eye on the dogs—they're getting vicious. They'd just as soon pull a fellow down as not, if they get a chance."

"And I was president of an Epworth once, and taught in the Sunday school." Having irrelevantly delivered himself of this, Mason fell into a dreamy contemplation of his steaming moccasins, but was aroused by Ruth filling his cup. "Thank God, we've got slathers of tea! I've seen it growing, down in Tennessee. What wouldn't I give for a hot corn pone just now! Never mind, Ruth; you won't starve much longer, nor wear moccasins either."

The woman threw off her gloom at this, and in her eyes welled up a great love for her white lord—the first white man she had ever seen—the first man whom she had known to treat a woman as something better than a mere animal or beast of burden.

"Yes, Ruth," continued her husband, having recourse to the macaronic jargon in which it was alone possible for them to understand each other; "wait till we clean up and pull for the Outside. We'll take the White Man's canoe and go to the Salt Water. Yes, bad water, rough water—great mountains dance up and down all the time. And so big, so far, so far away—you travel ten sleep, twenty sleep, forty sleep" (he graphically enumerated the days on his fingers), "all the time water, bad water. Then you come to great village, plenty people, just the same mosquitoes next summer. Wigwams oh, so high—ten, twenty pines. Hi-yu skookum!"

He paused impotently, cast an appealing glace at Malemute Kid, then laboriously placed the twenty pines, end on end, by sign language. Malemute Kid smiled with cheery cynicism; but Ruth's eyes were wide with wonder, and with pleasure; for she half believed he was joking, and such condescension pleased her poor woman's heart.

"And then you step into a—a box, and pouf! Up you go." He tossed his empty cup in the air by way of illustration, and as he deftly caught it, cried: "And biff! Down you come. Oh, great medicine-men! You go Fort Yukon, I go Arctic City—twenty-five sleep—big string, all the time—I catch him string—I say 'Hello, Ruth! How are ye?'—and you say, 'Is that my good husband?'—and I say 'Yes,'—and you say, 'No can bake good bread, no more soda,'—then I say, 'Look in cache, under flour; good-by.' You look and catch plenty soda. All the time you Fort Yukon, me Arctic City. Hi-yu medicine-man!"

Ruth smiled so ingenuously at the fairy story that both men burst into laughter. A row among the dogs cut short the wonders of the Outside, and by the time the snarling combatants were separated, she had lashed the sleds and all was ready for the trail.

*   *   *

"Mush! Baldy! Hi! Mush on!" Mason worked his whip smartly, and as the dogs whined low in the traces, broke out the sled with the gee-pole. Ruth followed with the second team, leaving Malemute Kid, who had helped her start, to bring up the rear. Strong man, brute that he was, capable of felling an ox at a blow, he could not bear to beat the poor animals, but humored them as a dog-driver rarely does—nay, almost wept with them in their misery.

"Come, mush on there, you poor sore-footed brutes!" he murmured, after several ineffectual attempts to start the load. But his patience was at last rewarded, and though whimpering with pain, they hastened to join their fellows.

No more conversation; the toil of the trail will not permit such extravagance. And of all deadening labors, that of the Northland trail is the worst. Happy is the man who can weather a day's travel at the price of silence, and that on a beaten track.

And of all heart-breaking labors, that of breaking trail is the worst. At every step the great webbed shoe sinks till the snow is level with the knee. Then up, straight up, the deviation of a fraction of an inch being a certain precursor of disaster, the snowshoe must be lifted till the surface is cleared;

then forward, down, and the other foot is raised perpendicu-
larly for the matter of half a yard. He who tries this for the
first time, if haply he avoids bringing his shoes in dangerous
propinquity and measures not his length on the treacherous
footing, will give up exhausted at the end of a hundred yards;
he who can keep out of the way of the dogs for a whole day
may well crawl into his sleeping-bag with a clear conscience
and a pride which passeth all understanding; and he who
travels twenty sleeps on the Long Trail is a man whom the
gods may envy.

The afternoon wore on, and with awe, born of the White
Silence, the voiceless travelers bent to their work. Nature has
many tricks wherewith she convinces man of his finity—the
ceaseless flow of the tides, the fury of the storm, the shock of
the earthquake, the long roll of heaven's artillery—but the
most tremendous, the most stupefying of all, is the passive
phase of the White Silence. All movement ceases, the sky
clears, the heavens are as brass; the slightest whisper seems
sacrilege, and man becomes timid, affrighted at the sound of
his own voice. Sole speck of life journeying across the ghostly
wastes of a dead world, he trembles at his audacity, realizes
that his is a maggot's life, nothing more. Strange thoughts
arise unsummoned, and the mystery of all things strives for
utterance. And the fear of death, of God, of the universe,
comes over him—the hope of the Resurrection and the Life,
the yearning for immortality, the vain striving of the imprisoned essence—it is then, if ever, man walks alone with God.

So wore the day away. The river took a great bend, and
Mason headed his team for the cut-off across the narrow neck
of land, but the dogs balked at the high bank. Again and again,

though Ruth and Malemute Kid were shoving on the sled, they slipped back. Then came the concerted effort. The miserable creatures, weak from hunger, exerted their last strength. Up—up—the sled poised on the top of the bank; but the leader swung the string of dogs behind him to the right, fouling Mason's snowshoes. The result was grievous. Mason was whipped off his feet; one of the dogs fell in the traces; and the sled toppled back dragging everything to the bottom again.

Slash! The whip fell among the dogs savagely, especially upon the one which had fallen.

"Don't Mason," entreated Malemute Kid; "the poor devil's on its last legs. Wait and we'll put my team on."

Mason deliberately withheld the whip till the last word had fallen, then out flashed the long lash, completely curling about the offending creature's body. Carmen—for it was Carmen—cowered in the snow, cried piteously, then rolled over on her side.

It was a tragic moment, a pitiful incident of the trail—a dying dog, two comrades in anger. Ruth glanced solicitously from man to man. But Malemute Kid restrained himself, though there was a world of reproach in his eyes, and bending over the dog, cut the traces. No word was spoken. The teams were double-spanned and the difficulty overcome; the sleds were under way again, the dying dog dragging herself along in the rear. As long as an animal can travel, it is not shot, and this last chance is accorded it—the crawling into camp, if it can, in the hope of a moose being killed.

Already penitent for his angry action, but too stubborn to make amends, Mason toiled on at the head of the cavalcade, little dreaming that danger hovered in the air. The timber clustered thick in the sheltered bottom, and through this they threaded their way. Fifty feet or more from the trail towered a lofty pine. For generations it had stood there, and for generations destiny had had this one end in view—perhaps the same had been decreed of Mason.

He stooped to fasten the loosened thong of his moccasin. The sleds came to a halt and the dogs lay down in the snow without a whimper. The stillness was weird; not a breath rustled the frost-encrusted forest; the cold and silence of outer space had chilled the heart and smote the trembling lips of nature. A sigh pulsed through the air—they did not seem to actually hear it, but rather felt it, like the premonition of movement in a motionless void. Then the great tree, burdened with its weight of years and snow, played its last part in the tragedy of life. He heard the warning crash and attempted to spring up, but almost erect, caught the blow squarely on the shoulder.

The sudden danger, the quick death—how often had Malemute Kid faced it! The pine needles were still quivering as he gave his commands and sprang into action. Nor did the Indian girl faint or raise her voice in idle wailing, as might many of her white sisters. At his order, she threw her weight on the end of a quickly extemporized handspike, easing the pressure and listening to her husband's groans, while Malemute Kid attacked the tree with his axe. The steel rang merrily as it bit into the frozen trunk, each stroke being accompanied by a forced, audible respiration, the "Huh!" "Huh!" of the woodsman.

At last the Kid laid the pitiable thing that was once a man in the snow. But worse than his comrade's pain was the dumb anguish in the woman's face, the blended look of hopeful, hopeless query. Little was said; those of the Northland are early taught the futility of words and the inestimable value of deeds. With the temperature at sixty-five below zero, a man cannot lie many minutes in the snow and live. So the sled-lashings were cut, and the sufferer, rolled in furs, laid on a couch of boughs. Before him roared a fire, built of the very wood which wrought the mishap. Behind and partially over him was stretched the primitive fly—a piece of canvas, which caught the radiating heat and threw it back and down upon him—a trick which men may know who study physics at the fount.

And men who have shared their bed with death know when the call is sounded. Mason was terribly crushed. The most cursory examination revealed it. His right arm, leg, and back, were broken; his limbs were paralyzed from the hips; and the likelihood of internal injuries was large. An occasional moan was his only sign of life.

No hope; nothing to be done. The pitiless night crept slowly by—Ruth's portion, the despairing stoicism of her race, and Malemute Kid adding new lines to his face of bronze. In fact, Mason suffered least of all, for he spent his time in Eastern Tennessee, in the Great Smoky Mountains, living over the scenes of his childhood. And most pathetic was the melody of his long-forgotten Southern vernacular, as he raved of swimming-holes and coon-hunts and watermelon raids. It was as Greek to Ruth, but the Kid understood and felt—felt as only one can feel who has been shut out for years from all that civilization means.

Morning brought consciousness to the stricken man, and Malemute Kid bent closer to catch his whispers.

"You remember when we foregathered on the Tanana, four years come next ice-run? I didn't care so much for her then. It was more like she was pretty, and there was a smack of excitement about it, I think. But d' ye know, I've come to think a heap of her. She's been a good wife to me, always at my shoulder in the pinch. And when it comes to trading, you know there isn't her equal. D' ye recollect the time she shot the Moosehorn Rapids to pull you and me off that rock, the bullets whipping the water like hailstones?—and the time of the famine at Nuklukyeto?—or when she raced the ice-run to bring the news? Yes, she's been a good wife to me, better 'n that other one. Didn't know I'd been there? Never told you, eh? Well, I tried it once, down in the States. That's why I'm here. Been raised together, too. I came away to give her a chance for divorce. She got it.

"But that's got nothing to do with Ruth. I had thought of cleaning up and pulling for the Outside next year—her and I—but it's too late. Don't send her back to her people, Kid. It's beastly hard for a woman to go back. Think of it!—nearly four years on our bacon and beans and flour and dried fruit, and then to go back to her fish and caribou. It's not good for her to have tried our ways, to come to know they're better 'n her people's, and then return to them. Take care of her, Kid—why don't you—but no, you always fought shy of them—and you never told me why you came to this country. Be kind to her, and send her back to the States as soon as you can. But fix it so as she can come back—liable to get homesick, you know.

"And the youngster—it's drawn us closer, Kid. I only hope it is a boy. Think of it!—flesh of my flesh, Kid. He mustn't stop in this country. And if it's a girl, why she can't. Sell my furs; they'll fetch at least five thousand, and I've got as much more with the company. And handle my interests with yours. I think that bench claim will show up. See that he gets a good school; and Kid, above all, don't let him come back. This country was not made for white men.

"I'm a gone man, Kid. Three or four sleeps at the best. You've got to go on. You must go on! Remember, it's my wife, it's my boy—O God! I hope it's a boy! You can't stay by me— and I charge you, a dying man, to pull on."

"Give me three days," pleaded Malemute Kid. "You may change for the better; something may turn up."

"No."

"Just three days."

"You must pull on."

"Two days."

"It's my wife and my body, Kid. You would not ask it."

"One day."

"No, no! I charge—"

"Only one day. We can shave it through on the grub, and I might knock over a moose."

"No—all right; one day, but not a minute more. And Kid, don't—don't leave me to face it alone. Just a shot, one pull on the trigger. You understand. Think of it! Think of it! Flesh of my flesh, and I'll never live to see him!

"Send Ruth here. I want to say good-by and tell her that she must think of the boy and not wait till I'm dead. She might refuse to go with you if I didn't. Good-by, old man; good-by.

"Kid! I say—a—sink a hole above the pup, next to the slide. I panned out forty cents on my shovel there.

"And Kid!" He stooped lower to catch the last faint words, the dying man's surrender of his pride. "I'm sorry—for—you know—Carmen."

Leaving the girl crying softly over her man, Malemute Kid slipped into his *parka* and snowshoes, tucked his rifle under his arm, and crept away into the forest. He was no tyro in the stern sorrows of the Northland, but never had he faced so stiff a problem as this. In the abstract, it was a plain, mathematical proposition—three possible lives as against one doomed one. But now he hesitated. For five years, shoulder to shoulder, on the rivers and trails, in the camps and mines, facing death by field and flood and famine, had they knitted the bonds of their comradeship. So close was the tie that he had often been conscious of a vague jealousy of Ruth, from the first time she had come between. And now it must be severed by his own hand.

Though he prayed for a moose, just one moose, all game seemed to have deserted the land, and nightfall found the exhausted man crawling into camp, light-handed, heavy-hearted. An uproar from the dogs and shrill cries from Ruth hastened him.

Bursting into the camp, he saw the girl in the midst of the snarling pack, laying about her with an axe. The dogs had broken the iron rule of their masters and were rushing the grub. He joined the issue with his rifle reversed, and the hoary game of natural selection was played out with all the ruthlessness of its primeval environment. Rifle and axe went up and down, hit or missed with monotonous regularity; lithe bodies flashed, with wild eyes and dripping fangs; and man and beast fought for supremacy to the bitterest conclusion.

Then the beaten brutes crept to the edge of the firelight, licking their wounds, voicing their misery to the stars.

The whole stock of dried salmon had been devoured, and perhaps five pounds of flour remained to tide them over two hundred miles of wilderness. Ruth returned to her husband, while Malemute Kid cut up the warm body of one of the dogs, the skull of which had been crushed by the axe. Every portion was carefully put away, save the hide and offal, which were cast to his fellows of the moment before.

Morning brought fresh trouble. The animals were turning on each other. Carmen, who still clung to her slender thread of life, was downed by the pack. The lash fell among them unheeded. They cringed and cried under the blows, but refused to scatter till the last wretched bit had disappeared—bones, hide, hair, everything.

Malemute Kid went about his work, listening to Mason, who was back in Tennessee, delivering tangled discourses and wild exhortations to his brethren of other days.

Taking advantage of neighboring pines, he worked rapidly, and Ruth watched him make a cache similar to those sometimes used by hunters to preserve their meat from the wolverines and dogs. One after the other, he bent the tops of two small pines toward each other and nearly to the ground, making them fast with thongs of moose hide. Then he beat the dogs into submission and harnessed them to two of the sleds, loading the same with everything but the furs which enveloped Mason. These he wrapped and lashed tightly about him, fastening either end of the robes to the bent pines. A single stroke of his hunting-knife would release them and send the body high in the air.

Ruth had received her husband's last wishes and made no struggle. Poor girl, she had learned the lesson of obedience well. From a child, she had bowed, and seen all women bow, to the lords of creation, and it did not seem in the nature of things for woman to resist. The Kid permitted her one outburst of grief, as she kissed her husband—her own people had no such custom—then led her to the foremost sled and helped her into her snowshoes. Blindly, instinctively, she took the gee-pole and whip, and "mushed" the dogs out on the trail. Then he returned to Mason, who had fallen into a coma; and long after she was out of sight, crouched by the fire, waiting, hoping, praying for his comrade to die.

It is not pleasant to be alone with painful thoughts in the White Silence. The silence of gloom is merciful, shrouding one as with protection and breathing a thousand intangible sympathies; but the bright White Silence, clear and cold, under steely skies, is pitiless.

An hour passed—two hours—but the man would not die. At high noon, the sun, without raising its rim above the southern horizon, threw a suggestion of fire athwart the heavens, then quickly drew it back. Malemute Kid roused and dragged himself to his comrade's side. He cast one glance about him. The White Silence seemed to sneer, and a great fear came upon him. There was a sharp report; Mason swung into his aerial sepulcher; and Malemute Kid lashed the dogs into a wild gallop as he fled across the snow.

from: *The Call of the Wild*

For the Love of a Man

When John Thornton froze his feet in the previous December, his partners had made him comfortable and left him to get well, going on themselves up the river to get out a raft of saw-logs for Dawson. He was still limping slightly at the time he rescued Buck, but with the continued warm weather even the slight limp left him. And here, lying by the riverbank through the long spring days, watching the running water, listening lazily to the songs of birds and the hum of nature, Buck slowly won back his strength.

A rest comes very good after one has traveled three thousand miles, and it must be confessed that Buck waxed lazy as his wounds healed, his muscles swelled out, and the flesh came back to cover his bones. For that matter, they were all loafing—Buck, John Thornton and Skeet and Nig—waiting for the raft to come that was to carry them down to Dawson.

Skeet was a little Irish setter who early made friends with Buck, who, in a dying condition, was unable to resent her first advances. She had the doctor trait which some dogs possess; and as a mother cat washes her kittens, so she washed and cleansed Buck's wounds. Regularly, each morning after he had finished his breakfast, she performed her self-appointed task, till he came to look for her ministrations as much as he did for Thornton's. Nig, equally friendly, though less demonstrative, was a huge black dog, half bloodhound and half deerhound, with eyes that laughed and a boundless good nature.

To Buck's surprise these dogs manifested no jealousy toward him. They seemed to share the kindliness and largeness of John Thornton. As Buck grew stronger they enticed him into all sorts of ridiculous games, in which Thornton himself could not forbear to join; and in this fashion Buck romped through his convalescence and into a new existence. Love, genuine passionate love, was his for the first time. This he had never experienced at Judge Miller's down in the sun-kissed Santa Clara Valley. With the Judge's sons, hunting and tramping, it had been a working partnership; with the Judge's grandsons, a sort of pompous guardianship; and with the Judge himself, a stately and dignified friendship. But love that was feverish and burning, that was adoration, that was madness, it had taken John Thornton to arouse.

This man had saved his life, which was something; but, further, he was the ideal master. Other men saw to the welfare of their dogs from a sense of duty and business expediency; he saw to the welfare of his as if they were his own children, because he could not help it. And he saw further. He never forgot a kindly greeting or a cheering word, and to sit down for a long talk with them ("gas" he called it) was as much his delight as theirs. He had a way of taking Buck's head roughly between his hands, and resting his own head upon Buck's, of shaking him back and forth, the while calling him ill names that to Buck were love names. Buck knew no greater joy than that rough embrace and the sound of murmured oaths, and at each jerk back and forth it seemed that his heart would be shaken out of his body so great was its ecstasy. And when, released, he sprang to his feet, his mouth laughing, his eye eloquent, his throat vibrant with unuttered sound, and in that fashion remain without movement, John Thornton would reverently exclaim, "God! You can all but speak!"

Buck had a trick of love expression that was akin to hurt. He would often seize Thornton's hand in his mouth and close so fiercely that the flesh bore the impress of his teeth for some time afterward. And as Buck understood the oaths to be love words, so the man understood this feigned bite for a caress.

For the most part, however, Buck's love was expressed in adoration. While he went wild with happiness when Thornton touched him or spoke to him, he did not seek these tokens. Unlike Skeet, who was wont to shove her nose under Thornton's hand and nudge and nudge till petted, or Nig, who would stalk up and rest his great head on Thornton's knee, Buck was content to adore at a distance. He would lie by the hour, eager, alert, at Thornton's feet, looking up into his face, dwelling upon it, studying it, following with keenest interest each fleeting expression, every movement or change of feature. Or, as chance might have it, he would lie farther away, to the side or rear, watching the outlines of the man and the occasional movements of his body. And often, such was the communion in which they lived, the strength of Buck's gaze would draw John Thornton's head around, and he would return the gaze, without speech, his heart shining out of his eyes as Buck's heart shone out.

For a long time after his rescue, Buck did not like Thornton to get out of his sight. From the moment he left the tent to when he entered it again, Buck would follow at his heels. His transient masters since he had come into the Northland had bred in him a fear that no master could be permanent. He was afraid that Thornton would pass out of his life as Perrault and François and the Scotch half-breed had passed out. Even in the night, in his dreams, he was haunted by this fear. At such times he would shake off sleep and creep through the chill to the flap of the tent, where he would stand and listen to the sound of his master's breathing.

But in spite of this great love he bore John Thornton, which seemed to bespeak the soft civilizing influence, the strain of the primitive, which the Northland had aroused in him, remained alive and active. Faithfulness and devotion, things born of fire and roof, were his; yet he retained his wildness and wiliness. He was a thing of the wild, come in from the wild to sit by John Thornton's fire, rather than a dog of the soft Southland stamped with the marks of generations of civilization. Because of his very great love, he could not steal from this man, but from any other man, in any other camp, he did not hesitate an instant; while the cunning with which he stole enabled him to escape detection.

His face and body were scored by the teeth of many dogs, and he fought as fiercely as ever and more shrewdly. Skeet and Nig were too good-natured for quarrelling—besides, they belonged to John Thornton; but the strange dog, no matter what the breed or valor, swiftly acknowledged Buck's supremacy or found himself struggling for life with a terrible antagonist. And Buck was merciless. He had learned well the law of club and fang, and he never forewent an advantage or drew back from a foe he had started on the way to Death. He had lessoned from Spitz, and from the chief fighting dogs of the police and mail, and knew there was no middle course. He must master or be mastered; while to show mercy was a weakness. Mercy did not exist in the primordial life. It was misunderstood for fear, and such misunderstandings made for death. Kill or be killed, eat or be eaten, was the law; and this mandate, down out of the depths of Time, he obeyed.

He was older than the days he had seen and the breaths he had drawn. He linked the past with the present, and the eternity behind him throbbed through him in a mighty rhythm to which he swayed as the tides and seasons swayed. He sat by John Thornton's fire, a broad-breasted dog, white-fanged and long-furred; but behind him were the shades of all manner of dogs, half-wolves and wild wolves, urgent and prompting, tasting the savor of the meat he ate, thirsting for the water he drank, scenting the wind with him, listening with him and telling him the sounds made by the wild life in the forest, dictating his moods, directing his actions, lying down to sleep with him when he lay down, and dreaming with him and beyond him and becoming themselves the stuff of his dreams.

So peremptorily did these shades beckon him that each day mankind and the claims of mankind slipped farther from him. Deep in the forest a call was sounding, and as often as he heard this call, mysteriously thrilling and luring, he felt compelled to turn his back upon the fire and the beaten earth around it, and to plunge into the forest, and on and on, he knew not where or why; nor did he wonder where or why, the call sounding imperiously, deep in the forest. But as often as he gained the soft unbroken earth and the green shade, the love for John Thornton drew him back to the fire again.

Thornton alone held him. The rest of mankind was as nothing. Chance travelers might praise or pet him; but he was cold under it all, and from a too demonstrative man he would get up and walk away. When Thornton's partners, Hans and Pete, arrived on the long-expected raft, Buck refused to notice them till he learned they were close to Thornton; after that he tolerated them in a passive sort of way, accepting favors from them as though he favored them by accepting. They were of the same large type as Thornton, living close to the earth, thinking simply and seeing clearly; and ere they swung the raft into the big eddy by the saw-mill at Dawson, they understood Buck and his ways, and did not insist upon an intimacy such as obtained with Skeet and Nig.

For Thornton, however, his love seemed to grow and grow. He, alone among men, could put a pack upon Buck's back in the summer traveling. Nothing was too great for Buck to do, when Thornton commanded. One day (they had grub-staked themselves from the proceeds of the raft and left Dawson for the head-waters of the Tanana) the men and dogs were sitting on the crest of a cliff which fell away, straight down, to naked bed-rock three hundred feet below. John Thornton was sitting near the edge, Buck at his shoulder. A thoughtless whim seized Thornton, and he drew the attention of Hans and Pete to the experiment he had in mind.

"Jump, Buck!" he commanded, sweeping his arm out over the chasm. The next instant he was grappling with Buck on the extreme edge, while Hans and Pete were dragging them back into safety.

"It's uncanny," Pet said, after it was over and they had caught their speech.

Thornton shook his head. "No, it is splendid, and it is terrible, too. Do you know, it sometimes makes me afraid."

"I'm not hankering to be the man that lays hands on you while he's around," Pete announced conclusively, nodding his head toward Buck.

"Py Jingo!" was Hans's contribution. "Not mineself either."

It was at Circle City, ere the year was out, that Pete's apprehensions were realized. "Black" Burton, a man evil-tempered and malicious, had been picking a quarrel with a tenderfoot at the bar, when Thornton stepped good-naturedly between. Buck, as was his custom, was lying in a corner, head on paws, watching his master's every action. Burton struck out, without warning, straight from the shoulder. Thornton was sent spinning, and saved himself from falling only by clutching the rail of the bar.

Those who were looking on heard what was neither bark nor yelp, but a something which is best described as a roar, and they saw Buck's body rise up in the air as he left the floor for Burton's throat. The man saved his life by instinctively throwing out his arm, but was hurled backward to the floor with Buck on top of him. Buck loosed his teeth from the flesh of the arm and drove in again for the throat. This time the man succeeded only in partly blocking, and his throat was torn open. Then the crowd was upon Buck, and he was driven off;

but while a surgeon checked the bleeding, he prowled up and down, growling furiously, attempting to rush in, and being forced back by an array of hostile clubs. A "miners' meeting," called on the spot, decided that the dog had sufficient provocation, and Buck was discharged. But his reputation was made, and from that day his name spread through every camp in Alaska.

Later on, in the fall of the year, he saved John Thornton's life in quite another fashion. The three partners were lining a long and narrow poling-boat down a bad stretch of rapids on the Forty-Mile Creek. Hans and Pete moved along the bank, snubbing with a thin Manila rope from tree to tree, while Thornton remained in the boat, helping its descent by means of a pole, and shouting directions to the shore. Buck, on the bank, worried and anxious, kept abreast of the boat, his eyes never off his master.

At a particularly bad spot, where a ledge of barely submerged rocks jutted out into the river, Hans cast off the rope, and, while Thornton poled the boat out into the stream, ran down the bank with the end in his hand to snub the boat when it had cleared the ledge. This it did, and was flying down-stream in a current as swift as a mill-race, when Hans checked it with the rope and checked too suddenly. The boat flirted over and snubbed in to the bank bottom up, while Thornton, flung sheer out of it, was carried down-stream toward the worst part of the rapids, a stretch of wild water in which no swimmer could live.

Buck had sprung in on the instant; and at the end of three hundred yards, amid a mad swirl of water, he overhauled Thornton. When he felt him grasp his tail, Buck headed for the bank, swimming with all his splendid strength. But the progress shoreward was slow; the progress down-stream amazingly rapid. From below came the fatal roaring where the wild current went wilder and was rent in shreds and spray by the rocks which thrust through like the teeth of an enormous comb. The suck of the water as it took the beginning of the last steep pitch was frightful, and Thornton knew that the shore was impossible. He scraped furiously over a rock, bruised across a second, and struck a third with crushing force. He clutched its slippery top with both hands, releasing Buck, and above the roar of the churning water shouted: "Go, Buck! Go!"

Buck could not hold his own, and swept on down-stream, struggling desperately, but unable to win back. When he heard Thornton's command repeated, he partly reared out of the water, throwing his head high, as though for a last look, then turned obediently toward the bank. He swam powerfully and was dragged ashore by Pete and Hans at the very point where swimming ceased to be possible and destruction began.

They knew that the time a man could cling to a slippery rock in the face of that driving current was a matter of minutes, and they ran as fast as they could up the bank to a point far above where Thornton was hanging on. They attached the line with which they had been snubbing the boat to Buck's neck and shoulders, being careful that it should neither strangle him nor impede his swimming, and launched him into the stream. He struck out boldly, but not straight enough into the stream. He discovered the mistake too late, when Thornton was abreast of him and a bare half-dozen strokes away while he was being carried helplessly past.

Hans promptly snubbed with the rope, as though Buck were a boat. The rope thus tightening on him in the sweep of the current, he was jerked under the surface, and under the surface he remained till his body struck against the bank and he was hauled out. He was half drowned, and Hans and Pete threw themselves upon him, pounding the breath into him and the water out of him. He staggered to his feet and fell down. The faint sound of Thornton's voice came to them, and though they could not make out the words of it, they knew that he was in his extremity. His master's voice acted on Buck like an electric shock. He sprang to his feet and ran up the bank ahead of the men to the point of his previous departure.

Again the rope was attached and he was launched, and again he struck out, but this time straight into the stream. He had miscalculated once, but he would not be guilty of it a second time. Hans paid out the rope, permitting no slack, while Pete kept it clear of coils. Buck held on till he was on a line straight above Thornton; then he turned, and with the speed of an express train headed down upon him. Thornton saw him coming, and, as Buck struck him like a battering ram, with the whole force of the current behind him, he reached up and closed with both arms around the shaggy neck. Hans snubbed the rope around the tree and Buck and Thornton were jerked under the water. Strangling, suffocating, sometimes one uppermost and sometimes the other, dragging over the jagged bottom, smashing against rocks and snags, they veered in to the bank.

Thornton came to, belly downward and being violently propelled back and forth across a drift log by Hans and Pete.

His first glance was for Buck, over whose limp and apparently lifeless body Nig was setting up a howl, while Skeet was licking the wet face and closed eyes. Thornton was himself bruised and battered, and he went carefully over Buck's body, when he had been brought around, finding three broken ribs.

"That settles it," he announced. "We camp right here." And camp they did, till Buck's ribs knitted and he was able to travel.

That winter, at Dawson, Buck performed another exploit, not so heroic, perhaps, but one that put his name many notches higher on the totem-pole of Alaskan fame. This exploit was particularly gratifying to the three men; for they stood in need of the outfit which it furnished, and were enabled to make a long-desired trip into the virgin East, where miners had not yet appeared. It was brought out by a conversation in the Eldorado Saloon, in which men waxed boastful of their favorite dogs. Buck, because of his record, was the target for these men, and Thornton was driven stoutly to defend him. At the end of half an hour one man stated that his dog could start a sled with five hundred pounds and walk off with it; a second bragged six hundred for his dog; and third, seven hundred.

"Pooh! Pooh!" said John Thornton; "Buck can start a thousand pounds."

"And break it out? And walk off with it for a hundred yards?" demanded Matthewson, a Bonanza King, he of the seven hundred vaunt.

"And break it out, and walk off with it for a hundred yards," John Thornton said coolly.

"Well," Matthewson said, slowly and deliberately, so that all could hear, "I've got a thousand dollars that says he can't. And there it is." So saying, he slammed a sack of gold dust of the size of a bologna sausage down upon the bar.

Nobody spoke, Thornton's bluff, if bluff it was, had been called. He could feel a flush of warm blood creeping up his face. His tongue had tricked him. He did not know whether Buck could start a thousand pounds. Half a ton! The enormousness of it appalled him. He had great faith in Buck's strength and had often thought him capable of starting such a load; but never, as now, had he faced the possibility of it, the eyes of a dozen men fixed upon him, silent and waiting. Further, he had no thousand dollars; nor had Hans or Pete.

"I've got a sled standing outside now, with twenty fifty-pound sacks of flour on it," Matthewson went on with brutal directness; "so don't let that hinder you."

Thornton did not reply. He did not know what to say. He glanced from face to face in the absent way of a man who has lost the power of thought and is seeking somewhere to find the thing that will start it going again. The face of Jim O'Brien, a Mastodon King and old-time comrade, caught his eyes. It was as a cue to him, seeming to rouse him to do what he would never have dreamed of doing.

"Can you lend me a thousand?" he asked, almost in a whisper.

"Sure," answered O'Brien, thumping down a plethoric sack by the side of Matthewson's. "Though it's little faith I'm having, John, that the beast can do the trick."

The Eldorado emptied its occupants into the street to see the test. The tables were deserted, and the dealers and game-keepers came forth to see the outcome of the wager and to lay odds. Several hundred men, furred and mittened, banked around the sled within easy distance. Matthewson's sled, loaded with a thousand pounds of flour, had been standing for a couple of hours, and in the intense cold (it was sixty below zero) the runners had frozen fast to the hard-packed snow. Men offered odds of two to one the Buck could not budge the sled. A quibble arose concerning the phrase "break out." O'Brien contended it was Thornton's privilege to knock the runners loose, leaving Buck to "break it out" from a dead standstill. Matthewson insisted that the phrase included breaking the runners from the frozen grip of the snow. A majority of men who had witnessed the making of the bet decided in his favor, whereat the odds went up to three to one against Buck.

There were no takers. Not a man believed him capable of the feat. Thornton had been hurried into the wager, heavy with doubt; and now that he looked at the sled itself, the concrete fact, with the regular team of ten dogs curled up in the snow before it, the more impossible the task appeared. Matthewson waxed jubilant.

"Three to one!" he proclaimed. "I'll lay you another thousand at that figure, Thornton. What d'ye say?"

Thornton's doubt was strong in his face, but his fighting spirit was aroused—the fighting spirit that soars above odds, fails to recognize the impossible, and is deaf to all save the clamor for battle. He called Hans and Pete to him. Their sacks were slim, and with his own the three partners could rake together only two hundred dollars. In the ebb of their fortunes, this sum was their total capital; yet they laid it unhesitatingly against Matthewson's six hundred.

The team of ten dogs was unhitched, and Buck, with his own harness, was put into the sled. He had caught the contagion of the excitement, and he felt that in some way he must do a great thing for John Thornton. Murmurs of admiration at his splendid appearance went up. He was in perfect condition, without an ounce of superfluous flesh, and the one hundred and fifty pounds that he weighed were so many pounds of grit and virility. His furry coat shone with the sheen of silk. Down the neck and across the shoulders, his mane, in repose as it was, half bristled and seemed to lift with every movement, as though excess of vigor made each particular hair alive and active. The great breast and heavy fore legs were no more than in proportion with the rest of the body, where the muscles showed in tight rolls underneath the skin. Men felt these muscles and proclaimed them hard as iron, and the odds went down to two to one.

"Gad, sir! Gad, sir!" stuttered a member of the latest dynasty, a king of the Skookum Benches. "I offer you eight hundred for him, sir, before the test, sir; eight hundred just as he stands."

Thornton shook his head and stepped to Buck's side.

"You must stand off from him," Matthewson protested. "Free play and plenty of room."

The crowd fell silent; only could be heard the voice of the gamblers vainly offering two to one. Everybody acknowledged Buck a magnificent animal, but twenty fifty-pound sacks of flour bulked too large in their eyes for them to loosen their pouch-strings.

Thornton knelt down by Buck's side. He took his head in his two hands and rested cheek on cheek. He did not playfully shake him, as was his wont, or murmur soft love curses; but he whispered in his ear. "As you love me, Buck. As you love me," was what he whispered. Buck whined with suppressed eagerness.

The crowd was watching curiously. The affair was growing mysterious. It seemed like a conjuration. As Thornton got to his feet, Buck seized his mittened hand between his jaws, pressing in with his teeth and releasing slowly, half-reluctantly. It was the answer, in terms, not of speech, but of love. Thornton stepped well back.

"Now, Buck," he said.

Buck tightened the traces, then slacked them for a matter of several inches. It was the way he had learned.

"Gee!" Thornton's voice rang out, sharp in the tense silence.

Buck swung to the right, ending the movement in a plunge that took up the slack and with a sudden jerk arrested his one hundred and fifty pounds. The load quivered, and from under the runners arose a crisp crackling.

"Haw!" Thornton commanded.

Buck duplicated the maneuver, this time to the left. The crackling turned into a snapping, the sled pivoting and the runner slipping and grating several inches to the side. The sled was broken out. Men were holding their breaths, intensely unconscious of the fact.

"Now, MUSH!"

Thornton's command cracked out like a pistol-shot. Buck threw himself forward, tightening the traces with a jarring lunge. His whole body was gathered compactly together in the tremendous effort, the muscles writhing and knotting like live things under the silky fur. His great chest was low to the ground, his head forward and down, while his feet were flying like mad, the claws scarring the hard-packed snow in parallel grooves. The sled swayed and trembled, half-started forward. One of his feet slipped, and one man groaned aloud. Then the sled lurched ahead in what appeared a rapid succession of jerks, though it never really came to a dead stop again . . . half an inch . . . an inch . . . two inches. . . . The jerks perceptibly diminished; as the sled gained momentum, he caught them up, till it was moving steadily along.

Men gasped and began to breathe again, unaware that for a moment they had ceased to breathe. Thornton was running behind, encouraging Buck with short, cheery words. The distance had been measured off, and as he neared the pile of firewood which marked the end of the hundred yards, a cheer began to grow and grow, which burst into a roar as he passed the firewood and halted at command. Every man was tearing himself loose, even Matthewson. Hats and mittens were flying in the air. Men were shaking hands, it did not matter with whom, and bubbling over in a general incoherent babel.

But Thornton fell on his knees beside Buck. Head was against head, and he was shaking him back and forth. Those who hurried up heard him cursing Buck, and he cursed him long and fervently, and softly and lovingly.

"Gad, sir! Gad, sir!" spluttered the Skookum Bench king. "I'll give you a thousand for him, sir, a thousand, sir—twelve hundred, sir."

Thornton rose to his feet. His eyes were wet. The tears were streaming frankly down his cheeks. "Sir," he said to the

Skookum Bench king, "no, sir. You can go to hell, sir. It's the best I can do for you, sir."

Buck seized Thornton's hand in his teeth. Thornton shook him back and forth. As though animated by a common impulse, the onlookers drew back to a respectful distance; nor were they again indiscreet enough to interrupt.

To Build a Fire

Day had broken cold and gray, exceedingly cold and gray, when the man turned aside from the main Yukon trail and climbed the high earth-bank, where a dim and little-traveled trail led eastward through the fat spruce timberland. It was a steep bank, and he paused for breath at the top, excusing the act to himself by looking at his watch. It was nine o'clock. There was no sun nor hint of sun, though there was not a cloud in the sky. It was a clear day, and yet there seemed an intangible pall over the face of things, a subtle gloom that made the day dark, and that was due to the absence of sun. This fact did not worry the man. He was used to the lack of sun. It had been days since he had seen the sun, and he knew that a few more days must pass before that cheerful orb, due south, would just peep above the sky-line and dip immediately from view.

The man flung a look back along the way he had come. The Yukon lay a mile wide and hidden under three feet of ice. On top of this ice were as many feet of snow. It was all pure white, rolling in gentle undulations where the ice-jams of the freeze-up had formed. North and south, as far as his eye could see, it was unbroken white, save for a dark hair-line that curved and twisted from around the spruce-covered island. This dark hair-line was the trail—the main trail—that led south five hundred miles to the Chilcoot Pass, Dyea, and salt water; and that led north seventy miles to Dawson, and still on to the north a thousand miles to Nulato, and finally to St. Michael on Bering Sea, a thousand miles and a half a thousand more.

But all this—the mysterious, far-reaching hair-line trail, the absence of sun from the sky, the tremendous cold, and the strangeness and weirdness of it all—made no impression on the man. It was not because he was long used to it. He was a newcomer in the land, a *chechaquo*, and this was his first winter. The trouble with him was that he was without imagination. He was quick and alert in the things of life, but only in the things, and not in the significances. Fifty degrees below zero meant eighty-odd degrees of frost. Such fact impressed him as being cold and uncomfortable, and that was all. It did not lead him to meditate upon his frailty as a creature of temperature, and upon man's frailty in general, able only to live within certain narrow limits of heat and cold; and from there on it did not lead him to the conjectural field of immortality and man's place in the universe. Fifty degrees below zero stood for a bite of frost that hurt and that must be guarded against by the use of mittens, ear-flaps, warm moccasins, and thick socks. Fifty degrees below zero was to him just precisely fifty degrees below zero. That there should be anything more to it than that was a thought that never entered his head.

As he turned to go on, he spat speculatively. There was a sharp, explosive crackle that startled him. He spat again. And again, in the air, before it could fall to the snow, the spittle crackled. He knew that at fifty below spittle crackled on the snow, but this spittle had crackled in the air. Undoubtedly it was colder than fifty below—how much colder he did not know. But the temperature did not matter. He was bound for the old claim on the left fork of Henderson Creek, where the boys were already. They had come over across the divide from the Indian Creek country, while he had come the round-about way to take a look at the possibilities of getting out logs in the spring from the islands in the Yukon. He would be in to camp by six o'clock; a bit after dark, it was true, but the boys would be there, a fire would be going, and a hot supper would be ready. As for lunch, he pressed his hand against the pro-truding bundle under his jacket. It was also under his shirt, wrapped up in a handkerchief and lying against the naked skin. It was the only way to keep the biscuits from freezing. He smiled agreeably to himself as he thought of those bis-cuits, each cut open and sopped in bacon grease, and each en-closing a generous slice of fried bacon.

He plunged in among the big spruce trees. The trail was faint. A foot of snow had fallen since the last sled had passed over, and he was glad he was without a sled, travel-ing light. In fact, he carried nothing but the lunch wrapped in the handkerchief. He was surprised, however, at the cold. It certainly was cold, he concluded, as he rubbed his numb nose and cheek-bones with his mittened hand. He was a

warm-whiskered man, but the hair on his face did not pro-
tect the high check-bones and the eager nose that thrust itself aggressively into the frosty air.

At the man's heels trotted a dog, a big native husky, the
proper wolf-dog, gray-coated and without any visible or tem-
peramental difference from its brother, the wild wolf. The
animal was depressed by the tremendous cold. It knew that it
was not time for traveling. Its instinct told it a truer tale than
was told to the man by the man's judgment. In reality, it was
not merely colder than fifty below zero; it was colder than
sixty below, than seventy below. It was seventy-five below
zero. Since the freezing-point is thirty-two above zero, it
meant that one hundred and seven degrees of frost obtained.
The dog did not know anything about thermometers. Possibly in its brain there was no sharp consciousness of a condition of very cold such as was in the man's brain. But the brute
had its instinct. It experienced a vague but menacing apprehension that subdued it and made it slink along at the man's
heels, and that made it question eagerly every unwonted
movement of the man as if expecting him to go into camp or
to seek shelter somewhere and build a fire. The dog had
learned fire, and it wanted fire, or else to burrow under the
snow and cuddle its warmth away from the air.

The frozen moisture of its breathing had settled on its fur
in a fine powder of frost, and especially were its jowls, muzzle, and eyelashes whitened by its crystalled breath. The
man's red beard and mustache were likewise frosted, but
more solidly, the deposit taking the form of ice and increasing
with every warm, moist breath he exhaled. Also, the man was
chewing tobacco, and the muzzle of ice held his lips so rigidly

that he was unable to clear his chin when he expelled the juice. The result was that a crystal beard of the color and solidity of amber was increasing its length on his chin. If he fell down it would shatter itself, like glass, into brittle fragments. But he did not mind the appendage. It was the penalty all tobacco-chewers paid in that country, and he had been out before in two cold snaps. They had not been so cold as this, he knew, but by the spirit thermometer at Sixty Mile he knew they had been registered at fifty below and at fifty-five.

He held on through the level stretch of woods for several miles, crossed a wide flat of niggerheads [*sic*], and dropped down a bank to the frozen bed of a small stream. This was Henderson Creek, and he knew he was ten miles from the forks. He looked at his watch. It was ten o'clock. He was making four miles an hour, and he calculated that he would arrive at the forks at half-past twelve. He decided to celebrate that event by eating his lunch there.

The dog dropped in again at his heels, with a tail drooping discouragement, as the man swung along the creek-bed. The furrow of the old sled-trail was plainly visible, but a dozen inches of snow covered the marks of the last runners. In a month no man had come up or down that silent creek. The man held steadily on. He was not much given to thinking, and just then particularly he had nothing to think about save that he would eat lunch at the forks and that at six o'clock he would be in camp with the boys. There was nobody to talk to; and, had there been, speech would have been impossible because of the ice-muzzle on his mouth. So he continued monotonously to chew tobacco and to increase the length of his amber beard.

Once in a while the thought reiterated itself that it was very cold and that he had never experienced such cold. As he walked along he rubbed his cheek-bones and nose with the back of his mittened hand. He did this automatically, now and again changing hands. But rub as he would, the instant he stopped his cheekbones went numb, and the following instant the end of his nose went numb. He was sure to frost his cheeks; he knew that, and experienced a pang of regret that he had not devised a nose-strap of the sort Bud wore in cold snaps. Such a strap passed across the cheeks, as well, and saved them. But it didn't matter much, after all. What were frosted cheeks? A bit painful, that was all; they were never serious.

Empty as the man's mind was of thoughts, he was keenly observant, and he noticed the changes in the creek, the curves and bends and the timber-jams, and always he sharply noted where he placed his feet. Once, coming around a bend, he shied abruptly, like a startled horse, curved away from the place where he had been walking, and retreated several paces back along the trail. The creek he knew was frozen clear to the bottom—no creek could contain water in that arctic winter— but he knew also that there were springs that bubbled out from the hillsides and ran along under the snow and on top the ice of the creek. He knew that the coldest snaps never froze these springs, and he knew likewise their danger. They were traps. They hid pools of water under the snow that might be three inches deep, or three feet. Sometimes a skin of ice half an inch thick covered them, and in turn was covered by the snow. Sometimes there were alternate layers of water and ice-skin, so that when one broke through he kept on breaking through for a while, sometimes wetting himself to the waist.

That was why he had shied in such panic. He had felt the give under his feet and heard the crackle of a snow-hidden ice-skin. And to get his feet wet in such a temperature meant trouble and danger. At the very least it meant delay, for he would be forced to stop and build a fire, and under its protection to bare his feet while he dried his socks and moccasins. He stood and studied the creek-bed and its banks, and decided that the flow of water came from the right. He reflected awhile, rubbing his nose and cheeks, then skirted to the left, stepping gingerly and testing the footing for each step. Once clear of the danger, he took a fresh chew of tobacco and swung along at his four-mile gait.

In the course of the next two hours he came upon several similar traps. Usually the snow above the hidden pools had a sunken, candied appearance that advertised the danger. Once again, however, he had a close call; and once, suspecting danger, he compelled the dog to go on in front. The dog did not want to go. It hung back until the man shoved it forward, and then it went quickly across the white, unbroken surface. Suddenly it broke through, floundered to one side, and got away to firmer footing. It had wet its forefeet and legs, and almost immediately the water that clung to it turned to ice. It made quick efforts to lick the ice off its legs, then dropped down in the snow and began to bite out the ice that had formed between the toes. This was a matter of instinct. To permit the ice to remain would mean sore feet. It did not know this. It merely obeyed the mysterious prompting that arose from the deep crypts of its being. But the man knew, having achieved a judgment on the subject, and he removed the mitten from his right hand and helped tear out the ice-particles. He did not expose his fingers more than a minute, and was astonished at the swift numbness than smote them. It certainly was cold. He pulled on the mitten hastily, and beat the hand savagely across his chest.

At twelve o'clock the day was at its brightest. Yet the sun was too far south on its winter journey to clear the horizon. The bulge of the earth intervened between it and Henderson Creek, where the man walked under a clear sky at noon and cast no shadow. At half-past twelve, to the minute, he arrived at the forks of the creek. He was pleased at the speed he had made. If he kept it up, he would certainly be with the boys by six. He unbuttoned his jacket and shirt and drew forth his lunch. The action consumed no more than a quarter of a minute, yet in that brief moment the numbness laid hold of the exposed fingers. He did not put the mitten on, but, instead, struck the fingers a dozen sharp smashes against his leg. Then he sat down on a snow-covered log to eat. The sting that followed upon the striking of his fingers against his leg ceased so quickly that he was startled. He had had no chance to take a bite of biscuit. He struck the fingers repeatedly and returned them to the mitten, baring the other hand for the purpose of eating. He tried to take a mouthful, but the ice-muzzle prevented. He had forgotten to build a fire and thaw out. He chuckled at his foolishness, and as he chuckled he noted the numbness creeping into the exposed fingers. Also, he noted that the stinging, which had first come to his toes when he sat down, was already passing away. He wondered whether the toes were warm or numb. He moved them inside the moccasins and decided that they were numb.

He pulled the mitten on hurriedly and stood up. He was a bit frightened. He stamped up and down until the stinging returned into the feet. It certainly was cold, was his thought. That man from Sulphur Creek had spoken the truth when telling how cold it sometimes got in the country. And he had laughed at him at the time! That showed one must not be too sure of things. There was no mistake about it, it *was* cold. He strode up and down, stamping his feet and threshing his arms, until reassured by the returning warmth. Then he got out matches and proceeded to make a fire. From the undergrowth, where high water of the previous spring had lodged a supply a seasoned twigs, he got his fire-wood. Working carefully from a small beginning, he soon had a roaring fire, over which he thawed the ice from his face and in the protection of which he ate his biscuits. For the moment the cold of space was outwitted. The dog took satisfaction in the fire, stretching out close enough for warmth and far enough away to escape being singed.

When the man had finished, he filled his pipe and took his comfortable time over a smoke. Then he pulled on his mittens, settled the ear-flaps of his cap firmly about his ears, and took the creek trail up the left fork. The dog was disappointed and yearned back toward the fire. This man did not know cold. Possibly all the generations of his ancestry had been ignorant of cold, of real cold, of cold one hundred and seven degrees below freezing-point. But the dog knew; all its ancestry knew, and it had inherited the knowledge. And it knew that it was not good to walk abroad in such fearful cold. It was the time to lie snug in a hole in the snow and wait for a curtain of cloud to be drawn across the face of outer space whence this cold came. On the other hand, there was no keen intimacy between the dog and the man. The one was the toil-slave of the other, and the only caresses it had ever received were the caresses of the whiplash and of harsh and menacing throat-sounds that threatened the whip-lash. So the dog made no effort to communicate its apprehension to the man. It was not concerned in the welfare of the man; it was for its own sake that it yearned back toward the fire. But the man whistled, and spoke to it with the sound of whiplashes, and the dog swung in at the man's heels and followed after.

The man took a chew of tobacco and proceeded to start a new amber beard. Also, his moist breath quickly powdered with white his mustache, eyebrows, and lashes. There did not seem to be so many springs on the left fork of the Henderson, and for half an hour the man saw no signs of any. And then it happened. At a place where there were no signs, where the soft, unbroken snow seemed to advertise solidity beneath, the man broke through. It was not deep. He wet himself halfway to the knees before he floundered out to the firm crust.

He was angry, and cursed his luck aloud. He had hoped to get into camp with the boys at six o'clock, and this would delay him an hour, for he would have to build a fire and dry out his footgear. This was imperative at that low temperature—he knew that much; and he turned aside to the bank, which he climbed. On top, tangled in the underbrush about the trunks of several small spruce trees, was a high-water deposit of dry fire-wood—sticks and twigs, principally, but also larger portions of seasoned branches and fine, dry, last-year's grasses. He threw down several large pieces on top of the snow. This served for a foundation and prevented the young flame from drowning itself in the snow it otherwise would melt. The flame he got by touching a match to a small shred of birch-bark that he took from his pocket. This burned even more readily than paper. Placing it on the foundation, he fed the young flame with wisps of dry grass and with the tiniest dry twigs.

He worked slowly and carefully, keenly aware of his danger. Gradually, as the flame grew stronger, he increased the size of the twigs with which he fed it. He squatted in the snow, pulling the twigs out from their entanglement in the brush and feeding directly to the flame. He knew there must be no failure. When it is seventy-five below zero, a man must not fail in his first attempt to build a fire—that is, if his feet are wet. If his feet are dry, and he fails, he can run along the trail for half a mile and restore his circulation. But the circulation of wet and freezing feet cannot be restored by running when it is seventy-five below. No matter how fast he runs, the wet feet will freeze the harder.

All this the man knew. The old-timer on Sulphur Creek had told him about it the previous fall, and now he was appreciating the advice. Already all sensation had gone out of his feet. To build the fire he had been forced to remove his mittens, and the fingers had quickly gone numb. His pace of four miles an hour had kept his heart pumping blood to the surface of his body and to all the extremities. But the instant he stopped, the action of the pump eased down. The cold of space smote the unprotected tip of the planet, and he, being on that unprotected tip, received the full force of the blow. The blood of his body recoiled before it. The blood was alive, like the dog, and like the dog it wanted to hide away and cover itself up from the fearful cold. So long as he walked four miles an hour, he pumped that blood, willy-nilly, to the surface; but now it ebbed away and sank down into the recesses of his body. The extremities were the first to feel its absence. His wet feet froze the faster, and his exposed fingers numbed the faster, though they had not yet begun to freeze. Nose and cheeks were already freezing, while the skin of all his body chilled as it lost its blood.

But he was safe. Toes and nose and cheeks would be only touched by the frost, for the fire was beginning to burn with strength. He was feeding it with twigs the size of his finger. In another minute he would be able to feed it with branches the size of his wrist, and then he could remove his wet foot-gear, and, while it dried, he could keep his naked feet warm by the fire, rubbing them at first, of course, with snow. The fire was a success. He was safe. He remembered the advice of the old-timer on Sulphur Creek and smiled. The old-timer had been very serious in laying down the law that no man must travel alone in the Klondike after fifty below. Well, here he was; he had had the accident; he was alone; and he had saved himself. Those old-timers were rather womanish, some of them, he thought. All a man had to do was to keep his head, and he was all right. Any man who was a man could travel alone. But it was surprising, the rapidity with which his cheeks and nose were freezing. And he had not thought his fingers could go lifeless in so short a time. Lifeless they were, for he could scarcely make them move together to grip a twig, and they seemed remote from his body and from him. When he touched a twig, he had to look and see whether or not he had hold of it. The wires were pretty well down between him and his finger-ends.

All of which counted for little. There was the fire, snapping and crackling and promising life with every dancing flame. He started to untie his moccasins. They were coated with ice, the thick German socks were like sheaths of iron halfway to the knees; and the moccasin strings were like rods of steel all twisted and knotted as by some conflagration. For a moment he tugged with his numb fingers, then, realizing the folly of it, he drew his sheath-knife.

But before he could cut the strings, it happened. It was his own fault or, rather, his mistake. He should not have built the fire under the spruce tree. He should have built it in the open. But it had been easier to pull the twigs from the brush and drop them directly on the fire. Now the tree under which he had done this carried a weight of snow on its boughs. No wind had blown for weeks, and each bough was fully freighted. Each time he had pulled a twig he had communicated a slight agitation to the tree—an imperceptible agitation, so far as he was concerned, but an agitation sufficient to bring about the disaster. High up in the tree one bough capsized its load of snow. This fell on the boughs beneath, capsizing them. This process continued spreading out and involving the whole tree. It grew like an avalanche, and it descended without warning upon the man and the fire, and the fire was blotted out! Where it had burned was a mantle of fresh and disordered snow.

The man was shocked. It was as though he had just heard his own sentence of death. For a moment he sat and stared at the spot where the fire had been. Then he grew very calm. Perhaps the old-timer on Sulphur Creek was right. If he had only had a trail-mate he would have been in no danger now.

The trail-mate could have built the fire. Well, it was up to him to build the fire over again, and this second time there must be no failure. Even if he succeeded, he would most likely lose some toes. His feet must be badly frozen by now, and there would be some time before the second fire was ready.

Such were his thoughts, but he did not sit and think them. He was busy all the time they were passing through his mind. He made a new foundation for a fire, this time in the open, where no treacherous tree could blot it out. Next, he gathered dry grasses and tiny twigs from the high-water flot-sam. He could not bring his fingers together to pull them out, but he was able to gather them by the handful. In this way he got many rotten twigs and bits of green moss that were unde-sirable, but it was the best he could do. He worked methodi-cally, even collecting an armful of the larger branches to be used later when the fire gathered strength. And all the while the dog sat and watched him, a certain yearning wistfulness in its eyes, for it looked upon him as the fire-provider, and the fire was slow in coming.

When all was ready, the man reached in his pocket for a second piece of birch-bark. He knew the bark was there, and, though he could not feel it with his fingers, he could hear its crisp rustling as he fumbled for it. Try as he would, he could not clutch hold of it. And all the time, in his consciousness, was the knowledge that each instant his feet were freezing. This thought tended to put him in a panic, but he fought against it and kept calm. He pulled on his mittens with his teeth, and threshed his arms back and forth, beating his hands with all his might against his sides. He did this sitting down, and he stood up to do it; and all the while the dog sat in the snow, its wolf-brush of a tail curled around warmly over its forefeet, its sharp wolf-ears pricked forward intently as it watched the man. And the man, as he beat and threshed with his arms and hands, felt a great surge of envy as he regarded the creature that was warm and secure in its natural covering.

After a time he was aware of the first faraway signals of sensation in his beaten fingers. The faint tingling grew stronger till it evolved into a stinging ache that was excruciating, but which the man hailed with satisfaction. He stripped the mitten from his right hand and fetched forth the birch-bark. The exposed fingers were quickly going numb again. Next he brought out his bunch of sulphur matches. But the tremendous cold had already driven the life out of his fingers. In his effort to separate one match from the others, the whole bunch fell in the snow. He tried to pick it out of the snow, but failed. The dead fingers could neither touch nor clutch. He was very careful. He drove the thought of his freezing feet, and nose, and cheeks, out of his mind, devoting his whole soul to the matches. He watched, using the sense of vision in place of that of touch, and when he saw his fingers on each side the bunch, he closed them—that is, he willed to close them, for the wires were down, and the fingers did not obey. He pulled the mitten on the right hand, and beat it fiercely against his knee. Then, with both mittened hands, he scooped the bunch of matches along with much snow, into his lap. Yet he was no better off.

After some manipulation he managed to get the bunch between the heels of his mittened hands. In this fashion he carried it to his mouth. The ice crackled and snapped when by a violent effort he opened his mouth. He drew the lower jaw in, curled the upper lip out of the way, and scraped the bunch with his upper teeth in order to separate a match. He succeeded in getting one, which he dropped on his lap. He was no better off. He could not pick it up. Then he devised a way. He picked it up in his teeth and scratched it on his leg. Twenty times he scratched before he succeeded in lighting it. As it flamed he held it with his teeth to the birch-bark. But the burning brimstone went up his nostrils and into his lungs, causing his to cough spasmodically. The match fell into the snow and went out.

The old-timer on Sulphur Creek was right, he thought in the moment of controlled despair that ensued: after fifty below, a man should travel with a partner. He beat his hands, but failed in exciting any sensation. Suddenly he bared both hands, removing the mittens with his teeth. He caught the whole bunch between the heels of his hands. His arm-muscles not being frozen enabled him to press the hand-heels tightly against the matches. Then he scratched the bunch along his leg. It flared into flame, seventy sulphur matches at once! There was no wind to blow them out. He kept his head to one side to escape the strangling fumes, and held the blazing bunch to the birch-bark. As he so held it, he became aware of sensation in his hand. His flesh was burning. He could smell it. Deep down below the surface he could feel it. The sensation developed into pain that grew acute. And still he endured it, holding the flame of the matches clumsily to the bark that would not light readily because his own burning hands were in the way, absorbing most of the flame.

At last, when he could endure no more, he jerked his hands apart. The blazing matches fell sizzling into the snow, but the birch-bark was alight. He began laying dry grasses and the tiniest twigs on the flame. He could not pick and choose, for he had to lift the fuel between the heels of his hands. Small pieces of rotten wood and green moss clung to the twigs, and he bit them off as well as he could with his teeth. He cherished the flame carefully and awkwardly. It meant life, and it must not perish. The withdrawal of blood from the surface of his body now made him begin to shiver, and he grew more awkward. A large piece of green moss fell squarely on the little fire. He tried to poke it out with his fingers, but his shivering frame made him poke too far, and he disrupted the nucleus of the little fire, the burning grasses and tiny twigs separating and scattering. He tried to poke them together again, but in spite of the tenseness of the effort, his shivering got away with him, and the twigs were hopelessly scattered. Each twig gushed a puff of smoke and went out. The fire-provider had failed. As he looked apathetically about him, his eyes chanced on the dog, sitting across the ruins of the fire from him, in the snow, making restless, hunching movements, slightly lifting one forefoot and then the other, shifting its weight back and forth on them with wistful eagerness.

The sight of the dog put a wild idea into his head. He remembered the tale of the man, caught in a blizzard, who killed a steer and crawled inside the carcass, and so was saved. He would kill the dog and bury his hands in the warm body until the numbness went out of them. Then he could build another fire. He spoke to the dog, calling it to him; but in his voice was a strange note of fear that frightened the animal, who had never known the man to speak in such way before. Something was the matter, and its suspicious nature sensed danger—it knew not what danger, but somewhere, somehow, in its brain arose an apprehension of the man. It flattened its ears down at the sound of the man's voice, and its restless, hunching movements and the liftings and shiftings of its forefeet became more pronounced; but it would not come to the man. He got on his hands and knees and crawled toward the dog. This unusual posture again excited suspicion, and the animal sidled mincingly away.

The man sat up in the snow for a moment and struggled for calmness. Then he pulled on his mittens, by means of his teeth, and got upon his feet. He glanced down at first in order to assure himself that he was really standing up, for the absence of sensation in his feet left him unrelated to the earth. His erect position in itself started to drive the webs of suspicion from the dog's mind; and when he spoke peremptorily, with the sound of whiplashes in his voice, the dog rendered its customary allegiance and came to him. As it came within reaching distance, the man lost his control. His arms flashed out to the dog, and he experienced genuine surprise when he discovered that his hand could not clutch, that there was neither bend nor feeling in the fingers. He had forgotten for the moment that they were frozen and that they were freezing more and more. All this happened quickly, and before the animal could get away, he encircled its body with his arms. He sat down in the snow, and in this fashion held the dog, while it snarled and whined and struggled.

But it was all he could do, hold its body encircled in his arms and sit there. He realized that he could not kill the dog. There was no way to do it. With his helpless hands he could neither draw nor hold his sheath knife nor throttle the animal. He released it, and it plunged wildly away, with tail between

its legs, and still snarling. It halted forty feet away and surveyed him curiously, with ears sharply pricked forward. The
man looked down at his hands in order to locate them, and
found them hanging on the ends of his arms. It struck him as
curious that one should have to use his eyes in order to find
out where his hands were. He began threshing his arms back
and forth, beating the mittened hands against his sides. He
did this for five minutes, violently, and his heart pumped
enough blood up the surface to put a stop to his shivering. But
no sensation was aroused in the hands. He had an impression
that they hung like weights on the ends of his arms, but when
he tried to run the impression down, he could not find it.

A certain fear of death, dull and oppressive, came to him.
The fear quickly became poignant as he realized that it was
no longer a mere matter of freezing his fingers and toes, or of
losing his hands and feet, but that it was a matter of life and
death with the chances against him. This threw him into a
panic, and he turned and ran up the creek-bed along the old,
dim trail. The dog joined in behind and kept up with him.
He ran blindly, without intention, in fear such as he had
never known in his life. Slowly, as he ploughed and floundered through the snow, he began to see things again—the
banks of the creek, the old timber-jams, the leafless aspens,
and the sky. The running made him feel better. He did not
shiver. Maybe, if he ran on, his feet would thaw out; and, anyway, if he ran far enough, he would reach camp and the boys.
Without doubt he would lose some fingers and toes and some
of his face; but the boys would take care of him, and save the
rest of him when he got there. And at the same time there
was another thought in his mind that said he would never get

to the camp and the boys; that it was too many miles away, that the freezing had too great a start on him, and that he would soon be stiff and dead. This thought he kept in the background and refused to consider. Sometimes it pushed itself forward and demanded to be heard, but he thrust it back and strove to think of other things.

It struck him as curious that he could run at all on feet so frozen that he could not feel them when they struck the earth and took the weight of his body. He seemed to himself to skim along above the surface, and to have no connection with the earth. Somewhere he had once seen a winged Mercury, and he wondered if Mercury felt as he felt when skimming over the earth.

His theory of running until he reached camp and the boys had one flaw in it: he lacked the endurance. Several times he stumbled, and finally he tottered, crumpled up, and fell. When he tried to rise, he failed. He must sit and rest, he decided, and next time he would merely walk and keep on going. As he sat and regained his breath, he noted that he was feeling quite warm and comfortable. He was not shivering, and it even seemed that a warm flow had come to his chest and trunk. And yet, when he touched his nose or cheeks, there was no sensation. Running would not thaw them out. Nor would it thaw out his hands and feet. Then the thought came to him that the frozen portions of his body must be extending. He tried to keep this thought down, to forget it, to think of something else; he was aware of the panicky feeling that it caused, and he was afraid of the panic. But the thought asserted itself, and persisted, until it produced a vision of his body totally frozen. This was too much, and he made another wild run along the trail. Once he slowed down to a walk, but the thought of the freezing extending itself made him run again.

And all the time the dog ran with him, at his heels. When he fell down a second time, it curled its tail over its forefeet and sat in front of him, facing him, curiously eager and intent. The warmth and security of the animal angered him, and he cursed it till it flattened down its ears appeasingly. This time the shivering came more quickly upon the man. He was losing in his battle with the frost. It was creeping into his body from all sides. The thought of it drove him on, but he ran no more than a hundred feet, when he staggered and pitched headlong. It was his last panic. When he had recovered his breath and control, he sat up and entertained in his mind the conception of meeting death with dignity. However, the conception did not come to him in such terms. His idea of it was that he had been making a fool of himself, running around like a chicken with its head cut off—such was the simile that occurred to him. Well, he was bound to freeze anyway, and he might as well take it decently. With this new-found peace of mind came the first glimmerings of drowsiness. A good idea, he thought, to sleep off to death. It was like taking an anesthetic. Freezing was not so bad as people thought. There were lots worse ways to die.

He pictured the boys finding his body next day. Suddenly he found himself with them, coming along the trail and looking for himself. And, still with them, he came around a turn in the trail and found himself lying in the snow. He did not belong with himself any more, for even then he was out of himself, standing with the boys and looking at himself in the snow. It certainly was cold, was his thought. When he got back to the States he could tell the folks what real cold was. He drifted on from this to a vision of the old-timer on Sulphur Creek. He could see him quite clearly, warm and comfortable, and smoking a pipe.

"You were right, old hoss; you were right," the man mumbled to the old-timer of Sulphur Creek.

Then the man drowsed off into what seemed to him the most comfortable and satisfying sleep he had ever known. The dog sat facing him and waiting. The brief day drew to a close in a long, slow twilight. There were no signs of a fire to be made, and besides, never in the dog's experience had it known a man to sit like that in the snow and make no fire. As the twilight drew on, its eager yearning for the fire mastered it, and with a great lifting and shifting of forefeet, it whined softly, then flattened its ears down in anticipation of being chidden by the man. But the man remained silent. Later, the dog whined loudly. And still later it crept close to the man and caught the scent of death. This made the animal bristle and back away. A little longer it delayed, howling under the stars that leaped and danced and shone brightly in the cold sky. Then it turned and trotted up the trail in the direction of the camp it knew, where were the other food-providers and fire-providers.

from: "The League of the Old Men"

Imber looked very tired. The fatigue of hopelessness and age was in his face. His shoulders drooped depressingly, and his eyes were lack-luster. His mop of hair should have been white, but sun and weatherbeat had burned and bitten it so that it hung limp and lifeless and colorless. He took no interest in what went on around him. The courtroom was jammed with the men of the creeks and trails, and there was an ominous note in the rumble and grumble of their low-pitched voices, which came to his ears like the growl of the sea from deep caverns.

He sat close by a window, and his apathetic eyes rested now and again on the dreary scene without. The sky was overcast, and a gray drizzle was falling. It was flood-time on the Yukon. The ice was gone, and the river was up in the town. Back and forth on the main street, in canoes and poling-boats, passed the people that never rested. Often he saw these boats turn aside from the street and enter the flooded square that marked the Barracks' parade ground. Sometimes they disappeared beneath him, and he heard them jar against the house-logs and their occupants scramble in through the window. After that came the slush of water against men's legs as they waded across the lower room and mounted the stairs. Then they appeared in the doorway, with doffed hats and dripping sea-boots, and added themselves to the waiting crowd.

And while they centered their looks on him, and in grim anticipation enjoyed the penalty he was to pay, Imber looked at them, and mused on their ways, and on their Law that never slept, but went on unceasing, in good times and bad, in flood and famine, through trouble and terror and death, and which would go on unceasing, it seemed to him, to the end of time.

A man rapped sharply on a table, and the conversation droned away into silence. Imber looked at the man. He seemed one in authority, yet Imber divined the square-browed man who sat by a desk farther back to be the one chief over them all and over the man who had rapped. Another man by the same table uprose and began to read aloud from many fine sheets of paper. At the top of each sheet he cleared his throat, at the bottom moistened his fingers. Imber did not understand his speech, but the others did, and he knew that it made them angry. Sometimes it made them very angry, and once a man cursed him, in single syllables, stinging and tense, till a man at the table rapped him to silence.

For an interminable period the man read. His monotonous, sing-song utterance lured Imber to dreaming, and he was dreaming deeply when the man ceased. A voice spoke to him in his own Whitefish tongue, and he roused up, without surprise, to look upon the face of his sister's son, a young man who had wandered away years agone to make his dwelling with the whites.

"Thou does not remember me," he said by way of greeting.

"Nay," Imber answered. "Thou art Howkan who went away. Thy mother be dead."

"She was an old woman," said Howkan.

But Imber did not hear, and Howkan, with hand upon his shoulder, roused him again.

"I shall speak to thee what the man has spoken, which is the tale of the troubles thou has done and which thou hast told, O fool, to the Captain Alexander. And thou shalt understand and say if it be true talk or talk not true. It is so commanded."

Howkan had fallen among the mission folk and been taught by them to read and write. In his hands he held the many fine sheets from which the man had read aloud, and which had been taken down by a clerk when Imber first made confession, through the mouth of Jimmy, to Captain Alexander. Howkan began to read. Imber listened for a space, when a wonderment rose up in his face and he broke in abruptly.

"That be my talk, Howkan. Yet from thy lips it comes when thy ears have not heard."

Howkan smirked with self-appreciation. His hair was parted in the middle. "Nay, from the paper it comes, O Imber. Never have my ears heard. From the paper it comes, through my eyes, into my head, and out of my mouth to thee. Thus it comes."

"Thus it comes? It be there in the paper?" Imber's voice sank in whisperful awe as he crackled the sheets 'twixt thumb and finger and stared at the charactery scrawled thereon. "It be a great medicine, Howkan, and thou art a worker of wonders."

"It be nothing, it be nothing," the young man responded carelessly and pridefully. He read at hazard from the document: *"In that year, before the break of the ice, came an old man and a boy who was lame of one foot. These also did I kill, and the old man made much noise—"*

"It be true," Imber interrupted breathlessly. "He made much noise and would not die for a long time. But how dost thou know, Howkan? The chief man of the white men told thee, mayhap? No one beheld me, and him alone have I told."

Howkan shook his head with impatience. "Have I not told thee it be there in the paper, O fool?"

Imber stared hard at the ink-scrawled surface. "As the hunter looks upon the snow and says, Here but yesterday there passed a rabbit; and here by the willow scrub it stood and listened, and heard, and was afraid; and here it turned upon its trail; and here it went with great swiftness, leaping wide; and here, with greater swiftness and wider leapings, came a lynx; and here, where the claws cut deep into the snow, the lynx made a very great leap; and here it struck, with the rabbit under and rolling belly up; and here leads off the trail of the lynx alone, and there is no more rabbit—as the hunter looks upon the markings of the snow and says thus and so and here, dost thou, too, look upon the paper and say thus and so and here be the things old Imber hath done?"

"Even so," said Howkan. "And now do thou listen, and keep thy woman's tongue between thy teeth till thou art called upon for speech."

Thereafter, and for a long time, Howkan read to him the confession, and Imber remained musing and silent. At the end, he said:

"It be my talk, and true talk, but I am grown old, Howkan, and forgotten things come back to me which were well for the head man there to know. First, there was the man who came over the Ice Mountains, with cunning traps made of iron, who sought the beaver of the Whitefish. Him I slew. And there were three men seeking gold on the Whitefish long ago. Them also I slew, and left them to the wolverines. And at the Five Fingers there was a man with a raft and much meat."

At the moments when Imber paused to remember, Howkan translated and a clerk reduced to writing. The courtroom listened stolidly to each unadorned little tragedy, till Imber told of a red-haired man whose eyes were crossed and whom he had killed with a remarkably long shot.

"Hell," said a man in the forefront of the onlookers. He said it soulfully and sorrowfully. He was red-haired. "Hell," he repeated. "That was my brother Bill." And at regular intervals throughout the session, his solemn "hell" was heard in the courtroom; nor did his comrades check him, nor did the man at the table rap him to order.

Imber's head drooped once more, and his eyes went dull, as though a film rose up and covered them from the world. And he dreamed as only age can dream upon the colossal futility of youth.

Later, Howkan roused him again, saying: "Stand up, O Imber. It be commanded that thou tellest why you did these troubles, and slew these people, and at the end journeyed here seeking the Law."

Imber rose feebly to his feet and swayed back and forth. He began to speak in a low and faintly rumbling voice, but Howkan interrupted him.

"This old man, he is damn crazy," he said in English to the square-browed man. "His talk is foolish and like that of a child."

"We will hear his talk which is like that of a child," said the square-browed man. "And we will hear it, word for word, as he speaks it. Do you understand?"

Howkan understood, and Imber's eyes flashed, for he had witnessed the play between his sister's son and the man in authority. And then began the story, the epic of a bronze patriot which might well itself be wrought into bronze for the generations unborn. The crowd fell strangely silent, and the square-browed judge leaned head on hand and pondered his soul and the soul of his race. Only was heard the deep tones of Imber, rhythmically alternating with the shrill voice of the interpreter, and now and again, like the bell of the lord, the wondering and meditative "Hell" of the red-haired man.

"I am Imber of the Whitefish people." So ran the interpretation of Howkan, whose inherent barbarism gripped hold of him, and who lost his mission culture and veneered civilization as he caught the savage ring and rhythm of old Imber's tale. "My father was Otsbaok, a strong man. The land was warm with sunshine and gladness when I was a boy. The people did not hunger after strange things, nor hearken to new voices, and the ways of their fathers were their ways. The women found favor in the eyes of the young men, and the young men looked upon them with content. Babes hung at the breasts of the women, and they were heavy-hipped with increase of the tribe. Men were men in those days. In peace and plenty, and in war and famine, they were men.

"At that time there was more fish in the water than now, and more meat in the forest. Our dogs were wolves, warm with thick hides and hard to the frost and storm. And as with our dogs so with us, for we were likewise hard to the frost and storm. And when the Pellys came into our land we slew them and were slain. For we were men, we Whitefish, and our fathers and our fathers' fathers had fought against the Pellys and determined the bounds of the land.

"As I say, with our dogs, so with us. And one day came the first white man. He dragged himself, so, on hand and knee, in the snow. And his skin was stretched tight, and his bones were sharp beneath. Never was such a man, we thought, and we wondered of what strange tribe he was, and of its land. And he was weak, most weak, like a little child, so that we gave him a place by the fire, and warm furs to lie upon, and we gave him food as little children are given food.

"And with him was a dog, large as three of our dogs, and very weak. The hair of this dog was short, and not warm, and the tail was frozen so that the end fell off. And this strange dog we fed, and bedded by the fire, and fought from it our dogs, which else would have killed him. And what of the moose meat and the sun-dried salmon, the man and dog took strength to themselves; and what of the strength they became big and unafraid. And the man spoke loud words and laughed at the old men and young men, and looked boldly upon the maidens. And the dog fought with our dogs, and for all of his short hair and softness slew three of them in one day.

"When we asked the man concerning his people, he said, 'I have many brothers,' and laughed in a way that was not good. And when he was in his full strength he went away, and with him went Noda, daughter to the chief. First, after that, was one of our bitches brought to pup. And never was there such a breed of dogs—big-headed, thick-jawed, and short-haired, and helpless. Well do I remember my father, Otsbaok, a strong man. His face was black with anger at such helplessness, and he took a stone, so, and so, and there was no more helplessness. And two summers after that came Noda back to us with a man-child in the hollow of her arm.

"And that was the beginning. Came a second white man, with short-haired dogs, which he left behind him when he went. And with him went six of our strongest dogs, for which, in trade, he had given Koo-So-Tee, my mother's brother, a wonderful pistol that fired with great swiftness six times. And Koo-So-Tee was very big, what of the pistol, and laughed at our bows and arrows. 'Woman's things,' he called them, and went forth against the bald-face grizzly, with the pistol in his hand. Now it be known that it is not good to hunt the bald-face with a pistol, but how were we to know? And how was Koo-So-Tee to know? So he went against the bald-face, very brave, and fired the pistol with great swiftness six times; and the bald-face but grunted and broke in his breast like it were an egg, and like honey from a bee's nest dripped the brains of Koo-So-Tee upon the ground. He was a good hunter, and there was no one to bring meat to his squaw and children. And we were bitter, and we said, 'That which for the white men is well, is for us not well.' And this be true. There be many white men and fat, but their ways have made us few and lean.

"Came the third white man, with great wealth of all manner of wonderful foods and things. And twenty of our strongest dogs he took from us in trade. Also, what of presents and great promises, ten of our young hunters did he take with him on a journey which fared no man knew where. It is said they died in the snow of the Ice Mountains where man has never been, or in the Hills of Silence which are beyond the edge of the earth. Be that as it may, dogs and young hunters were seen never again by the Whitefish people.

"And more white men came with the years, and ever, with pay and presents, they led the young men away with them. And sometimes the young men came back with strange tales of dangers and toils in the lands beyond the Pellys, and sometimes they did not come back. And we said: 'If they be unafraid of life, these white men, it is because they have many lives; but we be few by the Whitefish, and the young men shall go away no more.' But the young men did go away; and the young women went also; and we were very wroth.

"It be true, we ate flour, and salt pork, and drank tea which was a great delight; only, when we could not get tea, it was very bad and we became short of speech and quick of anger. So we grew to hunger for the things the white men brought in trade. Trade! Trade! All the time was it trade! One winter we sold our meat for clocks that would not go, and watches with broken guts, and files worn smooth, and pistols without cartridges and worthless. And then came famine, and we were without meat, and two score died ere the break of spring.

" 'Now we are grown weak,' we said; 'and the Pellys will fall upon us, and our bounds be overthrown.' But as it fared with us, so had it fared with the Pellys, and they were too weak to come against us.

"My father, Otsbaok, a strong man, was now old and very wise. And he spoke to the chief, saying: 'Behold, our dogs be worthless. No longer are they thick-furred and strong, and they die in the frost and harness. Let us go into the village and kill them, saving only the wolf ones, and these let us tie out in the night that they may mate with the wild wolves of the forest. Thus shall we have dogs warm and strong again.'

"And his word was harkened to, and we Whitefish became known for our dogs, which were the best in the land. But known we were not for ourselves. The best of our young men and women had gone away with the white men to wander on trail and river to far places. And the young women came back old and broken, as Noda had come, or they came not at all. And the young men came back to sit by our fires for a time, full of ill speech and rough ways, drinking evil drinks and gambling through long nights and days, with a great unrest always in their hearts, till the call of the white men came to them and they went away again to the unknown places. And they were without honor and respect, jeering the old-time customs and laughing in the faces of chief and shamans.

"As I say, we were become a weak breed, we Whitefish. We sold our warm skins and furs for tobacco and whiskey and thin cotton things that left us shivering in the cold. And the coughing sickness came upon us, and men and women coughed and sweated through the long nights, and the hunters on trail spat blood upon the snow. And now one, and now another, bled swiftly from the mouth and died. And the women bore few children, and those they bore were weak and given to sickness. And other sicknesses came to us from the white men, the like of which we had never known and could not understand. Smallpox, likewise measles, have I heard these sicknesses named, and we died of them as die the salmon in the still eddies when in the fall their eggs are spawned and there is no longer need for them to live.

"And yet, and here be the strangeness of it, the white men come as the breath of death; all their ways lead to death, their nostrils are filled with it; and yet they do not die. Theirs the whiskey, and tobacco, and short-haired dogs; theirs the many sicknesses, the smallpox and measles, the coughing and mouth-bleeding; theirs the white skin, and softness to the frost and storm; and theirs the pistols that shoot six times very swift and are worthless. And yet they grow fat on their many ills, and prosper, and lay a heavy hand over all the world and tread mightily upon its peoples. And their women, too, are soft as little babes, most breakable and never broken, the mothers of men. And out of all this softness, and sickness, and weakness, come strength, and power, and authority. They be gods, or devils, as the case may be. I do not know. What do I know, I, old Imber of the Whitefish? Only do I know that they are past understanding, these white men, far-wanderers and fighters over the earth that they be.

"As I say, the meat in the forest became less and less. It be true, the white man's gun is most excellent and kills a long way off; but of what worth the gun, when there is no meat to kill? When I was a boy on the Whitefish there was moose on every hill, and each year came the caribou uncountable. But now the hunter may take the trail ten days and not one moose gladdens his eyes, while the caribou uncountable come no more at all. Small worth the gun, I say, killing a long way off, when there be nothing to kill.

"And I, Imber, pondered upon these things, watching the while the Whitefish, and the Pellys, and all the tribes of the land, perishing as perished the meat of the forest. Long I pondered. I talked with the shamans and the old men who were wise. I went apart that the sounds of the village might not disturb me, and I ate no meat so that my belly should not press upon me, and make me slow of eye and ear. I sat long and sleepless in the forest, wide-eyed for the sign, my ears patient and keen for the word that was to come. And I wandered alone in the blackness of night to the river bank, where was wind-moaning and sobbing of water, and where I sought wisdom from the ghosts of old shamans in the trees and dead and gone.

"And in the end, as in a vision, came to me the short-haired and detestable dogs, and the way seemed plain. By the wisdom of Otsbaok, my father and a strong man, had the blood of our own wolf-dogs been kept clean, wherefore had they remained warm of hide and strong in the harness. So I returned to my village and made oration to the men. 'A very large tribe, and doubtless there is no longer meat in their land, and they are come among us to make a new land for themselves. But they weaken us, and we die. They are a very hungry folk. Already has our meat gone from us, and it were well, if we would live, that we deal by them as we have dealt by their dogs.'

"And further oration I made, counseling fight. And the men of the Whitefish listened, and some said one thing, and some another, and some spoke of other and worthless things, and no man made brave talk of deeds and war. But while the young men were weak as water and afraid, I watched that the old men sat silent, and that in their eyes fires came and went. And later, when the village slept and no one knew, I drew the old men away into the forest and made more talk. And now we were agreed, and we remembered the good young days, and the free land, and the times of plenty, and the gladness and sunshine; and we called ourselves brothers, and swore great secrecy, and a mighty oath to cleanse the land of the evil breed that had come upon it. It be plain we were fools, but how were we to know, we old men of the Whitefish?

"And to hearten the others, I did the first deed. I kept guard upon the Yukon till the first canoe came down. In it were two white men, and when I stood upright upon the bank and raised my hand they changed their course and drove in to me. And the man in the bow lifted his head, so, that he might know wherefore I wanted him, my arrow sang through the air straight to his throat, and he knew. The second man, who held paddle in the stern, had his rifle half to his shoulder when the first of my three spear-casts smote him.

"'These be the first,' I said, when the old men had gathered to me. 'Later we will bind together all the old men of all the tribes, and after that the young men who remain strong, and the work will become easy.'

"And then the two dead white men we cast into the river. And of the canoe, which was a very good canoe, we made a fire, and a fire, also, of the things within the canoe. But first we looked at the things, and they were pouches of leather which we cut open with our knives. And inside these pouches were many papers, like that from which thou has read, O Howkan, with markings on them which we marveled at and could not understand. Now, I am become wise, and I know them for the speech of men as though hast told me."

A whisper and buzz went around the courtroom when Howkan finished interpreting the affair of the canoe, and one man's voice spoke up: "That was the lost '91 mail, Peter James and Delaney bringing it in and last spoken at Le Barge by Matthews going out." The clerk scratched steadily away, and another paragraph was added to the history of the North.

"There be little more," Imber went on slowly. "It be there on the paper, the things we did. We were old men, and we did not understand. Even I, Imber, do not now understand. Secretly we slew, and continued to slay, for with our years we were crafty and we had learned the swiftness of going without haste. When the white men came among us with black looks and rough words, and took away six of the young men with irons binding them helpless, we knew we must slay wider and farther. And one by one we old men departed up river and down to the unknown lands. It was a brave thing. Old we were, and unafraid, but the fear of far places is a terrible fear to men who are old.

"So we slew, without haste and craftily. On the Chilcoot and in the Delta we slew, from the passes to the sea, wherever the white men camped or broke their trails. It be true, they died, but it was without worth. Ever did they come over the mountains, ever did they grow and grow, while we, being old, became less and less. I remember, by the Caribou Crossing, the camp of a white man. He was a very little white man, and three of the old men came upon him in his sleep. And the next day I came upon the four of them. The white man alone still breathed, and there was breath in him to curse me once and well before he died.

"And so it went, now one old man, and now another. Sometimes the word reached us long after of how they died, and sometimes it did not reach us. And the old men of the other tribes were weak and afraid, and would not join with us. As I say, one by one, till I alone was left. I am Imber, of the Whitefish people. My father was Otsbaok, a strong man. There are no Whitefish now. Of the old men I am the last. The young men and young women are gone away, some to live with the Pellys, some with the Salmons, and more with the white men. I am very old, and very tired, and it being vain fighting the Law, as thou sayest, Howkan, I am come seeking the Law."

"O Imber, thou art indeed a fool," said Howkan.

But Imber was dreaming. The square-browed judge like-wise dreamed, and all his race rose up before him in a mighty phantasmagoria—his steel-shod, mail-clad race, the lawgiver and world-maker among the families of men. He saw it dawn red-flickering across the dark forests and sullen seas; he saw it blaze, bloody and red, to full and triumphant noon; and down the shaded slope he saw the blood-red sands dropping into night. And through it all he observed the Law, pitiless and potent, ever unswerving and ever ordaining, greater than the motes of men who fulfilled it or were crushed by it, even as it was greater than he, his heart speaking for softness.

II

The Great Faithless Sea

The achievement of a difficult feat is successful adjustment to a sternly exacting environment. The more difficult the feat, the greater the satisfaction at its accomplishment.

It is good to ride the tempest and feel godlike. I dare to assert that for a finite speck of pulsating jelly to feel godlike is a far more glorious feeling than for a god to feel godlike.

Sheep Camp, 1897, on the trail north. The young man in the center is thought to be Jack London.

Chilkoot Pass: the way to the gold fields.

Panning for
gold, 1897.

Miner's cabin,
Yukon Territory.

Dawson, Yukon
Territory, site of Jack
London's final spree
before leaving for the
states via the Yukon
River.

Dawson in November. Ice on the Yukon has trapped
some river steamers.

The only way to go during winter in the Yukon.

Jack and Charmian on board the *Snark*.

Underway at last.

"Finding one's way about."

Jack in Hawaii with the *Snark* in background.

Jack in a South
Seas outrigger.

Jack's writing table;
Solomon Islands.

Charmian in the
Solomons.

Charmian London,
"mate woman."

Jack at his ranch
in Sonoma, California.

Jack sitting for Xavier Martinez in
Glen Ellen, California.

Jack London leaving
the steamship to go
ashore in Korea to
cover the Russo–
Japanese War.

from: *The Cruise of the* Snark

(The Cruise of the Snark is Jack London's account of the building of his yacht and the beginnings of his projected round the world voyage. Ed.)

The Inconceivable and the Monstrous

"Spare no money," I said to Roscoe. "Let everything on the *Snark* be of the best. And never mind decoration. Plain pine boards is good enough finishing for me. But put the money into the construction. Let the *Snark* be as staunch and strong as any boat afloat. Never mind what it costs to make her staunch and strong; you see that she is made staunch and strong, and I'll go on writing and earning the money to pay for it."

And I did . . . as well as I could; for the *Snark* ate up money faster than I could earn it. In fact, every little while I had to borrow money with which to supplement my earnings.

Now I borrowed one thousand dollars, now I borrowed two thousand dollars, and now I borrowed five thousand dollars. And all the time I went on working every day and sinking the earnings in the venture. I worked Sundays as well, and I took no holidays. But it was worth it. Every time I thought of the *Snark* I knew she was worth it.

For know, gentle reader, the staunchness of the *Snark*. She is forty-five feet long on the waterline. Her garboard strake is three inches thick; her planking two and a half inches thick; her deck-planking two inches thick and in all her planking there are no butts. I know, for I ordered that planking especially from Puget Sound. Then the *Snark* has four water-tight compartments, which is to say that her length is broken by three water-tight bulkheads. Thus, no matter how large a leak the *Snark* may spring, only one compartment can fill with water. The other three compartments will keep her afloat, anyway, and, besides, will enable us to mend the leak. There is another virtue in these bulkheads. The last compartment of all, in the very stern, contains six tanks that carry over one thousand gallons of gasoline. Now gasoline is a very dangerous article to carry in bulk on a small craft far out on the wide ocean. But when the six tanks that do not leak are themselves contained in a compartment hermetically sealed off from the rest of the boat, the danger will be seen to be very small indeed.

The *Snark* is a sailboat. She was built primarily to sail. But incidentally, as an auxiliary, a seventy-horse-power engine was installed. This is a good strong engine. I ought to know. I paid for it to come all the way from New York. Then, on the deck, above the engine, is a windlass. It is a magnificent affair. It weighs several hundred pounds and takes up no end of deck room. You see, it is ridiculous to hoist up anchor by hand-power when there is a seventy-horse-power engine on board. So we installed the windlass, transmitting power to it from the engine by means of a gear and castings specially made in a San Francisco foundry.

The *Snark* was made for comfort, and no expense was spared in this regard. There is the bathroom, for instance, small and compact, it is true, but containing all the conveniences of a bathroom upon land. The bathroom is a beautiful dream of schemes and devices, pumps and levers, and sea-valves. Why, in the course of its building, I used to lie awake at nights thinking of that bathroom. And next to the bathroom come the lifeboat and the launch. They are carried on deck, and they take up what little space might have been left to us for exercise. But then, they beat life insurance; and the prudent man, even if he has built as staunch and strong a craft as the *Snark,* will see to it that he has a good lifeboat as well. And ours is a good one. It is a dandy. It was stipulated to cost one hundred and fifty dollars, and when I came to pay the bill, it turned out to be three hundred and ninety-five dollars. That shows how good a lifeboat it is.

I could go on at great length relating the various virtues and excellences of the *Snark,* but I refrain. I have bragged enough as it is, and I have bragged to a purpose, as will be seen before my tale is ended. And please remember its title, "The Inconceivable and Monstrous." It was planned that the *Snark* should sail on October 1, 1906. That she did not so sail was inconceivable and monstrous. There was no valid reason for not sailing except that she was not ready. She was promised on November first, on November fifteenth, on December first; and yet she was never ready. On December first Charmian and I left the sweet, clean Sonoma country and came down to live in the stifling city—but not for long, oh, no, only for two weeks, for we would sail on December fifteenth. And I guess we ought to know, for Roscoe said so, and it was on his advice that we came to the city to stay for two weeks. Alas, the two weeks went by, four weeks went by, six weeks went by, eight weeks went by, and we were farther away from sailing than ever. Explain it? Who?—me? I can't. It is the one thing in all my life that I have backed down on. There is no explaining it; if there were, I'd do it. I, who am an artisan of speech, confess my inability to explain why the *Snark* was not ready. As I have said, and I must repeat, it was inconceivable and monstrous.

The eight weeks became sixteen weeks, and then, one day, Roscoe cheered us up by saying: "If we don't sail before April first, you can use my head for a football."

Two weeks later he said, "I'm getting my head in training for that match."

"Never mind," Charmian and I said to each other, "think of the wonderful boat it is going to be when it is completed."

Whereat we would rehearse for our mutual encouragement the manifold virtues and excellences of the *Snark*. Also, I would borrow more money, and would get down closer to my desk and write harder, and I refused heroically to take a Sunday off and go out into the hills with my friends. I was building a boat, and by the eternal it was going to be a boat, and a boat spelled out all in capitals B-O-A-T; and no matter what it cost I didn't care. So long as it was a BOAT.

And, oh, there is one other excellence of the *Snark* upon which I must brag, namely, her bow. No sea could ever come over it. It laughs at the sea, that bow does; it challenges the sea; it snorts defiance at the sea. And withal it is a beautiful bow; the lines of it are dreamlike; I doubt if ever a boat was blessed with a more beautiful and at the same time a more capable bow. It was a bow made to punch storms. To touch that bow is to rest one's hand on the cosmic nose of things. To look at it is to realize that expense cut no figure where it was concerned. And every time our sailing was delayed, or a new expense was tacked on, we thought of that wonderful bow and were content.

The *Snark* is a small boat. When I figured seven thousand dollars as her generous cost, I was both generous and correct. I have built barns and houses, and I know the particular trait such things have of running past their estimated cost. This knowledge was mine, was already mine, when I estimated the probable cost of the building of the *Snark* at seven thousand dollars. Well, she cost thirty thousand. Now don't ask me, please. It is the truth. I signed the checks and raised the money. Of course there is no explaining it, inconceivable and monstrous is what it is, as you will agree, I know, ere my tale is done.

Then there was the matter of delay. I dealt with forty-seven different kinds of union men and with one hundred and fifteen different firms. And not one union man and not one firm of all the union men and all the firms ever delivered anything at the time agreed upon, nor was ever on time for anything except payday and bill collection. Men pledged me their immortal souls that they would deliver a certain thing on a certain date; as a rule, after such pledging, they rarely exceeded being three months late in delivery. And so it went, and Charmian and I consoled ourselves by saying what a splendid boat the *Snark* was, so staunch and strong; also we would get into the small boat and row around the *Snark* and gloat over her unbelievably wonderful bow.

"Think," I would say to Charmian, "of a gale off the China coast, and of the *Snark* hove to, that splendid bow of hers driving into the storm. Not a drop will come over that bow. She be as dry as a feather, and we'll be all below playing whist while the gale howls."

And Charmian would press my hand enthusiastically and exclaim: "It's all worth every bit of it—the delay, the expense, and worry, and all the rest. Oh, what a truly wonderful boat!"

Whenever I looked at the bow of the *Snark* or thought of her watertight compartments, I was encouraged. Nobody else, however, was encouraged. My friends began to make bets against the various sailing dates of the *Snark*. Mr. Wiget, who was left behind in charge of our Sonoma ranch, was the first to cash his bet. He collected on New Year's Day, 1907. After that the bets came fast and furious. My friends surrounded me like a gang of harpies, making bets against every sailing date that I set. I was rash, and I was stubborn. I bet, and I bet, and I continued to bet; and I paid them all. Why, the women-kind of my friends grew so brave that those among them who had never bet before began to bet with me. And I paid them, too.

"Never mind," said Charmian to me, "just think of that bow and of being hove to on the China Seas."

"You see," I said to my friends, when I paid the latest bunch of wagers, "neither trouble nor cash is being spared in making the *Snark* the most seaworthy craft that ever sailed out through the Golden Gate—that is what causes all the delay."

In the meantime editors and publishers with whom I had contracts pestered me with demands for explanations. But how could I explain to them when I was unable to explain to myself, or when there was nobody, not even Roscoe, to explain to me? The newspapers began to laugh at me and to publish rhymes anent the *Snark*'s departure with refrains like, "Not yet, but soon." And Charmian cheered me up by reminding me of the bow, and I went to a banker and borrowed five thousand more. There was one recompense for the delay, however. A friend of mine, who happens to be a critic, wrote a roast of me, of all I had done, and of all I was ever going to do; and he planned to have it published after I was out on the ocean. I was still on shore when it came out, and he has been busy explaining ever since.

And the time continued to go by. One thing was becoming apparent, namely, that it was impossible to finish the *Snark* in San Francisco. She had been so long in the building that she was beginning to break down and wear out. In fact, she had reached the stage where she was breaking down faster than she could be repaired. She had become a joke. Nobody took her seriously; least of all the men who worked on her. I said we would sail her just as she was and finish building her in Honolulu. Promptly she sprang a leak that had to be attended to before we could sail. I started her for the boat-ways. Before she got to them she was caught between two huge barges and received a vigorous crushing. We got her on the ways, and, part way along, the ways spread and dropped her through, stern-first, into the mud.

It was a pretty tangle, a job for wreckers, not boat-builders. There are two high tides every twenty-four hours, and at every high tide, night and day, for a week, there were two steam tugs pulling and hauling on the *Snark*. There she was, stuck, fallen between the ways and standing on her stern. Next, and while still in that predicament, we started to use the gears and castings made in the local foundry whereby power was conveyed to the windlass. It was the first time we ever tried to use that windlass. The castings had flaws; they shattered asunder, the gears ground together, and the windlass was out of commission. Following upon that, the seventy-horse-power engine went out of commission. This engine came from New York; so did its bed-plate; there was a flaw in the bed-plate; there were lots of flaws in the bed-plate; and the seventy-horse-power engine broke away from its shattered foundations, reared up in the air, smashed all connections and fastenings, and fell over on its side. And the *Snark* continued to stick between the spread ways, and the two tugs continued to haul vainly upon her.

"Never mind," said Charmian, "think of what a staunch, strong boat she is."

"Yes," said I, "and of that beautiful bow."

So we took heart and went at it again. The ruined engine was lashed down on its rotten foundation; the smashed castings and cogs of the power transmission were taken down and stored away—all for the purpose of taking them to Honolulu where repairs and new castings could be made. Somewhere in the dim past the *Snark* had received on the outside one coat of white paint. The intention of the color was still evident, however, when one got it in the right light. The *Snark* had never received any paint on the inside. On the contrary, she was coated inches thick with the grease and tobacco-juice of the multitudinous mechanics who had toiled upon her. Never mind, we said; the grease and filth could be planed off, and later, when we fetched Honolulu, the *Snark* could be painted at the same time she was being rebuilt.

By main strength and sweat we dragged the *Snark* off from the wrecked ways and laid her alongside the Oakland City Wharf. The drays brought all the outfit from home, the books and blankets and personal luggage. Along with this, everything else came on board in a torrent of confusion— wood and coal, water and water tanks, vegetables, provisions, oil, the lifeboat and the launch, all our friends, all the friends of our friends, to say nothing of the friends of the friends of our crew. Also there were reporters, and photographers, and strangers, and cranks, and finally, and over all, clouds of coal dust from the wharf.

We were to sail Sunday at eleven, and Saturday afternoon had arrived. The crowd on the wharf and the coal dust were thicker than ever. In one pocket I carried a checkbook, a fountain pen, a dater, and a blotter; in another pocket I carried between one and two thousand dollars in paper money and gold. I was ready for the creditors, cash for the small ones, checks for the large ones, and was waiting only for Roscoe to arrive with the balances of the accounts of the one hundred and fifteen firms who had delayed me so many months. And then—

And then the inconceivable and monstrous happened once more. Before Roscoe could arrive there arrived another man. He was a United States marshal. He tacked a notice on the

Snark's brave mast so that all on the wharf could read that the *Snark* had been libeled for debt. The marshal left a little old man in charge of the *Snark* and himself went away. I had no longer any control of the *Snark*, nor of her wonderful bow. The little old man was now her lord and master, and I learned that I was paying him three dollars a day for being lord and master. Also, I learned the name of the man who had libeled the *Snark*. It was Sellers; the debt was two hundred and thirty-two dollars; and the deed was no more than was to be expected from the possessor of such a name. Sellers! Ye gods! Sellers!

But who under the sun was Sellers? I looked in my checkbook and saw that two weeks before I had made him out a check for five hundred dollars. Other checkbooks showed me that during the many months of the building of the *Snark* I had paid him several thousand dollars. Then why in the name of common decency hadn't he tried to collect his miserable little balance instead of libeling the *Snark*? I thrust my hands into my pockets, and in one pocket encountered the checkbook and the dater and the pen, and in the other pocket the gold money and the paper money. There was the wherewithal to settle his pitiful account a few score of times and over—why hadn't he given me a chance? There was no explanation; it was merely the inconceivable and monstrous.

To make matters worse, the *Snark* had been libeled late Saturday afternoon; and though I sent lawyers and agents all over Oakland and San Francisco, neither United States judge, nor United States marshal, nor Mr. Sellers, nor Mr. Sellers' attorney, nor anybody could be found. They were all out of town for the weekend. And so the *Snark* did not sail Sunday morning at eleven. The little old man was still in charge, and he said no. And Charmian and I walked out on an opposite wharf and took consolation in the *Snark*'s wonderful bow and thought of all the gales and typhoons it would proudly punch.

"A bourgeois trick," I said to Charmian, speaking of Mr. Sellers and his libel, "a petty trader's panic. But never mind; our troubles will cease when once we are away from this and out on the wide ocean."

And in the end we sailed away, on Tuesday morning, April 23, 1907. We started rather lame, I confess. We had to hoist the anchor by hand, because the power transmission was a wreck. Also, what remained of our seventy-horse-power engine was lashed down for ballast on the bottom of the *Snark*. But what of such things? They could be fixed in Honolulu, and in the meantime think of the magnificent rest of the boat! It is true, the engine in the launch wouldn't run, and the lifeboat leaked like a sieve; but then they weren't the *Snark*; they were mere appurtenances. The things that counted were the watertight bulkheads, the solid planking without butts, the bathroom devices—they were the *Snark*. And then there was, greatest of all, that noble, wind-punching bow.

We sailed out through the Golden Gate and set our course south toward that part of the Pacific where we could hope to pick up with the northeast trades. And right away things began to happen. I had calculated that youth was the stuff for a voyage like that of the *Snark*, and I had taken three youths—the engineer, the cook and the cabin boy. My calculation was only two-thirds off; I had forgotten to calculate on seasick youth, and I had two of them, the cook and the cabin boy. They immediately took to their bunks, and that was the end of their usefulness for a week to come. It will be understood, from the foregoing, that we did not have the hot meals we might have had, nor were things kept clean and orderly down below. But it did not matter very much anyway, for we quickly discovered that our box of oranges had at some time been frozen; that our box of apples was mushy and spoiling; that the crate of cabbages, spoiled before it was ever delivered to us, had to go over the side instanter; that kerosene had been spilled on the carrots, and that the turnips were woody and the beets rotten, while the kindling was dead wood that wouldn't burn, and the coal, delivered in rotten potato sacks, had spilled all over the deck and was washing through the scuppers.

But what did it matter? Such things were mere accessories. There was the boat—she was all right, wasn't she? I strolled along the deck and in one minute counted fourteen butts in the beautiful planking ordered specially from Puget Sound in order that there should be no butts in it. Also, that deck leaked, and it leaked badly. It drowned Roscoe out of his bunk and ruined the tools in the engine room, to say nothing of the provisions it ruined in the galley. Also, the sides of the *Snark* leaked, and the bottom leaked, and we had to pump every day to keep her afloat. The floor of the galley is a couple of feet above the inside bottom of the *Snark;* and yet I have stood on the floor of the galley, trying to snatch a cold bite, and been wet to the knees by the water churning around inside four hours after the last pumping.

Then those magnificent watertight compartments that cost so much time and money—well, they weren't watertight after all. The water moved free as the air from one compartment to another; furthermore, a strong smell of gasoline from the after compartment leads me to suspect that some one or more of the half-dozen tanks stored there have sprung a leak. The tanks leak, and they are not hermetically sealed in their compartment. Then there was the bathroom with its pumps and levers and sea-valves—it went out of commission inside the first twenty-four hours. Powerful iron levers broke off short in one's hand when one tried to pump with them. The bathroom was the swiftest wreck of any portion of the *Snark*.

And the iron-work on the *Snark*, no matter what its source, proved to be mush. For instance, the bed-plate of the engine came from New York, and it was mush; so were the casting and gears for the windlass that came from San Francisco. And finally there was the wrought iron used in the rigging that carried away in all directions when the first strains were put upon it. Wrought iron, mind you, and it snapped like macaroni.

A gooseneck on the gaff of the mainsail broke short off. We replaced it with the gooseneck from the gaff of the storm trysail, and the second gooseneck broke off inside fifteen minutes of use, and, mind you, it had been taken from the gaff of the storm trysail, upon which we would have depended in time of storm. At the present moment the *Snark* trails her mainsail like a broken wing, the gooseneck being replaced by a rough lashing. We'll see if we can get honest iron in Honolulu.

Man had betrayed us and sent us to sea in a sieve, but the Lord must have loved us, for we had calm weather in which to learn that we must pump every day in order to keep afloat, and that more trust could be placed in a wooden toothpick than in the most massive piece of iron to be found on board.

145

As the staunchness and the strength of the *Snark* went glimmering, Charmian and I pinned our faith more and more to the *Snark*'s wonderful bow. There was nothing else left to pin to. It was all inconceivable and monstrous, we knew, but that bow, at least, was rational. And then, one evening, we started to heave to.

How shall I describe it? First of all, for the benefit of the tyro, let me explain that heaving to is a sea maneuver which, by means of short and balanced canvas, compels a vessel to ride bow on to wind and sea. When the wind is too strong, or the sea is too high, a vessel the size of the *Snark* can heave to with ease, whereupon there is no more work to do on deck. Nobody needs to steer. The lookout is superfluous. All hands can go below and sleep or play whist.

Well, it was blowing half of a small summer gale when I told Roscoe we'd heave to. Night was coming on. I had been steering nearly all day, and all hands on deck (Roscoe and Bert and Charmian) were tired, while all hands below were seasick. It happened that we had already put two reefs in the big mainsail. The flying jib and the jib were taken in, and a reef put in the fore-staysail. The mizzen was also taken in. About this time the flying jib-boom buried itself in a sea and broke short off. I started to put the wheel down in order to heave to. The *Snark* at that moment was rolling in the trough. She continued rolling in the trough. I put the spokes down harder and harder. She never budged from the trough. (The trough, gentle reader, is the most dangerous position of all to lay a vessel.) I put the wheel hard down, and still the *Snark* rolled in the trough. Eight points [90 degrees] was the nearest I could get her to the wind. I had Roscoe and Bert come in on the main sheet. The *Snark* rolled on in the trough, now putting her rail under on one side and now under on the other side.

Again the inconceivable and monstrous was showing its grizzly head. It was grotesque, impossible. I refused to believe it. Under double reefed mainsail and single reefed staysail the *Snark* refused to heave to. We flattened the mainsail down. It did not alter the *Snark*'s course a tenth of a degree. We slacked the mainsail off with no more result. We set a storm trysail on the mizzen and took in the mainsail. No change. The *Snark* roiled on in the trough. That beautiful bow of hers refused to come up and face the wind.

Next we took in the reefed staysail. Thus, the only bit of canvas left on her was the storm trysail on the mizzen. If anything would bring her bow up to the wind, that would. Maybe you won't believe me when I say it failed, but I do say it failed. And I say it failed because I saw it fail, and not because I believe it failed. I don't believe it did fail. It is unbelievable, and I am not telling you what I believe; I am telling you what I saw.

Now, gentle reader, what would you do if you were on a small boat, rolling in the trough of the sea, a trysail on that small boat's stern that was unable to swing the bow up into the wind? Get out the sea-anchor. It's just what we did. We had a patent one, made to order and warranted not to dive. Imagine a hoop of steel that serves to keep open the mouth of a large, conical canvas bag, and you have a sea anchor. Well, we made a line fast to the sea anchor and to the bow of the *Snark* and then dropped the sea anchor overboard. It promptly dived. We had a tripping line on it, so we tripped the sea anchor and hauled it in. We attached a big timber as a float and dropped the sea anchor over again. This time it floated. The line to the bow grew taut. The trysail on the mizzen tended to swing the bow into the wind, but, in spite of this tendency, the *Snark* calmly took that sea anchor in her teeth and went on ahead, dragging it after her, still in the trough of the sea. And there you are. We even took in the trysail, hoisted the full mizzen in its place and hauled the full mizzen down flat, and the *Snark* wallowed in the trough and dragged the sea anchor behind her. Don't believe me. I don't believe it myself. I am merely telling you what I saw.

Now I leave it to you. Who ever heard of a sailing boat that wouldn't heave to?—that wouldn't heave to with a sea anchor to help it? Out of my brief experience with boats I know I never did. And I stood on deck and looked on the face of the inconceivable and monstrous—the *Snark* that wouldn't heave to. A stormy night with broken moonlight had come on. There was a splash of wet in the air, and up to windward there was a promise of rain squalls; and then there was the trough of the sea, cold and cruel in the moonlight, in which the *Snark* complacently rolled. And then we took in the sea anchor and the mizzen, hoisted the reefed staysail, ran the *Snark* off before it and went below—not to the hot meal that should have awaited us, but to skate across the slush and slime on the cabin floor, where cook and cabin boy lay like dead men in their bunks, and to lie down in our own bunks, with our clothes on ready for a call, and to listen to the bilge water spouting knee high on the galley floor.

In the Bohemian Club of San Francisco there are some crack sailors. I know, because I heard them pass judgment on the *Snark* during the process of her building. They found only one vital thing the matter with her, and on this they were all agreed, namely, that she could not run. She was all right in every particular, they said, except that I'd never be able to run her before a stiff wind and sea. "Her lines," they explained enigmatically, "it is the fault of her lines. She simply cannot be made to run, that is all." Well, I wish I'd only had those crack sailors of the Bohemian Club on board the *Snark* the other night to see for themselves their one, vital, unanimous judgment absolutely reversed. Run? It is the one thing the *Snark* does to perfection. Run? She ran with a sea anchor fast forward and a full mizzen flattened down aft. Run? At the present moment, as I write this, we are bowling along before it, at a six knot clip, in the northeast trades. Quite a tidy bit of sea is running. There is nobody at the wheel; the wheel is not even lashed and is set over a half-spoke of weather helm. To be precise, the wind is northeast, the *Snark*'s mizzen is furled, her mainsail is over to starboard, her head sheets are hauled flat, and the *Snark*'s course is south southwest. And yet there are men who have sailed the seas for forty years and who hold that no boat can run before it without being steered. They'll call me a liar when they read this; it's what they called Captain Slocum when he said the same of his *Spray*.

As regards the future of the *Snark* I'm all at sea. I don't know. If I had the money or the credit, I'd build another *Snark* that WOULD heave to. But I am at the end of my resources. I've got to put up with the present *Snark* or quit—and I can't quit. So I guess I'll have to try to get along with heaving the *Snark* to stern first. I am waiting for the next gale to see how it will work. I think it can be done. It all depends on how her stern takes the seas. And who knows but that some wild morning on the China Seas, some gray-beard skipper will stare, rub his incredulous eyes and stare again, at the spectacle of a weird, small craft very much like the *Snark*, hove to stern first and riding out the gale?

from: *The Cruise of the* Snark

Finding One's Way About

"But," our friends objected, "how dare you go to sea without a navigator on board? You're not a navigator, are you?"

I had to confess that I was not a navigator, that I had never looked through a sextant in my life, and that I doubted if I could tell a sextant from a nautical almanac. And when they asked if Roscoe was a navigator, I shook my head. Roscoe resented this. He had glanced at the "Epitome," bought for our voyage, knew how to use logarithm tables, had seen a sextant at some time, and, what of this and of his seafaring ancestry, he concluded that he did know navigation. But Roscoe was wrong, I still insist. When a young boy he came from Maine to California by way of the Isthmus of Panama, and that was the only time in his life that he was out of sight of land. He had never gone to a school of navigation, nor passed an examination in the same; nor had he sailed the deep sea and learned the art from some other navigator. He was a San Francisco Bay yachtsman, where land is always only several miles away and the art of navigation is never employed.

So the *Snark* started on her long voyage without a navigator. We beat through the Golden Gate on April 23, and headed for the Hawaiian Islands, twenty-one hundred sea-miles away as the gull flies. And the outcome was our justification. We arrived. And we arrived, furthermore, without any trouble, as you shall see; that is, without any trouble to amount to anything. To begin with, Roscoe tackled the navigating. He had the theory all right, but it was the first time he had ever applied it, as was evidenced by the erratic behavior of the *Snark*. Not but what the *Snark* was perfectly steady on the sea; the pranks she cut were on the chart. On a day with a light breeze she would make a jump on the chart that advertised "a wet sail and a flowing sheet," and on a day when she just raced over the ocean, she scarcely changed her position on the chart. Now when one's boat has logged six knots for twenty-four consecutive hours, it is incontestable that she has covered one hundred and forty-four miles of ocean. The ocean was all right, and so was the patent log; as for speed, one saw it with his own eyes. Therefore the thing that was not all right was the figuring that refused to boost the *Snark* along over the chart. Not that this happened every day, but that it did happen. And it was perfectly proper and no more than was to be expected from a first attempt at applying a theory.

The acquisition of the knowledge of navigation has a strange effect on the minds of men. The average navigator speaks of navigation with deep respect. To the layman navigation is a deep and awful mystery, which feeling has been generated in him by the deep and awful respect for navigation that the layman has seen displayed by navigators. I have known frank, ingenuous, and modest young men, open as the day, to learn navigation and at once betray secretiveness, reserve, and self-importance as if they had achieved some tremendous intellectual attainment. The average navigator impresses the layman as a priest of some holy rite. With bated breath, the amateur yachtsman navigator invites one in to look at his chronometer. And so it was that our friends suffered such apprehension at our sailing without a navigator.

During the building of the *Snark*, Roscoe and I had an agreement, something like this: "I'll furnish the books and instruments," I said, "and you study up navigation now. I'll be too busy to do any studying. Then, when we get to sea, you can teach me what you have learned." Roscoe was delighted. Furthermore, Roscoe was as frank and ingenuous and modest as the young men I have described. But when we got out to sea and he began to practice the holy rite, while I looked on admiringly, a change, subtle and distinctive, marked his bearing. When he shot the sun at noon, the flow of achievement wrapped him in lambent flame. When he went below, figured out his observation, and then returned on deck and announced our latitude and longitude, there was an authoritative ring in his voice that was new to all of us. But that was not the worst of it. He became filled with incommunicable information. And the more he discovered the reason for the erratic jumps of the *Snark* over the chart, and the less the *Snark* jumped, the more incommunicable and holy and awful became his information. My mild suggestions that it was about time that I began to learn, met with no hearty response, with no offers on his part to help me. He displayed not the slightest intention of living up to our agreement.

Now this was not Roscoe's fault; he could not help it. He had merely gone the way of all the men who learned navigation before him. By an understandable and forgivable confusion of values, plus a loss of orientation, he felt weighted by responsibility, and experienced the possession of power that was like unto that of a god. All his life Roscoe had lived on land, and therefore in sight of land. Being constantly in sight of land, with landmarks to guide him, he had managed, with occasional difficulties, to steer his body around and about the earth. Now he found himself on the sea, wide-stretching, bounded only by the eternal circle of the sky. This circle looked always the same. There were no landmarks. The sun rose to the east and set to the west and the stars wheeled through the night. But who may look at the sun or the stars and say, "My place on the face of the earth at the present moment is four and three-quarter miles to the west of Jones's Cash Store of Smithersville?" or "I know where I am now, for the Little Dipper informs me that Boston is three miles away on the second turning to the right?" And yet that was precisely what Roscoe did. That he was astounded by the achievement, is putting it mildly. He stood in reverential awe of himself; he had performed a miraculous feat. The act of finding himself on the face of the waters became a rite, and he felt himself a superior being to the rest of us who knew not this rite and were dependent on him for being shepherded across the heaving and limitless waste, the briny highroad that connects the continents and whereon there are no mile-stones. So, with the sextant he made obeisance to the sun-god, he consulted ancient tomes and tables of magic characters, muttered prayers in a strange tongue that sounded like INDEXERRORPARALLAXREFRACTION, made cabalistic signs on paper, added and carried one, and then, on a piece of holy script called the Grail—I mean the Chart—he placed his finger on a certain space conspicuous for its blankness and said, "Here we are." When we looked at the blank space and asked, "And where is that?" he answered in the cipher-code of the higher priesthood, "31–15–47 north, 133–5–30 west." And we said, "Oh," and felt mighty small.

So I aver, it was not Roscoe's fault. He was like unto a god, and he carried us in the hollow of his hand across the blank spaces on the chart. I experienced a great respect for Roscoe; this respect grew so profound that had he commanded, "Kneel down and worship me," I know that I should have flopped down on the deck and yammered. But, one day, there came a still small thought to me that said: "This is not a god; this is Roscoe, a mere man like myself. What he has done, I can do. Who taught him? Himself. Go you and do likewise— be your own teacher." And right there Roscoe crashed, and he was high priest of the *Snark* no longer. I invaded the sanctuary and demanded the ancient tomes and magic tables, also the prayer-wheel—the sextant, I mean.

And now, in simple language, I shall describe how I taught myself navigation. One whole afternoon I sat in the cockpit, steering with one hand and studying logarithms with the other. Two afternoons, two hours each, I studied the general theory of navigation and the particular process of taking a meridian altitude. Then I took the sextant, worked out the index error, and shot the sun. The figuring from the data of this observation was child's play. In the "Epitome" and the "Nautical Almanac" were scores of cunning tables, all worked out by mathematicians and astronomers. It was like using interest tables and lightning-calculator tables such as you all know. The mystery was mystery no longer. I put my finger on the chart and announced that that was where we were. I was right too, or at least I was as right as Roscoe, who selected a spot a quarter of a mile away from mine. Even he was willing to split the distance with me. I had exploded the mystery, and yet, such was the miracle of it, I was conscious of new power in me, and I felt the thrill and tickle of pride. And when Martin asked me, in the same humble and re-spectful way I had previously asked Roscoe, as to where we were, it was with exaltation and spiritual chest-throwing that I answered in the cipher-code of the higher priesthood and heard Martin's self-abasing and worshipful "Oh." As for Charmian, I felt that in a new way I had proved my right to her; and I was aware of another feeling, namely, that she was a most fortunate woman to have a man like me.

I couldn't help it. I tell it as a vindication of Roscoe and all the other navigators. The poison of power was working in me. I was not as other men—most other men; I knew what they did not know—the mystery of the heavens, that pointed out the way across the deep. And the taste of power I had received drove me on. I steered at the wheel long hours with one hand, and studied mystery with the other. By the end of the week, teaching myself, I was able to do divers things. For instance, I shot the North Star, at night, of course; got its altitude, cor-rected for index error, dip, etc., and found our latitude. And this latitude agreed with the latitude of the previous noon corrected by dead reckoning up to that moment. Proud? Well, I was even prouder with my next miracle. I was going to turn in at nine o'clock. I worked out the problem, self-instructed, and learned what star of the first magnitude would be passing the meridian around half-past eight. This star proved to be Alpha Crucis. I had never heard of the star before. I looked it up on the star map. It was one of the stars of the Southern Cross. What! thought I; have we been sailing with the Southern Cross in the sky of nights and never known it? Dolts that we are! Gudgeons and moles! I couldn't believe it. I went over the problem again, and verified it. Charmian had the wheel from eight till ten that evening. I told her to keep her eyes open and look due south for the Southern Cross. And when the stars came out, there shone the Southern Cross low on the horizon. Proud? No medicine man nor high priest was ever prouder. Furthermore, with the prayer-wheel I shot Alpha Crucis and from its altitude worked out our latitude. And still furthermore, I shot the North Star, too, and it agreed with what had been told me by the Southern Cross. Proud? Why, the language of the stars was mine, and I listened and heard them telling me my way over the deep.

Proud? I was a worker of miracles. I forgot how easily I had taught myself from the printed page. I forgot that all the work (and a tremendous work, too) had been done by the masterminds before me, the astronomers and mathematicians, who had discovered and elaborated the whole science of navigation and made the tables in the "Epitome." I remembered only the everlasting miracle of it—that I had listened to the voices of the stars and been told my place upon the highway of the sea. Charmian did not know, Martin did not know, Tochigi, the cabin-boy, did not know. But I told them. I was God's messenger. I stood between them and infinity. I translated the high celestial speech into terms of their ordinary understanding. We were heaven-directed, and it was I who could read the sign-post of the sky!—I! I!

And now, in a cooler moment, I hasten to blab the whole simplicity of it, to blab on Roscoe and the other navigators and the rest of the priesthood, all for fear that I may become even as they, secretive, immodest, and inflated with self-esteem. And I want to say this now: any young fellow with ordinary gray matter, ordinary education, and with the slightest trace of the student-mind, can get the books and charts, and instruments and teach himself navigation. Now I must not be misunderstood. Seamanship is an entirely different matter. It is not learned in a day, nor in many days; it requires years. Also, navigating by dead reckoning requires long study and practice. But navigating by observations of the sun, moon, and stars, thanks to the astronomers and mathematicians, is child's play. Any average young fellow can teach himself in a week. And yet again I must not be misunderstood. I do not mean to say that at the end of a week a young fellow could take charge of a fifteen-thousand-ton steamer, driving twenty knots an hour through the brine, racing from land to land, fair weather and foul, clear sky or cloudy, steering by degrees on the compass card and making landfalls with most amazing precision. But what I do mean is just this: the average young fellow I have described can get into a staunch sail-boat and put out across the ocean, without knowing anything about navigation, and at the end of the week he will know enough to know where he is on the chart. He will be able to take a

meridian observation with fair accuracy, and from that observation, with ten minutes of figuring, work out his latitude and
longitude. And, carrying neither freight nor passengers, being
under no press to reach his destination, he can jog comfort-
ably along, and if at any time he doubts his own navigation
and fears an imminent landfall, he can heave to all night and
proceed in the morning.

Joshua Slocum sailed around the world a few years ago in
a thirty-seven-foot boat all by himself. I shall never forget, in
his narrative of the voyage, where he heartily indorsed the
idea of young men, in similar small boats, making similar voyage. I promptly indorsed his idea, and so heartily that I took
my wife along. While it certainly makes a Cook's tour look
like thirty cents, on top of that, on top of the fun and pleasure, it is a splendid education for a young man—oh, not a
mere education in the things of the world outside, of lands,
and peoples, and climates, but an education in the world inside, an education in one's self, a chance to learn one's own
self, to get on speaking terms with one's soul. Then there is
the training and the disciplining of it. First, naturally, the
young fellow will learn his limitations; and next, inevitably,
he will proceed to press back those limitations. And he cannot escape returning from such a voyage a bigger and better
man. And as for sport, it is a king's sport, taking one's self
around the world, doing it with one's own hands, depending
on no one but one's self, and at the end, back at the starting-
point, contemplating with inner vision the planet rushing
through space, and saying, "I did it; with my own hands I did
it. I went clear around that whirling sphere, and I can travel
alone, without any nurse of a sea captain to guide my steps

across the seas. I may not fly to other stars, but of this star I myself am master."

As I write these lines I lift my eyes and look seaward. I am on the beach of Waikiki on the island of Oahu. Far, in the azure sky, the trade-wind clouds drift low over the blue-green turquoise of the deep sea. Nearer, the sea is emerald and light olive-green. Then comes the reef, where the water is all slatey purple flecked with red. Still nearer are brighter greens and tans, lying in alternate stripes and showing where sand beds lie between the living coral banks. Through and over and out of these wonderful colors tumbles and thunders a magnificent surf. As I say, I lift my eyes to all this, and through the white crest of a breaker suddenly appears a dark figure, erect, a man-fish or a sea-god, on the very forward face of the crest where the top falls over and down, driving in toward shore, buried to his loins in smoking spray, caught up by the sea and flung landward, bodily, a quarter of a mile. It is a Kanaka on a surfboard. And I know that when I have finished these lines I shall be out in that riot of color and pounding surf, trying to bit those breakers even as he, and failing as he never failed, but living life as the best of us may live it. And the picture of that colored sea and that flying sea-god Kanaka becomes another reason for the young man to go west, and farther west, beyond the Baths of Sunset, and still west till he arrives home again.

But to return. Please do not think that I already know it all. I know only the rudiments of navigation. There is a vast deal yet for me to learn. On the *Snark* there is a score of fascinating books on navigation waiting for me. There is the danger-angle of Lecky, there is the line of Summer, which, when you know least of all where you are, shows most conclusively where you are, and where you are not. There are dozens and dozens of methods of finding one's location on the deep, and one can work years before he masters it all in all its fineness.

Even in the little we did learn there were slips that accounted for the apparently antic behavior of the *Snark*. On Thursday, May 16, for instance, the trade wind failed us. During the twenty-four hours that ended Friday at noon, by dead reckoning we had not sailed twenty miles. Yet here are our positions, at noon, for the two days, worked out from our observations:

Thursday—20 degrees 57 minutes 9 seconds N—152 degrees 40 minutes 30 seconds W. Friday—21 degrees 15 minutes 33 seconds N—154 degrees 12 minutes W.

The difference between the two positions was something like eighty miles. Yet we knew we had not traveled twenty miles. Now our figuring was all right. We went over it several times. What was wrong was the observation we had taken. To take a correct observation requires practice and skill, and especially so on a small craft like the *Snark*. The violently moving boat and the closeness of the observer's eye to the surface of the water are to blame. A big wave that lifts up a mile off is liable to steal the horizon away.

But in our particular case there was another perturbing factor. The sun, in its annual march north through the heavens, was increasing its declination. On the 19th parallel of north latitude in the middle of May the sun is nearly overhead. The angle of arc was between eighty-eight and eighty-nine degrees. Had it been ninety degrees it would have been straight overhead. It was on another day that we learned a few things about taking the altitude of the almost perpendicular sun. Roscoe started in drawing the sun down to the eastern horizon, and he stayed by that point of the compass despite the fact that the sun would pass the meridian to the south. I, on the other hand, started in to draw the sun down to south-east and strayed away to the south-west. You see, we were teaching ourselves. As a result, at twenty-five minutes past twelve by the ship's time, I called twelve o'clock by the sun. Now this signified that we had changed our location on the face of the world by twenty-five minutes, which was equal to something like six degrees of longitude, or three hundred and fifty miles. This showed the *Snark* had traveled fifteen knots per hour for twenty-four consecutive hours— and we had never noticed it! It was absurd and grotesque. But Roscoe, still looking east, averred that it was not yet twelve o'clock. He was bent on giving us a twenty-knot clip. Then we began to train our sextants rather wildly all around the horizon, and wherever we looked, there was the sun, puzzlingly close to the skyline, sometimes above it and sometimes below it. In one direction the sun was proclaiming morning, in another direction it was proclaiming afternoon. The sun was all right—we knew that; therefore we were all wrong. And the rest of the afternoon we spent in the cockpit reading up the matter in the books and finding out what was wrong. We missed the observation that day, but we didn't the next. We had learned.

And we learned well, better than for a while we thought we had. At the beginning of the second dog-watch one evening, Charmian and I sat down on the forecastle-head for a rubber of cribbage. Chancing to glance ahead, I saw cloud-capped mountains rising from the sea. We were rejoiced at the sight of land, but I was in despair over our navigation. I thought we had learned something, yet out position at noon, plus what we had run since, did not put us within a hundred miles of land. But there was the land, fading away before our eyes in the fires of sunset. The land was all right. There was no disputing it. Therefore our navigation was all wrong. But it wasn't. That land we saw was the summit of Haleakala, the House of the Sun, the greatest extinct volcano in the world. It towered ten thousand feet above the sea, and it was all of a hundred miles away. We sailed all night at a seven-knot clip, and in the morning the House of the Sun was still before us, and it took a few more hours of sailing to bring it abreast of us. "That island is Maui," we said, verifying by the chart. "That next island sticking out is Molokai, where the lepers are. And the island next to that is Oahu. There is Makapuu Head now. We'll be in Honolulu tomorrow. Our navigation is all right."

A Son of the Sun

I

The *Willi-Waw* lay in the passage between the shore-reef and the outer reef. From the latter came the low murmur of a lazy surf, but the sheltered stretch of water, not more than a hundred yards across to the white beach of pounded coral sand, was of glass-like smoothness. Narrow as was the passage, and anchored as she was in the shoalest place that gave room to swing, the *Willi-Waw*'s chain rode up-and-down a clean hundred feet. Its course could be traced over the bottom of living coral. Like some monstrous snake, the rusty chain's slack wandered over the ocean floor, crossing and recrossing itself several times and fetching up finally at the idle anchor. Big rock-cod, dun and mottled, played warily in and out of the coral. Other fish, grotesque of form and colour, were brazenly indifferent, even when a big fish-shark drifted sluggishly along and sent the rock-cod scuttling for their favorite crevices.

On deck, for'ard, a dozen blacks pottered clumsily at scraping the teak rail. They were as inexpert at their work as so many monkeys. In fact they looked very much like monkeys of some enlarged and prehistoric type. Their eyes had in them the querulous plaintiveness of the monkey, their faces were even less symmetrical than the monkey's, and, hairless of body, they were far more ungarmented than any monkey, for clothes they had none. Decorated they were as no monkey ever was. In holes in their ears they carried short clay pipes, rings of turtle shell, huge plugs of wood, rusty wire nails, and empty rifle cartridges. The caliber of a Winchester rifle was the smallest hole an ear bore; some of the largest holes were inches in diameter, and any single ear averaged from three to half a dozen holes. Spikes and bodkins of polished bone or petrified shell were thrust through their noses. On the chest of one hung a white doorknob, on the chest of another the handle of a china cup, on the chest of a third the brass cog-wheel of an alarm clock. They chattered in queer, falsetto voices, and, combined, did no more work than a single white sailor.

Aft, under an awning, were two white men. Each was clad in a six-penny undershirt and wrapped about the loins with a strip of cloth. Belted about the middle of each was a revolver and tobacco pouch. The sweat stood out on their skin in myriads of globules. Here and there the globules coalesced in tiny streams that dripped to the heated deck and almost immediately evaporated. The lean, dark-eyed man wiped his fingers wet with a stinging stream from his forehead and flung it from him with a weary curse. Wearily, and without hope, he gazed seaward across the outer-reef, and at the tops of the palms along the beach.

"Eight o'clock, an' hell don't get hot till noon," he complained. "Wisht to God for a breeze. Ain't we never goin' to get away?"

The other man, a slender German of five and twenty, with the massive forehead of a scholar and the tumble-home chin of a degenerate, did not trouble to reply. He was busy emptying powdered quinine into a cigarette paper. Rolling what was approximately fifty grains of the drug into a tight wad, he tossed it into his mouth and gulped it down without the aid of water.

"Wisht I had some whiskey," the first man panted, after a fifteen-minute interval of silence.

Another equal period elapsed ere the German announced, relevant of nothing.

"I'm rotten with fever. I'm going to quit you, Griffiths, when we get to Sydney. No more tropics for me. I ought to known better when I signed on with you."

"You ain't been much of a mate," Griffiths replied, too hot himself to speak heatedly. "When the beach at Guvutu heard I'd shipped you, they all laughed. 'What? Jacobsen?' they said. 'You can't hide a square face of trade gin or sulphuric acid that he won't smell out!' You've certainly lived up to your reputation. I ain't had a drink for a fortnight, what of your snoopin' my supply."

"If the fever was as rotten in you as me, you'd understand," the mate whimpered.

"I ain't kickin'," Griffiths answered. "I only wisht God'd send me a drink, or a breeze of wind, or something. I'm ripe for my next chill tomorrow."

The mate proffered him the quinine. Rolling a fifty-grain dose, he popped the wad into his mouth and swallowed it dry.

"God! God!" he moaned. "I dream of a land somewheres where they ain't no quinine. Damned stuff of hell! I've scoffed tons of it in my time."

Again he quested seaward for signs of wind. The usual trade-wind clouds were absent, and the sun, still low in its climb to meridian, turned all the sky to heated brass. One seemed to see as well as feel this heat, and Griffiths sought vain relief by gazing shoreward. The white beach was a searing ache to his eyeballs. The palm trees, absolutely still, outlined flatly against the unrefreshing green of the packed jungle, seemed so much cardboard scenery. The little black boys, playing naked in the dazzle of sand and sun, were an affront and a hurt to the sun-sick man. He felt a sort of relief when one, running, tripped and fell on all-fours in the tepid sea-water.

An exclamation from the blacks for'ard sent both men glancing seaward. Around the near point of land, a quarter of a mile away and skirting the reef, a long black canoe paddled into sight.

"Gooma boys from the next bight," was the mate's verdict.

One of the blacks came aft, treading the hot deck with the unconcern of one whose bare feet felt no heat. This, too, was a hurt to Griffiths, and he closed his eyes. But the next moment they were open wide.

"White fella marster stop along Gooma boy," the black said.

Both men were on their feet and gazing at the canoe. Aft could be seen the unmistakable sombrero of a white man. Quick alarm showed itself on the face of the mate.

"It's Grief," he said.

Griffiths satisfied himself by a long look, then ripped out a wrathful oath.

"What's he doing up here?" he demanded . . . of the mate, of the aching sea and sky, of the merciless blaze of sun, and of the whole superheated and implacable universe with which his fate was entangled.

The mate began to chuckle.

"I told you you couldn't get away with it," he said.

But Griffiths was not listening.

"With all his money, coming around like a rent collector," he chanted his outrage, almost in an ecstasy of anger. "He's loaded with money, he's stuffed with money, he's busting with money. I know for a fact he sold his Yringa plantations for three hundred thousand pounds. Bell told me so himself last time we were drunk at Guvutu. Worth millions and millions, and Shylocking me for what he wouldn't light his pipe with." He whirled on the mate. "Of course you told me so. Go on and say it, and keep on saying it. Now just what was it you did tell me so?"

"I told you you didn't know him, if you thought you could clear the Solomons without paying him. That man Grief is a devil, but he's straight. I know. I told you he'd throw a thousand quid away for the fun of it, and for sixpence fight like a shark for a rusty tin. I tell you I know. Didn't he give his *Balakula* to the Queensland Mission when they lost their *Evening Star* on San Cristobal?—and the *Balakula* worth three thousand pounds if she was worth a penny? And didn't he beat up Strothers till he laid abed a fortnight, all because of a difference of two pound ten in the account, and because Strothers got fresh and tried to make the gouge go through?"

"God strike me blind!" Griffiths cried in impotency of rage.

The mate went on with his exposition.

"I tell you only a straight man can buck a straight man like him, and the man's never hit the Solomons that could do it. Men like you and me can't buck him. We're too rotten, too rotten all the way through. You've got plenty more than twelve hundred quid below. Pay him, and get it over with."

But Griffiths gritted his teeth and drew his thin lips tightly across them.

"I'll buck him," he muttered—more to himself and the brazen ball of sun than to the mate. He turned and half started to go below, then turned back again. "Look here, Jacobsen. He won't be here for quarter of an hour. Are you with me? Will you stand by me?"

"Of course I'll stand by you. I've drunk all your whiskey, haven't I? What are you going to do?"

"I'm not going to kill him if I can help it. But I'm not going to pay. Take that flat."

Jacobsen shrugged his shoulders in calm acquiescence to fate, and Griffiths stepped to the companionway and went below.

II

Jacobsen watched the canoe across the low reef as it came abreast and passed on to the entrance of the passage. Griffiths, with ink-marks on right thumb and forefinger, returned on deck. Fifteen minutes later the canoe came alongside. The man with the sombrero stood up.

"Hello, Griffiths!" he said. "Hello, Jacobsen!" With his hand on the rail he turned to his dusky crew. "You fella boy stop along canoe altogether."

As he swung over the rail and stepped on deck a hint of cat-like litheness showed in the apparently heavy body. Like the other two, he was scantily clad. The cheap undershirt and white loin-cloth did not serve to hide the well put up body. Heavy muscled he was, but he was not lumped and hummocked by muscles. They were softly rounded, and, when they did move, slid softly and silkily under the smooth, tanned skin. Ardent suns had likewise tanned his face till it was swarthy as a Spaniard's. The yellow moustache appeared incongruous in the midst of such swarthiness, while the clear blue of the eyes produced a feeling of shock on the beholder. It was difficult to realize that the skin of this man had once been fair.

"Where did you blow in from?" Griffiths asked, as they shook hands. "I thought you were over in the Santa Cruz."

"I was," the newcomer answered. "But we made a quick passage. The *Wonder's* just around in the bight at Gooma, waiting for wind. Some of the bushmen reported a ketch here, and I just dropped around to see. Well, how goes it?"

"Nothing much. Copra sheds mostly empty, and not half a dozen tons of ivory nuts. The women all got rotten with fever and quit, and the men can't chase them back into the swamps. They're a sick crowd. I'd ask you to have a drink, but the mate finished off my last bottle. I wisht to God for a breeze of wind."

Grief, glancing with keen carelessness from one to the other, laughed.

"I'm glad the calm held," he said. "It enabled me to get around to see you. My supercargo dug up that little note of yours, and I brought it along."

The mate edged politely away, leaving his skipper to face his trouble.

"I'm sorry, Grief, damned sorry," Griffiths said, "but I ain't got it. You'll have to give me a little more time."

Grief leaned up against the companionway, surprise and pain depicted on his face.

"It does beat hell," he communed, "how men learn to lie in the Solomons. The truth's not in them. Now take Captain Jensen. I'd sworn by his truthfulness. Why, he told me only five days ago—do you want to know what he told me?"

Griffiths licked his lips.

"Go on."

"Why, he told me that you'd sold out—sold out everything, cleaned up, and was pulling out for the New Hebrides."

"He's a damned liar!" Griffiths cried hotly.

Grief nodded.

"I should say so. He even had the nerve to tell me that he'd bought two of your stations from you—Mauri and Kahula. Said he paid you seventeen hundred gold sovereigns, lock, stock and barrel, good will, trade-goods, credit, and copra."

Griffiths's eyes narrowed and glinted. The action was involuntary, and Grief noted it with a lazy sweep of his eyes.

"And Parsons, your trader at Hickimavi, told me that the Fulcrum Company had bought that station from you. Now what did he want to lie for?"

Griffiths, overwrought by sun and sickness, exploded. All his bitterness of spirit rose up in his face and twisted his mouth into a snarl.

"Look here, Grief, what's the good of playing with me that way? You know, and I know you know. Let it go at that. I *have* sold out, and I *am* getting away. And what are you going to do about it?"

Grief shrugged his shoulders, and no hint of resolve shadowed itself in his own face. His expression was as of one in a quandary.

"There's no law here," Griffiths pressed home his advantage. "Tulagi is a hundred and fifty miles away. I've got my clearance papers, and I'm on my own boat. There's nothing to stop me from sailing. You've got no right to stop me just because I owe you a little money. And by God! You can't stop me. Put that in your pipe."

The look of pained surprise on Grief's face deepened.

"You mean you're going to cheat me out of that twelve hundred, Griffiths?"

"That's just about the size of it, old man. And calling hard names won't help any. There's the wind coming. You'd better get overside before I pull out, or I'll tow your canoe under."

"Really, Griffiths, you sound almost right. I can't stop you." Grief fumbled in the pouch that hung on his revolver-belt and pulled out a crumpled official-looking paper. "But maybe this will stop you. And it's something for *your* pipe. Smoke up."

"What is it?"

"An admiralty warrant. Running to the New Hebrides won't save you. It can be served anywhere."

Griffiths hesitated and swallowed, when he had finished glancing at the document. With knit brows he pondered this new phase of the situation. Then, abruptly, as he looked up, his face relaxed into all frankness.

"You were cleverer than I thought, old man," he said. "You've got me hip and thigh. I ought to have known better than to try and beat you. Jacobsen told me I couldn't, and I wouldn't listen to him. But he was right, and so are you. I've got the money below. Come on down and we'll settle."

He started to go down, then stepped aside to let his visitor precede him, at the same time glancing seaward to where the dark flaw of wind was quickening the water.

"Heave short," he told the mate. "Get up sail and stand ready to break out."

As Grief sat down on the edge of the mate's bunk, close against and facing the tiny table, he noticed the butt of a revolver just projecting from under the pillow. On the table, which hung on hinges from the for'ard bulkhead, were pen and ink, also a battered log-book.

"Oh, I don't mind being caught in a dirty trick," Griffiths was saying defiantly. "I've been in the tropics too long. I'm a sick man, a damn sick man. And the whiskey, and the sun, and the fever have made me sick in morals, too. Nothing's too mean and low for me now, and I can understand why the niggers [*sic*] eat each other, and take heads, and such things. I could do it myself. So I call trying to do you out of that small account a pretty mild trick. Wisht I could offer you a drink."

Grief made no reply, and the other busied himself in attempting to unlock a large and much-dented cash-box. From on deck came falsetto cries and the creak and rattle of blocks as the black crew swung up mainsail and driver. Grief watched a large cockroach crawling over the greasy paint-work. Griffiths, with an oath of irritation, carried the cash-box to the companion-steps for better light. Here, on his feet, and bending over the box, his back to his visitor, his hands shot out to the rifle that stood beside the steps, and at the same moment he whirled about.

"Now don't you move a muscle," he commanded.

Grief smiled, elevated his eyebrows quizzically, and obeyed. His left hand rested on the bunk beside him; his right hand lay on the table. His revolver hung on his right hip in plain sight. But in his mind was recollection of the other revolver under the pillow.

"Huh!" Griffiths sneered. "You've got everybody in the Solomons hypnotized, but let me tell you, you ain't got me. Now I'm going to throw you off my vessel, along with your admiralty warrant, but first you've got to do something. Lift up that log-book."

The other glanced curiously at the log-book, but did not move.

"I tell you I'm a sick man, Grief; and I'd as soon shoot you as smash a cockroach. Lift up that log-book, I say."

Sick he did look, his lean face working nervously with the rage that possessed him. Grief lifted the book and set it aside. Beneath lay a written sheet of tablet paper.

"Read it," Griffiths commanded. "Read it aloud."

Grief obeyed; but while he read, the fingers of his left hand began an infinitely slow and patient crawl toward the butt of the weapon under the pillow.

"On board the ketch Willi-Waw, *Bombi Bight, Island, Anna, Solomon Islands,"* he read. *"Know all men by these presents that I do hereby sign off and release in full, for due value received, all debts whatsoever owing to me by Harrison J. Griffiths, who has this day paid to me twelve hundred pounds sterling."*

"With that receipt in my hands," Griffiths grinned, "your admiralty warrant's not worth the paper it's written on. Sign it."

"It won't do any good, Griffiths," Grief said. "A document signed under compulsion won't hold before the law."

"In that case, what objection have you to signing it then?"

"Oh, none at all, only that I might save you heaps of trouble by not signing it."

Grief's fingers had gained the revolver, and, while he talked, with his right hand he played with the pen and with his left began slowly and imperceptibly drawing the weapon to his side. As his hand finally closed upon it, second finger on trigger and forefinger laid past the cylinder and along the barrel, he wondered what luck he would have at left-handed snap-shooting.

"Don't consider me," Griffiths gibed. "And just remember Jacobsen will testify that he saw me pay the money over. Now sign, sign in full, at the bottom, David Grief, and date it."

From on deck came the jar of sheet-blocks and the rat-tat-tat of the reef-points against the canvas. In the cabin they could feel the *Willi-Waw* heel, swing into the wind, and right. David Grief still hesitated. From for'ard came the jerking rattle of headsail halyards through the sheaves. The little vessel heeled, and through the cabin walls came the gurgle and wash of water.

"Get a move on!" Griffiths cried. "The anchor's out."

The muzzle of the rifle, four feet away, was bearing directly on him, when Grief resolved to act. The rifle wavered as Griffiths kept his balance in the uncertain puffs of the first of the wind. Grief took advantage of the wavering, made as if to sign the paper, and at the same instant, like a cat, exploded into swift and intricate action. As he ducked low and leaped forward with his body, his left hand flashed from under the screen of the table, and so accurately timed was the single stiff pull on the self-cocking trigger that the cartridge discharged as the muzzle came forward. Not a whit behind was Griffiths. The muzzle of his weapon dropped to meet the ducking body, and, shot at snap direction, rifle and revolver went off simultaneously.

Grief felt the sting and sear of a bullet across the skin of his shoulder, and knew that his own shot had missed. His forward rush carried him to Griffiths before another shot could be fired, both of whose arms, still holding the rifle, he locked with a low tackle about the body. He shoved the revolver muzzle, still in his left hand, deep into the other's abdomen. Under the press of his anger and the sting of his abraded skin, Grief's finger was lifting the hammer, when the wave of anger passed and he recollected himself. Down the companionway came indignant cries from the Gooma boys in his canoe.

Everything was happening in seconds. There was apparently no pause in his actions as he gathered Griffiths in his

177

arms and carried him up the steep steps in a sweeping rush. Out into the blinding glare of sunshine he came. A black stood grinning at the wheel, and the *Willi-Waw*, heeled over from the wind, was foaming along. Rapidly dropping astern was his Gooma canoe. Grief turned his head. From amidships, revolver in hand, the mate was springing toward him. With two jumps, still holding the helpless Griffiths, Grief leaped to the rail and overboard.

Both men were grappled together as they went down; but Grief, with a quick updraw of his knees to the other's chest, broke the grip and forced him down. With both feet on Griffiths's shoulder, he forced him still deeper, at the same time driving himself to the surface. Scarcely had his head broken into the sunshine when two splashes of water, in quick succession and within a foot of his face, advertised that Jacobsen knew how to handle a revolver. There was a chance for no third shot, for Grief, filling his lungs with air, sank down. Under water he struck out, nor did he come up till he saw the canoe and the bubbling paddles overhead. As he climbed aboard, the *Willi-Waw* went into the wind to come about.

"Washee-washee!" Grief cried to his boys. "You fella make-um beach quick fella time!"

In all shamelessness, he turned his back on the battle and ran for cover. The *Willi-Waw*, compelled to deaden way in order to pick up its captain, gave Grief his chance for a lead. The canoe struck the beach full-tilt, with every paddle driving, and they leaped out and ran across the sand for the trees. But before they gained the shelter, three times the sand kicked into puffs ahead of them. Then they drove into the green safety of the jungle.

Grief watched the *Willi-Waw* haul up close, go out the passage, then slack its sheets as it headed south with the wind abeam. As it went out of sight past the point he could see the top-sail being broken out. One of the Gooma boys, a black, nearly fifty years of age, hideously marred and scarred by skin diseases and old wounds, looked up into his face and grinned.

"My word," the boy commented, "that fella skipper too much, cross along you."

Grief laughed, and led the way back across the sand to the canoe.

III

How many millions David Grief was worth no man in the Solomons knew, for his holdings and ventures were everywhere in the great South Pacific. From Samoa to New Guinea and even to the north of the Line his plantations were scattered. He possessed pearling concessions in the Paumotus. Though his name did not appear, he was in truth the German company that traded in the French Marquesas. His trading stations were in strings in all the groups, and his vessels that operated them were many. He owned atolls so remote and tiny that his smallest schooners and ketches visited the solitary agents but once a year.

In Sydney, on Castlereagh Street, his offices occupied three floors. But he was rarely in those offices. He preferred always to be on the go amongst the island, nosing out new investments, inspecting and shaking up old ones, and rubbing shoulders with fun and adventure in a thousand strange guises. He bought the wreck of the great steamship *Gavonne* for a song, and in salving it achieved the impossible and cleaned up a quarter of a million. In the Louisiades he planted the first commercial rubber, and in Bora-Bora he ripped out the South Sea cotton and put the jolly islanders at the work of planting cacao. It was he who took the deserted island of Lallu-Ka, colonized it with Polynesians from the Ontong-Java Atoll, and planted four thousand acres to cocoanuts. And it was he who reconciled the warring chiefstocks of Tahiti and swung the great deal of the phosphate island of Hikihu.

His own vessels recruited his contract labor. They brought Santa Cruz boys to the New Hebrides, New Hebrides boys to the Banks, and the head-hunting cannibals of Malaita to the plantations of New Georgia. From Tonga to the Gilberts and on to the far Louisiades his recruiters combed the islands for labor. His keels ploughed all ocean stretches. He owned three steamers on regular island runs, though he rarely elected to travel in them, preferring the wilder and more primitive way of wind and sail.

At least forty years of age, he looked no more than thirty. Yet beachcombers remembered his advent among the islands a score of years before, at which time the yellow moustache was already budding silkily on his lip. Unlike other white men in the tropics, he was there because he liked it. His protective skin pigmentation was excellent. He had been born to the sun. One he was in ten thousand in the matter of sun-resistance. The invisible and high-velocity light waves failed to bore into him. Other white men were pervious. The sun drove through their skins, ripping and smashing tissues and nerves, till they became sick in mind and body, tossed most of the Decalogue overboard, descended to beastliness, drank themselves into quick graves, or survived so savagely that war vessels were sometimes sent to curb their license.

But David Grief was a true son of the sun, and he flourished in all its ways. He merely became browner with the passing of the years, though in the brown was the hint of golden tint that glows in the skin of the Polynesian. Yet his blue eyes retained their blue, his moustache its yellow, and the lines of his face were those which had persisted through the centuries in his English race. English he was in blood, yet those that thought they knew contended he was at least American born. Unlike them, he had not come out to the South Seas seeking hearth and saddle of his own. In fact, he had brought hearth and saddle with him. His advent had been in the Paumotus. He arrived on board a tiny schooner yacht, master and owner, a youth questing romance and adventure along the sun-washed path of the tropics. He also arrived in a hurricane, the giant waves of which deposited him and yacht and all in the thick of a cocoanut grove three hundred yards beyond the surf. Six months later he was rescued by a pearling cutter. But the sun had got into his blood. At Tahiti, instead of taking a steamer home, he bought a schooner, outfitted her with trade-goods and divers, and went for a cruise through the Dangerous Archipelago.

As the golden tint burned into his face it poured molten out of the ends of his fingers. His was the golden touch, but he played the game, not for the gold, but for the game's sake. It was a man's game, the rough contacts and fierce give and take of the adventurers of his own blood and of half the bloods of Europe and the rest of the world, and it was a good game; but over and beyond was his love of all the other things that go to make up a South Seas rover's life—the smell of the reef; the infinite exquisiteness of the shoals of living coral in the mirror-surfaced lagoons; the crashing sunrises of raw colors spread with lawless cunning; the palm-tufted islets set in turquoise deeps; the tonic wine of the trade-winds; the heave and send of the orderly, crested seas; the moving deck beneath his feet, the straining canvas over-head; the flower-garlanded, golden-glowing men and maids of Polynesia, half-children and half-gods; and even the howling savages of Melanesia, head-hunters and man-eaters, half-devil and all beast.

And so, favored child of the sun, out of munificence of energy and sheer joy of living, he, the man of many millions, forbore on his far way to play the game with Harrison J. Griffiths for a paltry sum. It was his whim, his desire, his expression of self and of the sun-warmth that poured through him. It was fun, a joke, a problem, a bit of play on which life was lightly hazarded for the joy of the playing.

IV

The early morning light found the *Wonder* lying close-hauled along the coast of Guadalcanal. She moved lazily through the water under the dying breath of the land breeze. To the east, heavy masses of clouds promised a renewal of the southeast trades, accompanied by sharp puffs and rain squalls. Ahead, lying along the same course as the *Wonder*, and being slowly overtaken, was a small ketch. It was not the *Willi-Waw*, how-ever, and Captain Ward, on the *Wonder*, putting down his glasses, named it the *Kauri*.

Grief, just on deck from below, sighed regretfully.

"If only it had been the *Willi-Waw*," he said.

"You do hate to be beaten," Denby, the supercargo, re-marked sympathetically.

"I certainly do." Grief paused and laughed with genuine mirth. "It's my firm conviction that Griffiths is a rogue and that he treated me quite scurvily yesterday. 'Sign,' he says, 'sign in full, at the bottom, and date it.' And Jacobsen, the lit-tle rat, stood in with him. It was rank piracy, the days of Bully Hayes all over again."

"If you weren't my employer, Mr. Grief, I'd like to give you a piece of my mind," Captain Ward broke in.

"Go on and spit it out," Grief encouraged.

"Well, then—." The captain hesitated and cleared his throat. "With all the money you've got, only a fool would take the risk you did with those two curs. What do you do it for?"

"Honestly, I don't know, Captain. I just want to, I suppose. And can you give me a better reason for anything you do?"

"You'll get your bally head shot off some fine day," Cap-tain Ward growled in answer, as he stepped to the binnacle and took the bearing of a peak which had just thrust its head through the clouds that covered Guadalcanal.

The land breeze strengthened in a last effort, and the *Wonder*, slipping swiftly through the water, ranged alongside the *Kauri* and began to go by. Greetings flew back and forth, then David Grief called out:

"Seen anything of the *Willi-Waw*?"

The captain, slouch-hatted and barelegged, with a rolling twist hitched the faded blue *lava-lava* tighter around his waist and spat tobacco juice over the side.

"Sure," he answered. "Griffiths lay at Savo last night, taking on pigs and yams and filling his water tanks. Looked like he was going for a long cruise, but he said no. Why? Did you want to see him?"

"Yes, but if you see him first, don't tell him you've seen me."

The captain nodded and considered and walked for'ard on his own deck to keep abreast of the faster vessel.

"Say!" he called. "Jacobsen told me they were coming down this afternoon to Gabera. Said they were going to lie there tonight and take on sweet potatoes."

"Gabera has the only leading lights in the Solomons," Grief said, when his schooner had drawn well ahead. "Is that right, Captain Ward?"

The captain nodded.

"And the little bight just around the point on this side, it's a rotten anchorage, isn't it?"

"No anchorage. All coral patches and shoals, and a bad surf. That's where the *Molly* went to pieces three years ago."

Grief stared straight before him with lusterless eyes for a full minute, as if summoning some vision to his inner sight. Then the corners of his eyes wrinkled and the ends of his yellow moustache lifted in a smile.

"We'll anchor at Gabera," he said. "And run in close to the little bight this side. I want you to drop me in a whaleboat as you go by. Also, give me six boys, and serve out rifles. I'll be back on board before morning."

The captain's face took on an expression of suspicion, which swiftly slid into one of reproach.

"Oh, just a little fun, skipper," Grief protested with the apologetic air of a schoolboy caught in mischief by an elder.

Captain Ward grunted, but Denby was all alertness.

"I'd like to go along, Mr. Grief," he said.

Grief nodded consent.

"Bring some axes and bush-knives," he said. "And, oh, by the way, a couple of bright lanterns. See they've got oil in them."

V

An hour before sunset the *Wonder* tore by the little bight. The wind had freshened, and a lively sea was beginning to make. The shoals toward the beach were already white with the churn of the water, while those farther out as yet showed no more sign than of discolored water. As the schooner went into the wind and backed her jib and staysail the whaleboat was swung out. Into leaped six breech-clouted Santa Cruz boys, each armed with a rifle. Denby, carrying the lanterns, dropped into the stern-sheets. Grief, following, paused at the rail.

"Pray for a dark night, skipper," he pleaded.

"You'll get it," Captain Ward answered. "There's no moon, anyway, and there won't be any sky. She'll be a bit squally, too."

The forecast sent a radiance into Grief's face, making more pronounced the golden tint of his sunburn. He leaped down beside the supercargo.

"Cast off!" Captain Ward ordered. "Draw the headsails! Put your wheel over! There! Steady! Take that course!"

The *Wonder* filled and ran on around the point for Gabera, while the whaleboat, pulling six oars and steered by Grief, headed for the beach. With superb boatsmanship he threaded the narrow, tortuous channel which no craft larger than a whaleboat could negotiate, until the shoals and patches showed seaward and they grounded on the quiet, rippling beach.

The next hour was filled with work. Moving about among the wild cocoanuts and jungle brush, Grief selected the trees.

"Chop this fella tree; chop that fella tree," he told his blacks. "No chop that other fella," he said with a shake of head.

In the end a wedge-shaped segment of the jungle was cleared. Near to the beach remained one long palm. At the apex of the wedge stood another. Darkness was falling as the lanterns were lighted, carried up the two trees, and made fast.

"That outer lantern is too high." David Grief studied it critically. "Put it down about ten feet, Denby."

VI

The *Willi-Waw* was tearing through the water with a bone in her teeth, for the breath of the passing squall was still strong. The blacks were swinging up the big mainsail, which had been lowered on the run when the puff was at its height. Jacobsen, supervising the operation, ordered them to throw the halyards down on deck and stand by, then went for'ard on the lee-bow and joined Griffiths. Both men stared with wide-strained eyes at the blank wall of darkness through which they were flying, their ears tense for the sound of surf on the invisible shore. It was by this sound that they were for the moment steering.

The wind fell lighter, the scud of clouds thinned and broke, and in the glimmer of starlight loomed the jungle-clad coast. Ahead, and well on the lee-bow, appeared a jagged rock-point. Both men strained to it.

"Amboy Point," Griffiths announced. "Plenty of water close up. Take the wheel, Jacobsen, till we set a course. Get a move on!"

Running aft, barefooted and barelegged, the rainwater dripping from his scant clothing, the mate displaced the black at the wheel.

"How's she heading?" Griffiths called.

"South-a-half-west!"

"Let her come up south-by-west! Got it?"

"Right on it!"

Griffiths considered the changed relation of Amboy Point to the *Willi-Waw*'s course.

"And a half west!" he cried.

"And a half west!" came the answer. "Right on it!"

"Steady! That'll do."

"Steady she is!" Jacobsen turned the wheel over to the savage. "You steer good fella, savve?" he warned. "No good fella I knock your damn black head off."

Again he went for'ard and joined the other, and again the cloud-scud thickened, the star-glimmer vanished, and the wind rose and screamed in another squall.

"Watch that mainsail!" Griffiths yelled in the mate's ear, at the same time studying the ketch's behavior.

Over she pressed, and lee-rail under, while he measured the weight of the wind and quested its easement. The tepid seawater, with here and there tiny globules of phosphorescence, washed about his ankles and knees. The wind screamed a higher note, and every shroud and stay sharply chorused an answer as the *Willi-Waw* pressed farther over and down.

"Down mainsail!" Griffiths yelled, springing to the peak-halyards, thrusting away the black who held on, and casting off the turn.

Jacobsen, at the throat-halyards, was performing the like office. The big sail rattled down, and the blacks, with shouts and yells, threw themselves on the battling canvas. The mate, finding one skulking in the darkness, flung his bunched knuckles into the creature's face and drove him to his work.

The squall held at its high pitch, and under her small canvas the *Willi-Waw* still foamed along. Again the two men stood for'ard and vainly watched the horizontal drive of rain.

"We're all right," Griffiths said. "This rain won't last. We can hold this course till we pick up the lights. Anchor in thirteen fathoms. You'd better overhaul forty-five on a night like this. After that get the gaskets on the mainsail. We won't need it."

Half an hour afterward his weary eyes were rewarded by a glimpse of two lights.

"There they are, Jacobsen. I'll take the wheel. Run down the fore-staysail and stand by to let go. Make the sailors jump."

Aft, the spokes of the wheel in his hands, Griffiths held the course till the two lights came in line, when he abruptly altered and headed directly in for them. He heard the tumble and roar of the surf, but decided it was farther away—as it should be, at Gabera.

He heard the frightened cry of the mate, and was grinding the wheel down with all his might, when the *Willi-Waw* struck. At the same instant her mainmast crashed over the bow. Five wild minutes followed. All hands held on while the hull upheaved and smashed down on the brittle coral and the warm seas swept over them. Grinding and crunching, the *Willi-Waw* worked itself clear over the shoal patch and came solidly to rest in the comparatively smooth and shallow channel beyond.

Griffiths sat down on the edge of the cabin, head bowed on chest, in silent wrath and bitterness. Once he lifted his face to glare at the two white lights, one above the other and perfectly in line.

"There they are," he said. "And this isn't Gabera. Then what the hell is it?"

Though the surf still roared and across the shoal flung its spray and upper wash over them, the wind died down and the stars came out. Shoreward came the sound of oars.

"What have you had—an earthquake?" Griffiths called out. "The bottom's all changed. I've anchored here a hundred times in thirteen fathoms. Is that you, Wilson?"

A whaleboat came alongside, and a man climbed over the rail. In the faint light Griffiths found an automatic Colt thrust into his face, and looking up, saw David Grief.

"No, you never anchored here before," Grief laughed. "Gabera's just around the point, where I'll be as soon as I've collected that little sum of twelve hundred pounds. We won't bother for the receipt. I've your note here, and I'll just return it."

"You did this!" Griffiths cried, springing to his feet in a sudden gust of rage. "You faked those leading lights! You've wrecked me, and by—"

"Steady! Steady!" Grief's voice was cool and menacing. "I'll trouble you for that twelve hundred, please."

To Griffiths, a vast impotence seemed to descend upon him. He was overwhelmed by a profound disgust—disgust for the sunlands and the sun-sickness, for the futility of all his endeavor, for this blue-eyed, golden tinted, superior man who had defeated him on all his ways.

"Jacobsen," he said, "will you open the cash-box and pay this—this bloodsucker—twelve hundred pounds?"

Make Westing

Whatever you do, make westing! make westing!
—Sailing directions for Cape Horn.

For seven weeks the *Mary Rogers* had been between 50° south in the Atlantic and 50° south in the Pacific, which meant that for seven weeks she had been struggling to round Cape Horn. For seven weeks she had been either in dirt or close to dirt save once, and then, following upon six days of excessive dirt, which she had ridden out under the shelter of the redoubtable Terra Del Fuego coast, she had almost gone ashore during a heavy swell in the dead calm that had suddenly fallen. For seven weeks she had wrestled with the Cape Horn graybeards, and in return been buffeted and smashed by them. She was a wooden ship, and her ceaseless straining had opened her seams, so that twice a day the watch took its turn at the pumps.

The *Mary Rogers* was strained, the crew was strained, and big Dan Cullen, master, was likewise strained. Perhaps he was strained most of all, for upon him rested the responsibility of that titanic struggle. He slept most of the time in his clothes, though he rarely slept. He haunted the deck at night, a great, burly, robust ghost, black with the sunburn of thirty years of sea and hairy as an orangutan. He, in turn, was haunted by one thought of action, a sailing direction for the Horn: *Whatever you do, make westing! make westing!* It was an obsession. He thought of nothing else, except, at times, to blaspheme God for sending such bitter weather.

Make westing! He hugged the Horn, and a dozen times lay hove to with the iron Cape bearing east-by-north, or north-north-east, a score of miles away. And each time the eternal west wind smote him back and he made easting. He fought gale after gale, south to 64°, inside the Antarctic drift ice, and pledged his immortal soul to the Powers of Darkness for a bit of westing, for a slant to take him around. And he made easting. In despair, he had tried to make the passage through the Straits of Le Maire. Halfway through, the wind hauled to the north'ard of northwest, the glass dropped to 28.88, and he turned and ran before a gale of cyclonic fury, missing, by a hairbreadth, piling up the *Mary Rogers* on the black-toothed rocks. Twice he had made west to the Diego Ramirez Rocks, one of the times saved between two snow squalls by sighting the gravestones of ships a quarter of a mile dead ahead.

Blow! Captain Dan Cullen instanced all his thirty years at sea to prove that never had it blown so before. The *Mary Rogers* was hove to at the time he gave the evidence, and to clinch it inside half an hour the *Mary Rogers* was hove down to the hatches. Her new maintopsail and brand new spencer were blown away like tissue paper; and five sails, furled and fast under double gaskets, were blown loose and stripped from the yards. And before morning the *Mary Rogers* was hove down twice again, and holes were knocked in her bulwarks to ease her decks from the weight of ocean that pressed her down.

On an average of once a week Captain Dan Cullen caught glimpses of the sun. Once, for ten minutes, the sun shone at midday, and ten minutes afterward a new gale was piping up, both watches were shortening sail, and all was buried in the obscurity of a driving snow squall. For a fortnight, once, Captain Dan Cullen was without a meridian or a chronometer sight. Rarely did he know his position within half of a degree, except when in sight of land; for sun and stars remained hidden behind the sky, and it was so gloomy that even at the best the horizons were poor for accurate observations. A gray gloom shrouded the world. The clouds were gray; the great driving seas were leaden gray; the smoking crests were a gray churning; even the occasional albatrosses were gray, while the snow flurries were not white, but gray under the somber pall of the heavens.

Life on board the *Mary Rogers* was gray—gray and gloomy. The faces of the sailors were blue-gray; they were afflicted with sea-cuts and sea boils and suffered exquisitely. They were shadows of men. For seven weeks, in the forecastle or on deck, they had not known what it was to be dry. They had forgotten what it was to sleep out a watch, and all watches it was, "All hands on deck!" They caught snatches of agonized sleep, and they slept in their oilskins ready for the everlasting call. So weak and worn were they that it took both watches to do the work of one. That was why both watches were on deck so much of the time. And no shadow of a man could shirk duty. Nothing less than a broken leg could enable a man to knock off work; and there were two such, who had been mauled and pulped by the seas that broke aboard.

One other man who was the shadow of a man was George Dorety. He was the only passenger on board, a friend of the firm, and he had elected to make the voyage for his health. But seven weeks of Cape Horn had not bettered his health. He gasped and panted in his bunk through the long, heaving nights; and when on deck he was so bundled up for warmth that he resembled a peripatetic old-clothes shop. At midday, eating at the cabin table in a gloom so deep that the swinging sea lamps burned always, he looked as blue-gray as the sickest, saddest man for'ard. Nor did gazing across the table at Captain Dan Cullen have any cheering effect upon him. Captain Cullen chewed and scowled and kept silent. The scowls were for God, and with every chew he reiterated the sole thought of his existence, which was *make westing*. He was a big hairy brute, and the sight of him was not stimulating to the other's appetite. He looked upon George Dorety as a Jonah, and told him so, once each meal, savagely transferring the scowl from God to the passenger and back again.

Nor did the mate prove a first aid to a languid appetite. Joshua Higgins by name, a seaman by profession and pull, but a pot-walloper by capacity, he was a loose-jointed, sniffling creature, heartless and selfish and cowardly, without a soul, in fear of his life of Dan Cullen, and a bully over the sailors, who knew that behind the mate was Captain Cullen, the lawgiver and compeller, the driver and the destroyer, the incarnation of a dozen bucko mates. In that wild weather at the southern end of the earth, Joshua Higgins ceased washing. His grimy face usually robbed George Dorety of what little appetite he managed to accumulate. Ordinarily this lavatorial dereliction would have caught Captain Cullen's eye and vocabulary, but in the present his mind was filled with making westing, to the exclusion of all other things not contributory thereto. Whether the mate's face was clean or dirty had no bearing upon westing. Later on, when 50° south in the Pacific had been reached, Joshua Higgins would wash his face very abruptly. In the meantime, at the cabin table, where gray twilight alternated with lamplight while the lamps were being filled, George Dorety sat between the two men, one a tiger and the other a hyena, and wondered why God had made them. The second mate, Matthew Turner, was a true sailor and a man, but George Dorety did not have the solace of his company, for he ate by himself, solitary, when they had finished.

On Saturday morning, July 24, George Dorety awoke to a feeling of life and headlong movement. On deck he found the *Mary Rogers* running off before a howling southeaster. Nothing was set but the lower topsails and the foresail. It was all she could stand, yet she was making fourteen knots, as Mr. Turner shouted in Dorety's ear when he came on deck. And it was all westing. She was going around the Horn at last . . . if the wind held. Mr. Turner looked happy. The end of the struggle was in sight. But Captain Cullen did not look happy. He scowled at Dorety in passing. Captain Cullen did not want God to know that he was pleased with that wind. He had a conception of a malicious God, and believed in his secret soul that if God knew it was a desirable wind, God would promptly efface it and send a snorter from the west. So he walked softly before God, smothering his joy down under scowls and muttered curses, and so fooling God, for God was the only thing in the universe of which Dan Cullen was afraid.

All Saturday and Saturday night the *Mary Rogers* raced her westing. Persistently she logged her fourteen knots, so that by Sunday morning she had covered three hundred and fifty miles. If the wind held, she would make around. If it failed, and the snorter came from anywhere between southwest and north, back the *Mary Rogers* would be hurled and be no better off than she had been seven weeks before. And on Sunday morning the wind *was* failing. The big sea was going down and running smooth. Both watches were on deck setting sail after sail as fast as the ship could stand it. And now Captain Cullen went around brazenly before God, smoking a big cigar, smiling jubilantly, as if the failing wind delighted him, while down underneath he was raging against God for taking the life out of the blessed wind. *Make westing!* So he would, if God would only leave him alone. Secretly, he pledged himself anew to the Powers of Darkness, if they would let him make westing. He pledged himself so easily because he did not believe in the Powers of Darkness. He really believed only in God, though he did not know it. And in his inverted theology God was really the Prince of Darkness. Captain Cullen was a devil-worshiper, but he called the devil by another name, that was all.

At midday, after calling eight bells, Captain Cullen ordered the royals on. The men went aloft faster than they had gone in weeks. Not alone were they nimble because of the westing, but a benignant sun was shining down and limbering their stiff bodies. George Dorety stood aft, near Captain Cullen, less bundled in clothes than usual, soaking in the grateful warmth as he watched the scene. Swiftly and abruptly the incident occurred. There was a cry from the foreroyal-yard of "Man overboard!" Somebody threw a life buoy over the side, and at the same instant the second mate's voice came aft, ringing and peremptory: "Hard down your helm!"

The man at the wheel never moved a spoke. He knew better, for Captain Dan Cullen was standing alongside of him. He wanted to move a spoke, to move all the spokes, to grind the wheel down, hard down, for his comrade drowning in the sea. He glanced at Captain Dan Cullen and Captain Dan Cullen gave no sign.

"Down! Hard down!" the second mate roared, as he sprang aft.

But he ceased springing and commanding, and stood still, when he saw Dan Cullen by the wheel. And big Dan Cullen puffed at his cigar and said nothing. Astern, and going astern fast, could be seen the sailor. He had caught the life buoy and was clinging to it. Nobody spoke. Nobody moved. The men aloft clung to the royal yards and watched with terror-stricken faces. And the *Mary Rogers* raced on, making her westing. A long, silent minute passed.

"Who was it?" Captain Cullen demanded.

"Mops, sir," eagerly answered the sailor at the wheel.

Mops topped a wave astern and disappeared temporarily in the trough. It was a large wave, but it was no graybeard. A small boat could live easily in such a sea, and in such a sea the *Mary Rogers* could easily come to. But she could not come to and make westing at the same time.

For the first time in all his years, George Dorety was see-ing a real drama of life and death—a sordid little drama in which the scales balanced an unknown sailor named Mops against a few miles of longitude. At first he had watched the man astern, but now he watched big Dan Cullen, hairy and black, vested with power of life and death, smoking a cigar.

Captain Dan Cullen smoked another long, silent minute. Then he removed the cigar from his mouth. He glanced aloft at the spars of the *Mary Rogers*, and overside at the sea.

"Sheet home the royals!" he cried.

Fifteen minutes later they sat at table, in the cabin, with food served before them. On one side of George Dorety sat Dan Cullen, the tiger, on the other side, Joshua Higgins, the hyena. Nobody spoke. On deck the men were sheeting home the skysails. George Dorety could hear their cries, while a persistent vision haunted him of a man called Mops, alive and well, clinging to a life buoy miles astern in that lonely ocean. He glanced at Captain Cullen, and experienced a feel-ing of nausea, for the man was eating his food with relish, al-most bolting it.

"Captain Cullen," Dorety said, "you are in command of this ship, and it is not proper for me to comment now upon what you do. But I wish to say one thing. There is a hereafter, and yours will be a hot one."

Captain Cullen did not even scowl. In his voice was regret as he said, "It was blowing a living gale. It was impossible to save the man."

"He fell from the royal yard," Dorety cried hotly. "You were setting the royals at the time. Fifteen minutes afterward you were setting the skysails."

"It was a living gale, wasn't it, Mr. Higgins?" Captain Cullen said, turning to the mate.

"If you'd brought her to, it'd have taken the sticks out of her," was the mate's answer. "You did the proper thing, Captain Cullen. The man hadn't a ghost of a show."

George Dorety made no answer, and to the meal's end no one spoke. After that, Dorety had his meals served in his stateroom. Captain Cullen scowled at him no longer, though no speech was exchanged between them, while the *Mary Rogers* sped north toward warmer latitudes. At the end of the week, Dan Cullen cornered Dorety on deck.

"What are you going to do when we get to 'Frisco?" he demanded bluntly.

"I am going to swear out a warrant for your arrest," Dorety answered quietly. "I am going to charge you with murder, and I am going to see you hanged for it."

"You're almighty sure of yourself," Captain Cullen sneered, turning on his heel.

A second week passed, and one morning found George Dorety standing in the coach house companionway at the for'ard end of the long poop, taking his first gaze around the deck. The *Mary Rogers* was reaching full-and-by, in a stiff breeze. Every sail was set and drawing, including the staysails. Captain Cullen strolled for'ard along the poop. He strolled carelessly, glancing at the passenger out of the corner of his eye. Dorety was looking the other way, standing with head and shoulders outside the companionway, and only the back of his head was to be seen. Captain Cullen, with swift eye, embraced the mainstaysail block and the head and estimated the distance. He glanced about him. Nobody was looking. Aft, Joshua Higgins, pacing up and down, had just turned his back and was going the other way. Captain Cullen bent over suddenly and cast the staysail sheet off from its pin. The heavy block hurtled through the air, smashing Dorety's head like an eggshell and hurtling on and back and forth as the staysail whipped and slatted in the wind. Joshua Higgins turned around to see what had carried away, and met the full blast of the vilest portion of Captain Cullen's profanity.

"I made the sheet fast myself," whimpered the mate in the first lull, "with an extra turn to make sure. I remember it distinctly."

"Made fast?" the Captain snarled back, for the benefit of the watch as it struggled to capture the flying sail before it tore to ribbons. "You couldn't make your grandmother fast, you useless hell's scullion. If you made that sheet fast with an extra turn, why in hell didn't it stay fast? That's what I want to know. Why in hell didn't it stay fast?"

The mate whined inarticulately.

"Oh, shut up!" was the final word of Captain Cullen.

Half an hour later he was as surprised as any when the body of George Dorety was found inside the companionway on the floor. In the afternoon, alone in his room, he doctored up the log.

"Ordinary seaman, Karl Brun," he wrote, *"lost overboard from foreroyal-yard in a gale of wind. Was running at the time, and for the safety of the ship did not dare come up to the wind. Nor could a boat have lived in the sea that was running."*

On another page, he wrote:

"Had often warned Mr. Dorety about the danger he ran because of his carelessness on deck. I told him, once, that some day he would get his head knocked off by a block. A carelessly fastened mainstaysail sheet was the cause of the accident, which was deeply to be regretted because Mr. Dorety was a favorite with all of us."

Captain Dan Cullen read over his literary effort with admiration, blotted the page, and closed the log. He lighted a cigar and stared before him. He felt the *Mary Rogers* lift, and heel, and surge along, and knew that she was making nine knots. A smile of satisfaction slowly dawned on his black and hairy face. Well, anyway, he had made his westing and fooled God.

from: *The Sea Wolf*

(The story is told from the point of view of Humphrey Van Weyden, an aristocratic, somewhat effete young man who was rescued after a shipwreck by Wolf Larsen, captain of the seal hunting vessel, Ghost. *Despite his protests, Van Weyden is put to work as a common sailor. The following two excerpts of the novel are taken from chapters ten and seventeen. Ed.)*

Chapter 10

My intimacy with Wolf Larsen increases—if by intimacy may be denoted those relations which exist between master and man, or, better yet, between king and jester. I am to him no more than a toy, and he values me no more than a child values a toy. My function is to amuse, and so long as I amuse all goes well; but let him become bored, or let him have one of his black moods come upon him, and at once I am relegated from cabin table to galley, while, at the same time, I am fortunate to escape with my life and a whole body.

The loneliness of the man is slowly being borne in upon me. There is not a man aboard but hates or fears him, nor is there a man whom he does not despise. He seems consuming with the tremendous power that is in him and that seems never to have found adequate expression in works. He is as Lucifer would be, were that proud spirit banished to a society of soulless, Tomlinsonian ghosts.

This loneliness is bad enough in itself, but, to make it worse, he is oppressed by the primal melancholy of the race. Knowing him, I review the old Scandinavian myths with clearer understanding. The white-skinned, fair-haired savages who created that terrible pantheon were of the same fiber as he. The frivolity of the laughter-loving Latins is no part of him. When he laughs it is from a humor that is nothing else than ferocious. But he laughs rarely; he is too often sad. And it is a sadness as deep-reaching as the roots of the race. It is the race heritage, the sadness which has made the race sober-minded, clean-lived, and fanatically moral, and which, in this latter connection, has culminated among the English in the Reformed Church and Mrs. Grundy.

In point of fact, the chief vent to this primal melancholy has been religion in its more agonizing forms. But the compensations of such religion are denied Wolf Larsen. His brutal materialism will not permit it. So, when his blue moods come on, nothing remains for him but to be devilish. Were he not so terrible a man, I could sometimes feel sorry for him, as instance three mornings ago, when I went into his stateroom to fill his water bottle and came unexpectedly upon him. He did not see me. His head was buried in his hands, and his shoulders were heaving convulsively as with sobs. He seemed torn, by some mighty grief. As I softly withdrew I could hear him groaning, "God! God! God!" Not that he was calling upon God; it was a mere expletive, but it came from his soul.

At dinner he asked the hunters for a remedy for headache, and by evening, strong man that he was, he was half-blind and reeling about the cabin.

"I've never been sick in my life, Hump," he said, as I guided him to his room. "Nor did I ever have a headache except the time my head was healing after having been laid open for six inches by a capstan-bar."

For three days this blinding headache lasted, and he suffered as wild animals suffer, as it seemed the way on ship to suffer, without plaint, without sympathy, utterly alone.

This morning, however, on entering his stateroom to make the bed and put things in order, I found him well and hard at work. Table and bunk were littered with designs and calculations. On a large transparent sheet, compass and square in hand, he was copying what appeared to be a scale of some sort or other.

"Hello, Hump," he greeted me genially. "I'm just finishing the finishing touches. Want to see it work?"

"But what is it?" I asked.

"A labor-saving device for mariners, navigation reduced to kindergarten simplicity," he answered gaily. "From today a child will be able to navigate a ship. No more long-winded calculations. All you need is one star in the sky on a dirty night to know instantly where you are. Look. I place the transparent scale on this star-map, revolving the scale on the North Pole.

On the scale I've worked out the circles of altitude and the lines of bearing. All I do is to put it on a star, revolve the scale till it is opposite those figures on the map underneath, and presto! There you are, the ship's precise location!"

There was a ring of triumph in his voice, and his eyes, clear blue this morning as the sea, were sparkling with light.

"You must be well up in mathematics," I said. "Where did you go to school?"

"Never saw the inside of one, worse luck," was the answer. "I had to dig it out for myself."

"And why do you think I have made this thing?" he demanded, abruptly. "Dreaming to leave footprints on the sands of time?" He laughed one of his horrible mocking laughs. "Not at all. To get it patented, to make money from it, to revel in piggishness . . . while other men do the work. That's my purpose. Also, I have enjoyed working it out."

"The creative joy," I murmured.

"I guess that's what it ought to be called. Which is another way of expressing the joy of life in that it is alive, the triumph of movement over matter, of the quick over the dead, the pride of the yeast because it is yeast and crawls."

I threw up my hands with helpless disapproval of his inveterate materialism and went about making the bed. He continued copying lines and figures upon the transparent scale. It was a task requiring the utmost nicety and precision, and I could not but admire the way he tempered his strength to the fineness and delicacy of the need.

When I had finished the bed, I caught myself looking at him in a fascinated sort of way. He was certainly a handsome man—beautiful in the masculine sense. And again, with never-failing wonder, I remarked the total lack of vicious-ness, or wickedness, or sinfulness, in his face. It was the face, I am convinced, of a man who did no wrong. And by this I do not wish to be misunderstood. What I mean is that it was the face of a man who either did nothing contrary to the dictates of his conscience, or who had no conscience. I am inclined to the latter way of accounting for it. He was a magnificent atavism, a man so purely primitive that he was of the type that came into the world before the development of the moral nature. He was not immoral, but merely unmoral.

As I have said, in the masculine sense his was a beautiful face. Smooth-shaven, every line was distinct, and it was cut as clear and sharp as a cameo; while sea and sun had tanned the naturally fair skin to a dark bronze which bespoke struggle and battle and added both to his savagery and his beauty. The lips were full, yet possessed of the firmness, almost harshness, which is characteristic of thin lips. The set of his mouth, his chin, his jaw, was likewise firm or harsh, with all the fierceness and indomitableness of the male—the nose also. It was the nose of a being born to conquer and com-mand. It just hinted of the eagle beak. It might have been Grecian, it might have been Roman, only it was a shade too massive for the one, a shade too delicate for the other. And while the whole face was the incarnation of fierceness and strength, the primal melancholy from which he suffered seemed to greaten the lines of mouth and eye and brow, seemed to give a largeness and completeness which other-wise the face would have lacked.

And so I caught myself standing idly and studying him. I cannot say how greatly the man had come to interest me. Who was he? What was he? How had he happened to be? All powers seemed his, all potentialities—why, then, was he no more than the obscure master of a seal-hunting schooner with a reputation for frightful brutality amongst the men who hunted seals?

My curiosity burst from me in a flood of speech.

"Why is it that you have not done great things in this world? With the power that is yours you might have risen to any height. Unpossessed of conscience or moral instinct, you might have mastered the world, broken it to your hand. And yet here you are, at the top of your life, where diminishing and dying begin, living an obscure and sordid existence, hunting sea animals for the satisfaction of woman's vanity and love of decoration, reveling in a piggishness, to use your own words, which is anything and everything except splendid. Why, with all that wonderful strength, have you not done something? There was nothing to stop you, nothing that could stop you. What was wrong? Did you lack ambition? Did you fall under temptation? What was the matter? What was the matter?"

He had lifted his eyes to me at the commencement of my outburst, and followed me complacently until I had done and stood before him breathless and dismayed. He waited a moment, as though seeking where to begin, and then said:

"Hump, do you know the parable of the sower who went forth to sow? If you will remember, some of the seed fell upon stony places, where there was not much earth, and forthwith they sprung up because they had no deepness of earth. And when the sun was up they were scorched, and because they had no root they withered away. And some fell among thorns, and the thorns sprung up and choked them."

"Well?" I said.

"Well?" he queried, half petulantly. "It was not well. I was one of those seeds."

He dropped his head to the scale and resumed the copying. I finished my work and had opened the door to leave, when he spoke to me.

"Hump, if you will look on the west coast of the map of Norway you will see an indentation called Romsdal Fiord. I was born within a hundred miles of that stretch of water. But I was not born Norwegian. I am a Dane. My father and mother were Danes, and how they ever came to that bleak bight of land on the west coast I do not know. I never heard. Outside of that there is nothing mysterious. They were poor people and unlettered. They came of generations of poor unlettered people—peasants of the sea who sowed their sons on the waves as has been their custom since time began. There is no more to tell."

"But there is," I objected. "It is still obscure to me."

"What can I tell you?" he demanded, with a recrudescence of fierceness. "Of the meagerness of a child's life? of fish diet and coarse living? of going out with the boats from the time I could crawl? of my brothers, who went away one by one to the deep-sea farming and never cane back? of myself, unable to read or write, cabin-boy at the mature age of ten on the coastwise, old-country ships? of the rough fare and rougher usage, where kicks and blows were bed and breakfast and took the place of speech, and fear and hatred and pain were my only soul-experience? I do not care to remember. A madness comes up in my brain even now as I think of it. But there were coastwise skippers I would have returned and killed when a man's strength came to me, only the lines of my life were cast at the time in other places. I did return, not long ago, but unfortunately the skippers were dead, all but one, a mate in the old days, a skipper when I met him, and when I left him a cripple who would never walk again."

"But you who read Spencer and Darwin and have never seen the inside of a school, how did you learn to read and write?" I queried.

"In the English merchant service. Cabin-boy at twelve, ship's boy at fourteen, ordinary seaman at sixteen, able seaman at seventeen, and cock of the fo'c'sle, infinite ambition and infinite loneliness, receiving neither help nor sympathy, I did it all for myself—navigation, mathematics, science, literature, and what not. And of what use has it been? Master and owner of a ship at the top of my life, as you say, when I am beginning to diminish and die. Paltry, isn't it? And when the sun was up I was scorched, and because I had no root I withered away."

"But history tells of slaves who rose to the purple," I chided.

"And history tells of opportunities that came to the slaves who rose to the purple," he answered grimly. "No man makes opportunity. All the great men ever did was to know it when it came to them. The Corsican knew. I have dreamed as greatly as the Corsican. I should have known the opportunity, but it never came. The thorns sprung up and choked me. And, Hump, I can tell you that you know more about me than any living man, except my own brother."

"And what is he? And where is he?"

"Master of the steamship *Macedonia*, seal-hunter," was the answer. "We will meet him most probably on the Japan coast. Men call him 'Death' Larsen."

"Death Larsen!" I involuntarily cried. "Is he like you?"

"Hardly. He is a lump of an animal without any head. He has all my—my—"

"Brutishness," I suggested.

"Yes—thank you for the word—all my brutishness, but he can scarcely read or write."

"And he has never philosophized on life," I added.

"No," Wolf Larsen answered, with an indescribable air of sadness. "And he is all the happier for leaving life alone. He is too busy living it to think about it. My mistake was in ever opening the books."

from: *The Sea Wolf*

Chapter 17

Strange to say, in spite of the general foreboding, nothing of especial moment happened on the *Ghost*. We ran on to the north and west till we raised the coast of Japan and picked up with the great seal herd. Coming from no man knew where in the illimitable Pacific, it was traveling north on its annual migration to the rookeries of Bering Sea. And north we traveled with it, ravaging and destroying, flinging the naked carcasses to the shark and salting down the skins so that they might later adorn the fair shoulders of the women of the cities.

It was wanton slaughter, and all for woman's sake. No man ate of the seal meat or the oil. After a good day's killing I have seen our decks covered with hides and bodies, slippery with fat and blood, the scuppers running red; masts, ropes, and rails spattered with the sanguinary color; and the men like butchers plying their trade, naked and red of arm and

hand, hard at work with ripping and flensing-knives, removing the skins from the pretty sea-creatures they had killed.

It was my task to tally the pelts as they came aboard from
the boats, to oversee the skinning and afterward the cleans-
ing of the decks and bringing things shipshape again. It was
not pleasant work. My soul and my stomach revolted at it;
and yet, in a way, this handling and directing of many men
was good for me. It developed what little executive ability I
possessed, and I was aware of a toughening or hardening
which I was undergoing and which could not be anything but
wholesome for "Sissy" Van Weyden.

One thing I was beginning to feel, and that was that I
could never again be quite the same man I had been. While
my hope and faith in human life still survived Wolf Larsen's
destructive criticism, he had nevertheless been a cause of
change in minor matters. He had opened up for me the world
of the real, of which I had known practically nothing and
from which I had always shrunk. I had learned to look more
closely at life as it was lived, to recognize that there were
such things as facts in the world, to emerge from the realm of
mind and idea and to place certain values on the concrete and
objective phases of existence.

I saw more of Wolf Larsen than ever when we had gained
the grounds. For when the weather was fair and we were in the
midst of the herd, all hands were away in the boats, and left on
board were only he and I, and Thomas Mugridge, who did not
count. But there was no play about it. The six boats, spreading
out fan-wise from the schooner until the first weather boat and
the last lee boat were anywhere from ten to twenty miles apart,
cruised along a straight course over the sea till nightfall or bad

weather drove them in. It was our duty to sail the *Ghost* well to leeward of the last lee boat, so that all the boats should have fair wind to run for us in case of squalls or threatening weather.

It is no slight matter for two men, particularly when a stiff wind has sprung up, to handle a vessel like the *Ghost*, steering, keeping lookout for the boats, and setting or taking in sail; so it devolved upon me to learn and learn quickly. Steering I picked up easily, but running aloft to the crosstrees and swinging my whole weight by my arms when I left the ratlines and climbed still higher, was more difficult. This, too, I learned, and quickly, for I felt somehow a wild desire to vindicate myself in Wolf Larsen's eyes, to prove my right to live in ways other than of the mind. Nay, the time came when I took joy in the run of the masthead and in the clinging on by my legs at that precarious height while I swept the sea with glasses in search of the boats.

I remember one beautiful day, when the boats left early and the reports of the hunters' guns grew dim and distant and died away as they scattered far and wide over the sea. There was just the faintest wind from the westward; but it breathed its last by the time we managed to get to leeward of the last lee boat. One by one—I was at the masthead and saw—the six boats disappeared over the bulge of the earth as they followed the seal into the west. We lay, scarcely rolling on the placid sea, unable to follow. Wolf Larsen was apprehensive. The barometer was down, and the sky to the east did not please him. He studied it with unceasing vigilance.

"If she comes out of there," he said, "hard and snappy, putting us to windward of the boats, it's likely there'll be empty bunks in steerage and fo'c'sle."

By eleven o'clock the sea had become glass. By mid-day, though we were well up in the northerly latitudes, the heat was sickening. There was no freshness in the air. It was sultry and oppressive, reminding me of what the old Californians term "earthquake weather." There was something ominous about it, and in intangible ways one was made to feel that the worst was about to come. Slowly the whole eastern sky filled with clouds that overtowered us like some black sierra of the infernal regions. So clearly could one see canyon, gorge, and precipice, and the shadows that lie therein, that one looked unconsciously for the white surf-line and bellowing caverns where the sea charges on the land. And still we rocked gently, and there was no wind.

"It's no squall," Wolf Larsen said, "Old Mother Nature's going to get up on her hind legs and howl for all that's in her, and it'll keep us jumping, Hump, to pull through with half our boats. You'd better run up and loosen the topsails."

"But if it is going to howl, and there are only two of us?" I asked, a note of protest in my voice.

"Why, we've got to make the best of the first of it and run down to our boats before our canvas is ripped out of us. After that I don't give a rap what happens. The sticks'll stand it, and you and I will have to, though we've plenty cut out for us."

Still the calm continued. We ate dinner, a hurried and anxious meal for me with eighteen men abroad on the sea and beyond the bulge of the earth and with that heaven-rolling mountain range of clouds moving slowly down upon us. Wolf Larsen did not seem affected, however; though I noticed, when we returned to the deck, a slight twitching of the nostrils, a perceptible quickness of movement. His face was stern, the lines of it had grown hard, and yet in his eyes— blue, clear blue this day—there was a strange brilliancy, a bright scintillating light. It struck me that he was joyous, in a ferocious sort of way; that he was glad there was an impending struggle; that he was thrilled and upborne with knowledge that one of the great moments of living, when the tide of life surges up in flood, was upon him.

Once, and unwitting that he did so or that I saw, he laughed aloud, mockingly and defiantly, at the advancing storm. I see him yet, standing there like a pygmy out of the "Arabian Nights" before the huge front of some malignant genie. He was daring destiny, and he was unafraid.

He walked to the galley. "Cooky, by the time you've finished pots and pans you'll be wanted on deck. Stand ready for a call."

"Hump," he said, becoming cognizant of the fascinated gaze I bent upon him, "this beats whiskey, and is where your Omar misses. I think he only half lived after all."

The western half of the sky had by now grown murky. The sun had dimmed and faded out of sight. It was two in the afternoon, and a ghostly twilight, shot through by wandering purplish lights, had descended upon us. In this purplish light Wolf Larsen's face glowed and glowed, and to my excited fancy he appeared encircled by a halo. We lay in the midst of an unearthly quiet, while all about us were signs and omens of oncoming sound and movement. The sultry heat had become unendurable. The sweat was standing on my forehead, and I could feel it trickling down my nose. I felt as though I should faint, and reached out to the rail for support.

And then, just then, the faintest possible whisper of air passed by. It was from the east, and like a whisper it came and went. The drooping canvas was not stirred, and yet my face had felt the air and been cooled.

"Cooky," Wolf Larsen called in a low voice. Thomas Mugridge turned a pitiable, scared face. "Let go that fore-boom tackle and pass it across, and when she's willing let go the sheet and come in snug with the tackle. And if you make a mess of it, it will be the last you ever make. Understand?

"Mr. Van Weyden, stand by to pass the head-sails over. Then jump for the topsails and spread them quick as God'll let you—the quicker you do it the easier you'll find it. As for Cooky, if he isn't lively bat him between the eyes."

I was aware of the compliment and pleased, in that no threat had accompanied my instructions. We were lying head to northwest, and it was his intention to jibe over all with the first puff.

"We'll have the breeze on our quarter," he explained to me. "By the last guns the boats were bearing away slightly to the south'ard."

He turned and walked aft to the wheel. I went forward and took my station at the jibs. Another whisper of wind, and another, passed by. The canvas flapped lazily.

"Thank Gawd she's not comin' all of a bunch, Mr. Van Weyden," was the Cockney's fervent ejaculation.

And I was indeed thankful, for I had by this time learned enough to know, with all our canvas spread, what disaster in such event awaited us. The whispers of wind became puffs, the sails filled, the *Ghost* moved. Wolf Larsen put the wheel hard up, to port, and we began to pay off. The wind was now dead astern, muttering and puffing stronger and stronger, and my head-sails were pounding lustily. I did not see what went on elsewhere, though I felt the sudden surge and heel of the schooner as the wind-pressures changed to the jibing of the fore- and main-sails. My hands were full with the flying-jib, jib, and staysail; and by the time this part of my task was accomplished the *Ghost* was leaping into the southwest, the wind on her quarter and all her sheets to starboard. Without pausing for breath, though my heart was beating like a trip-hammer from my exertions, I sprang to the topsails, and before the wind had become too strong we had them fairly set and were coiling down. Then I went aft for orders.

Wolf Larsen nodded approval and relinquished the wheel to me. The wind was strengthening steadily and the sea rising. For an hour I steered, each moment becoming more difficult. I had not the experience to steer at the gait we were going on a quartering course.

"Now take a run up with the glasses and raise some of the boats. We've made at least ten knots, and we're going twelve or thirteen now. The old girl knows how to walk."

I contented myself with the fore crosstrees, some seventy feet above the deck. As I searched the vacant stretch of water before me, I comprehended thoroughly the need for haste if we were to recover any of our men. Indeed, as I gazed at the heavy sea through which we were running, I doubted that there was a boat afloat. It did not seem possible that such frail craft could survive such stress of wind and water.

I could not feel the full force of the wind, for we were running with it; but from my lofty perch I looked down as though outside the *Ghost* and apart from her, and saw the shape of her outlined sharply against the foaming sea as she tore along instinct with life. Sometimes she would lift and send across some great wave, burying her starboard rail from view, and covering her deck to the hatches with the boiling ocean. At such moments, starting from a windward roll, I would go flying through the air with dizzying swiftness, as though I clung to the end of a huge, inverted pendulum, the arc of which, between the greater rolls, must have been seventy feet or more. Once, the terror of this giddy sweep overpowered me, and for a while I clung on, hand and foot, weak and trembling, unable to search the sea for the missing boats or to behold aught of the sea but that which roared beneath and strove to overwhelm the *Ghost*.

But the thought of the men in the midst of it steadied me, and in my quest for them I forgot myself. For an hour I saw nothing but the naked, desolate sea. And then, where a vagrant shaft of sunlight struck the ocean and turned its surface to wrathful silver, I caught a small black speck thrust skyward for an instant and swallowed up. I waited patiently. Again the tiny point of black projected itself through the wrathful blaze a couple of points off our port-bow. I did not attempt to shout, but communicated the news to Wolf Larsen by waving my arm. He changed the course, and I signaled affirmation when the speck showed dead ahead.

It grew larger, and so swiftly that for the first time I fully appreciated the speed of our flight. Wolf Larsen motioned for me to come down, and when I stood beside him at the wheel gave me instructions for heaving in.

"Expect all hell to break loose," he cautioned me, "but don't mind it. Yours is to do your own work and to have Cooky stand by the fore-sheet."

I managed to make my way forward, but there was little choice of sides, for the weather-rail seemed buried as often as the lee. Having instructed Thomas Mugridge as to what he was to do, I clambered into the fore rigging a few feet. The boat was now very close, and I could make out plainly that it was lying head to wind and sea and dragging on its mast and sail, which had been thrown overboard and made to serve as a sea-anchor. The three men were bailing. Each rolling mountain whelmed them from view, and I would wait with sickening anxiety, fearing that they would never appear again. Then, and with black suddenness, the boat would shoot clear through the foaming crest, bow pointed to the sky, and the whole length of her bottom showing, wet and dark, till she seemed on end. There would be a fleeting glimpse of the three men flinging water in frantic haste, when she would topple over and fall into the yawing valley, bow down and showing her full inside length to the stern up-reared almost directly above the bow. Each time that she reappeared was a miracle.

The *Ghost* suddenly changed her course, keeping away, and it came to me with a shock that Wolf Larsen was giving up the rescue as impossible. Then I realized that he was preparing to heave to, and dropped to the deck to be in readiness. We were now dead before the wind, the boat far away and abreast of us. I felt an abrupt easing of the schooner, a loss for the moment of all strain and pressure, coupled with a swift acceleration of speed. She was rushing around on her heel into the wind.

As she arrived at right angles to the sea, the full force of the wind (from which we had hitherto run away) caught us. I was unfortunately and ignorantly facing it. It stood up against me like a wall, filling my lungs with air which I could not expel. And as I choked and strangled, and as the *Ghost* wallowed for an instant, broadside on and rolling straight over and far into the wind, I beheld a huge sea rise far above my head. I turned aside, caught my breath, and looked again. The wave over-topped the *Ghost*, and I gazed sheer up and into it. A shaft of sunlight smote the over-curl, and I caught a glimpse of translucent, rushing green, backed by a milky smother of foam.

Then it descended, pandemonium broke loose, every-thing happened at once. I was struck a crushing, stunning blow, nowhere in particular and yet everywhere. My hold had been broken loose, I was under water, and the thought passed through my mind that this was the terrible thing of which I had heard, the being swept in the trough of the sea. My body struck and pounded as it was dashed helplessly along and turned over and over, and when I could hold my breath no longer, I breathed the stinging salt water into my lungs. But through it all I clung to the one idea—*I must get the jib backed over to windward.* I had no fear of death. I had no doubt but that I should come through somehow. And as this idea of fulfilling Wolf Larsen's order persisted in my dazed consciousness, I seemed to see him standing at the wheel in the midst of the wild welter, pitting his will against the will of the storm and defying it.

I brought up violently against what I took to be the rail, breathed, and breathed the sweet air again. I tried to rise, but struck my head and was knocked back on hands and knees. By some freak of the waters I had been swept clear under the forecastle-head and into the eyes. As I scrambled out on all fours, I passed of the body of Thomas Mugridge, who lay in a groaning heap. There was no time to investigate. I must get the jib backed over.

When I emerged on deck it seemed that the end of everything had come. On all sides there was a rending and crashing of wood and steel and canvas. The *Ghost* was being wrenched and torn to fragments. The foresail and fore topsail, emptied of the wind by the maneuver, and with no one to bring in the sheet in time, were thundering into ribbons, the heavy boom threshing and splintering from rail to rail. The air was thick with flying wreckage, detached ropes and stays were hissing and coiling like snakes, and down through it all crashed the gaff of the foresail.

The spar could not have missed me by many inches, while it spurred me to action. Perhaps the situation was not hopeless. I remembered Wolf Larsen's caution. He had expected all hell to break loose, and here it was. And where was he? I caught sight of him toiling at the main sheet, heaving it in and flat with his tremendous muscles, the stern of the schooner lifted high in the air and his body outlined against a white surge of sea sweeping past. All this, and more—a whole world of chaos and wreck—in possibly fifteen seconds I had seen and heard and grasped.

I did not stop to see what had become of the small boat, but sprang to the jib-sheet. The jib itself was beginning to slap, partially filling and emptying with sharp reports; but with a turn of the sheet and the application of my whole strength each time it slapped, I slowly backed it. This I know: I did my best. I pulled till I burst open the ends of all my fingers; and while I pulled, the flying-jib and staysail split their cloths apart and thundered into nothingness.

Still I pulled, holding what I gained each time with a double turn until the next slap gave me more. Then the sheet gave with greater ease, and Wolf Larsen was beside me, heaving in alone while I was busied taking up the slack.

"Make fast!" he shouted. "And come on!"

As I followed him, I noted that in spite of rack and ruin a rough order obtained. The *Ghost* was hove to. She was still in working order, and she was still working. Though the rest of her sails were gone, the jib, backed to windward, and the mainsail hauled down flat, were themselves holding, and holding her bow to the furious sea as well.

I looked for the boat, and while Wolf Larsen cleared the boat-tackles, saw it lift to leeward on a big sea and not a score of feet away. And, so nicely had he made his calculation, we drifted fairly down upon it, so that nothing remained to do but hook the tackles to either end and hoist it aboard. But this was not done so easily as it is written.

In the bow was Kerfoot, Oofty-Oofty in the stern, and Kelly amidships. As we drifted closer, the boat would rise on a wave while we sank in the trough, till almost straight above me I could see the heads of the three men craned overside and looking down. Then, the next moment, we would lift and soar upward while they sank far down beneath us. It seemed incredible that the next surge should not crush the *Ghost* down upon the tiny eggshell.

But, at the right moment, I passed the tackle to the Kanaka, while Wolf Larsen did the same thing forward to Kerfoot. Both tackles were hooked in a trice, and the three men, deftly timing the roll, made a simultaneous leap aboard the schooner. As the *Ghost* rolled her side out of water, the boat was lifted snugly against her, and before the return roll came, we had heaved it in over the side and turned it bottom up on the deck. I noticed blood spouting from Kerfoot's left hand. In some way the third finger had been crushed to a pulp. But he gave no sign of pain, and with his single right hand helped us lash the boat in its place.

"Stand by to let that jib over, you Oofty!" Wolf Larsen commanded, the very second we had finished with the boat. "Kelly, come aft and slack off the main-sheet! You, Kerfoot, go for'ard and see what's become of Cooky! Mr. Van Weyden, run aloft again, and cut away any stray stuff on your way!"

And having commanded, he went aft with his peculiar tigerish leaps, to the wheel. While I toiled up the fore-shrouds the *Ghost* slowly paid off. This time, as we went into the trough of the sea and were swept, there were no sails to carry away. And halfway to the crosstrees and flattened against the rigging by the full force of the wind so that it would have been impossible for me to have fallen, the *Ghost* almost on her beam ends and the masts parallel with the water, I looked, not down, but at almost right angles from the perpendicular, to the deck of the *Ghost*. But I saw, not the deck, but where the deck should have been, for it was buried beneath a wild tumbling of water. Out of this water I could see the two masts rising, and that was all. The *Ghost*, for the moment, was buried beneath the sea. As she squared off more and more, escaping from the side pressure, she righted herself and broke her deck, like a whale's back, through the ocean surface.

Then we raced, and wildly, across the wild sea, the while I hung like a fly in the crosstrees and searched for the other boats. In half an hour I sighted the second one, swamped and bottom up, to which were desperately clinging Jock Horner, fat Louis, and Johnson. This time I remained aloft, and Wolf Larsen succeeded in heaving to without being swept. As before, we drifted down upon it. Tackles were made fast and lines flung to the men, who scrambled aboard like monkeys. The boat itself was crushed and splintered against the schooner's side as it came inboard; but the wreck was securely lashed, for it could be patched and made whole again.

Once more the *Ghost* bore away before the storm, this time so submerging herself that for some seconds I thought she would never reappear. Even the wheel, quite a deal higher than the waist, was covered and swept again and again. At such moments I felt strangely alone with God, alone with him and watching the chaos of his wrath. And then the wheel would reappear, and Wolf Larsen's broad shoulders, his hands gripping the spokes and holding the schooner to the course of his will, himself an earth-god, dominating the storm, flinging its descending waters from him and riding it to his own ends. And oh, the marvel of it! The marvel of it! That tiny men should live and breathe and work, and drive so frail a contrivance of wood and cloth through so tremendous an elemental strife!

As before, the *Ghost* swung out of the trough, lifting her deck again out of the sea, and dashed before the howling blast. It was now half-past five, and half an hour later, when the last of the day lost itself in a dim and furious twilight, I sighted a third boat. It was bottom up, and there was no sign of its crew. Wolf Larsen repeated his maneuver, holding off and then rounding up to windward and drifting down upon it. But this time he missed by forty feet, the boat passing astern.

"Number four boat!" Oofty-Oofty cried, his keen eyes reading its number in the one second when it lifted clear of the foam and upside down.

It was Henderson's boat, and with him had been lost Holyoak and Williams, another of the deep-water crowd. Lost they indubitably were; but the boat remained, and Wolf Larsen made one more reckless effort to recover it. I had come down to the deck, and I saw Horner and Kerfoot vainly protest against the attempt.

"By God, I'll not be robbed of my boat by any storm that ever blew out of hell!" he shouted, and though we four stood with our heads together that we might hear, his voice seemed faint and far, as though removed from us an immense distance.

"Mr. Van Weyden!" he cried, and I heard through the tumult as one might hear a whisper. "Stand by that jib with Johnson and Oofty! The rest of you tail aft to the main sheet! Lively now! Or I'll sail you all into Kingdom Come! Understand?"

And when he put the wheel hard over and the *Ghost*'s bow swung off, there was nothing for the hunters to do but obey and make the best of a risky chance. How great the risk I realized when I was once more buried beneath the pounding seas and clinging for life to the pin-rail at the foot of the foremast. My fingers were torn loose, and I swept across to the side and over the side into the sea. I could not swim, but before I could sink I was swept back again. A strong hand gripped me, and when the *Ghost* finally emerged, I found that

I owed my life to Johnson. I saw him looking anxiously about him, and noted that Kelly, who had come forward at the last moment, was missing.

This time, having missed the boat and not being in the same position as in the previous instances, Wolf Larsen was compelled to resort to a different maneuver. Running off before the wind with everything to starboard, he came about and returned close-hauled on the port tack.

"Grand!" Johnson shouted in my ear, as we successfully came through the attendant deluge, and I knew he referred, not to Wolf Larsen's seamanship, but to the performance of the *Ghost* herself.

It was now so dark that there was no sign of the boat; but Wolf Larsen held back through the frightful turmoil as if guided by unerring instinct. This time, though we were continually half-buried, there was no trough in which to be swept, and we drifted squarely down upon the up-turned boat, badly smashing it as it was heaved inboard.

Two hours of terrible work followed, in which all hands of us—two hunters, three sailors, Wolf Larsen, and I—reefed, first one and then the other, the jib and mainsail. Hove to under this short canvas, our decks were comparatively free of water, while the *Ghost* bobbed and ducked amongst the combers like a cork.

I had burst open the ends of my fingers at the very first, and during the reefing I had worked with tears of pain running down my cheeks. And when all was done, I gave up like a woman and rolled upon the deck in the agony of exhaustion.

In the meantime Thomas Mugridge, like a drowned rat, was being dragged out from under the forecastle head where he had cravenly ensconced himself. I saw him pulled aft to the cabin and noted with a shock of surprise that the galley had disappeared. A clean space of deck showed where it had stood.

In the cabin I found all hands assembled, sailors as well, and while coffee was being cooked over the small stove we drank whiskey and crunched hardtack. Never in my life had food been so welcome. And never had hot coffee tasted so good. So violently did the *Ghost* pitch and toss and tumble that it was impossible for even the sailors to move about without holding on, and several times, after a cry of "Now she takes it!" we were heaped upon the wall of the port cabins as though it had been the deck.

"To hell with a lookout," I heard Wolf Larsen say when we had eaten and drunk our fill. "There's nothing can be done on deck. If anything's going to run us down we couldn't get out of its way. Turn in, all hands, and get some sleep."

The sailors slipped forward, setting the side-lights as they went, while the two hunters remained to sleep in the cabin, it not being deemed advisable to open the slide to the steerage companionway. Wolf Larsen and I, between us, cut off Kerfoot's crushed finger and sewed up the stump. Mugridge, who, during all the time he had been compelled to cook and serve coffee and keep the fire going, had complained of internal pains, now swore that he had a broken rib or two. On examination we found that he had three. But his case was deferred to next day, principally for the reason that I did not know anything about broken ribs and would first have to read it up.

"I don't think it was worth it," I said to Wolf Larsen, "a broken boat for Kelly's life."

"But Kelly didn't amount to much," was the reply. "Good night."

After all that had passed, suffering intolerable anguish in my finger ends, and with three boats missing, to say nothing of the wild capers the *Ghost* was cutting, I should have thought it impossible to sleep. But my eyes must have closed the instant my head touched the pillow, and in utter exhaustion I slept throughout the night, while the *Ghost*, lonely and undirected, fought her way through the storm.

The Seed of McCoy

The *Pyrenees*, her iron sides pressed low in the water by her cargo of wheat, rolled sluggishly, and made it easy for the man who was climbing aboard from out a tiny outrigger canoe. As his eyes came level with the rail, so that he could see inboard, it seemed to him that he saw a dim, almost indiscernible haze. It was more like an illusion, like a blurring film that had spread abruptly over his eyes. He felt an inclination to brush it away, and the same instant he thought that he was growing old and that it was time to send to San Francisco for a pair of spectacles.

As he came over the rail he cast a glance aloft at the tall masts, and, next, at the pumps. They were not working. There seemed nothing the matter with the big ship, and he wondered why she had hoisted the signal of distress. He thought of his happy islanders, and hoped it was not disease.

Perhaps the ship was short of water or provisions. He shook hands with the captain whose gaunt face and care-worn eyes made no secret of the trouble, whatever it was. At the same moment the newcomer was aware of a faint, indefinable smell. It seemed like that of burnt bread, but different.

He glanced curiously about him. Twenty feet away a weary-faced sailor was calking the deck. As his eyes lingered on the man, he saw suddenly arise from under his hands a faint spiral of haze that curled and twisted and was gone. By now he had reached the deck. His bare feet were pervaded by a dull warmth that wickedly penetrated the thick calluses. He knew now the nature of the ship's distress. His eyes roved swiftly forward, where the full crew of weary-faced sailors regarded him eagerly. The glance from his liquid brown eyes swept over them like a benediction, soothing them, wrapping them about as in the mantle of a great peace. "How long has she been afire, Captain?" he asked in a voice so gentle and unperturbed that it was as the cooing of a dove.

At first the captain felt the peace and content of it stealing in upon him, then the consciousness of all that he had gone through and was going through smote him, and he was resentful. By what right did this ragged beachcomber, in dungaree trousers and a cotton shirt, suggest such a thing as peace and content to him and his overwrought, exhausted soul? The captain did not reason this; it was the unconscious process of emotion that caused his resentment.

"Fifteen days," he answered shortly. "Who are you?"

"My name is McCoy," came the answer in tones that breathed tenderness and compassion.

"I mean, are you the pilot?"

McCoy passed the benediction of his gaze over the tall, heavy-shouldered man with the haggard, unshaven face who had joined the captain.

"I am as much a pilot as anybody," was McCoy's answer. "We are all pilots here, Captain, and I know every inch of these waters."

But the captain was impatient.

"What I want is some of the authorities. I want to talk with them, and blame quick."

"Then I'll do just as well."

Again that insidious suggestion of peace, and his ship a raging furnace beneath his feet! The captain's eyebrows lifted impatiently and nervously, and his fist clenched as if he were about to strike a blow with it.

"Who in hell are you?" he demanded.

"I am the chief magistrate," was the reply in a voice that was still the softest and gentlest imaginable.

The tall, heavy-shouldered man broke out in a harsh laugh that was partly amusement, but mostly hysterical. Both he and the captain regarded McCoy with incredulity and amazement. That this barefooted beachcomber should possess such high-sounding dignity was inconceivable. His cotton shirt, unbuttoned, exposed a grizzled chest and the fact that there was no undershirt beneath.

A worn straw hat failed to hide the ragged gray hair. Halfway down his chest descended an untrimmed patriarchal beard. In any slop shop, two shillings would have outfitted him complete as he stood before them.

"Any relation to the McCoy of the *Bounty*?" the captain asked.

"He was my great-grandfather."

"Oh," the captain said, then bethought himself. "My name is Davenport, and this is my first mate, Mr. Konig."

They shook hands.

"And now to business." The captain spoke quickly, the urgency of a great haste pressing his speech. "We've been on fire for over two weeks. She's ready to break all hell loose any moment. That's why I held for Pitcairn. I want to beach her, or scuttle her, and save the hull."

"Then you made a mistake, Captain," said McCoy. "You should have slacked away for Mangareva. There's a beautiful beach there, in a lagoon where the water is like a mill pond."

"But we're here, ain't we?" the first mate demanded. "That's the point. We're here, and we've got to do something."

McCoy shook his head kindly.

"You can do nothing here. There is no beach. There isn't even anchorage."

"Gammon!" said the mate. "Gammon!" he repeated loudly, as the captain signaled him to be more soft spoken. "You can't tell me that sort of stuff. Where d'ye keep your own boats, hey—your schooner, or cutter, or whatever you have? Hey? Answer me that."

McCoy smiled as gently as he spoke. His smile was a caress, an embrace that surrounded the tired mate and sought to draw him into the quietude and rest of McCoy's tranquil soul.

"We have no schooner or cutter," he replied. "And we carry our canoes to the top of the cliff?"

"You've got to show me," snorted the mate. "How d'ye get around to the other islands, heh? Tell me that."

"We don't get around. As governor of Pitcairn, I some-times go. When I was younger, I was away a great deal—sometimes on the trading schooners, but mostly on the missionary brig. But she's gone now, and we depend on pass-ing vessels. Sometimes we have had as high as six calls in one year. At other times, a year, and even longer, has gone by without one passing ship. Yours is the first in seven months."

"And you mean to tell me—," the mate began.

But Captain Davenport interfered.

"Enough of this. We're losing time. What is to be done, Mr. McCoy?"

The old man turned his brown eyes, sweet as a woman's, shoreward, and both captain and mate followed his gaze around from the lonely rock of Pitcairn to the crew clustering forward and waiting anxiously for the announcement of a de-cision. McCoy did not hurry. He thought smoothly and slowly, step by step, with the certitude of a mind that was never vexed or outraged by life.

"The wind is light now," he said finally. "There is a heavy current setting to the westward."

"That's what made us fetch to leeward," the captain in-terrupted, desiring to vindicate his seamanship.

"Yes, that is what fetched you to leeward," McCoy went on. "Well, you can't work up against this current today. And if you did, there is no beach. Your ship will be a total loss."

He paused, and the captain and mate looked despair at each other.

"But I will tell you what you can do. The breeze will freshen tonight around midnight—see those tails of clouds and that thickness to windward, beyond the point there?

That's where she'll come from, out of the southeast, hard. It is three hundred miles to Mangareva. Square away for it. There is a beautiful bed for your ship there."

The mate shook his head.

"Come in to the cabin, and we'll look at the chart," said the Captain.

McCoy found a stifling, poisonous atmosphere in the pent cabin. Stray waftures of invisible gases bit his eyes and made them sting. The deck was hotter, almost unbearably hot to his bare feet. The sweat poured out of his body. He looked almost with apprehension about him. This malignant, internal heat was astounding. It was a marvel that the cabin did not burst into flames. He had a feeling as if of being in a huge bake oven where the heat might at any moment increase tremendously and shrivel him up like a blade of grass.

As he lifted one foot and rubbed the hot sole against the leg of his trousers, the mate laughed in a savage, snarling fashion.

"The anteroom of hell," he said. "Hell herself is right down there under your feet."

"It's hot!" McCoy cried involuntarily, mopping his face with a bandana handkerchief.

"Here's Mangareva," the captain said, bending over the table and pointing to a black speck in the midst of the white blankness of the chart. "And here, in between, is another island. Why not run for that?"

McCoy did not look at the chart.

"That's Crescent Island," he answered. "It is uninhabited, and it is only two or three feet above water. Lagoon, but no entrance. No, Mangareva is the nearest place for your purpose."

"Mangareva it is then," said Captain Davenport, interrupting the mate's growling objection. "Call the crew aft, Mr. Konig."

The sailors obeyed, shuffling wearily along the deck and painfully endeavoring to make haste. Exhaustion was evident in every movement. The cook came out of his galley to hear, and the cabin boy hung about near him.

When Captain Davenport had explained the situation and announced his intention of running for Mangareva, an uproar broke out. Against a background of throaty rumbling arose inarticulate cries of rage, with here and there a distinct curse, or word, or phase. A shrill Cockney voice soared and dominated for a moment, crying: "Gawd! After bein' in 'ell for fifteen days—an' now 'e wants to sail this floatin' 'ell to sea again?"

The captain could not control them, but McCoy's gentle presence seemed to rebuke and calm them, and the muttering and cursing died away, until the full crew, save here and there an anxious face directed at the captain, yearned dumbly toward the green clad peaks and beetling coast of Pitcairn.

Soft as a spring zephyr was the voice of McCoy:

"Captain, I thought I heard some of them say they were starving."

"Ay," was the answer, "and so we are. I've had a sea biscuit and a spoonful of salmon in the last two days. We're on whack. You see, when we discovered the fire, we battened down immediately to suffocate the fire. And then we found how little food there was in the pantry. But it was too late. We didn't dare break out the lazarette. Hungry? I'm just as hungry as they are."

He spoke to the men again, and again the throat rumbling and cursing arose, their faces convulsed and animal-like with rage. The second and third mates had joined the captain, standing behind him at the break of the poop. Their faces were set and expressionless, they seemed bored, more than anything else, by this mutiny of their crew. Captain Davenport glanced questioningly at his first mate, and that person merely shrugged his shoulders in token of his helplessness.

"You see," the captain said to McCoy, "you can't compel sailors to leave the safe land and go to sea on a burning vessel. She has been their floating coffin for over two weeks now. They are worked out, and starved out, and they've got enough of her. We'll beat up for Pitcairn."

But the wind was light, the *Pyrenees'* bottom was foul, and she could not beat up against the strong westerly current. At the end of two hours she had lost three miles. The sailors worked eagerly, as if by main strength they could compel the *Pyrenees* against the adverse elements. But steadily, port tack and starboard tack, she sagged off to the westward. The captain paced restlessly up and down, pausing occasionally to survey the vagrant smoke wisps and to trace them back to the portions of the deck from which they sprang. The carpenter was engaged constantly in attempting to locate such places, and, when he succeeded, in calking them tighter and tighter.

"Well, what do you think?" the captain finally asked McCoy, who was watching the carpenter with all a child's interest and curiosity in his eyes.

McCoy looked shoreward, where the land was disappearing in the thickening haze.

"I think it would be better to square away for Mangareva. With that breeze that is coming, you'll be there tomorrow evening."

"But what if the fire breaks out? It is liable to do it any moment?"

"Have your boats ready in the falls. The same breeze will carry your boats to Mangareva if the ship burns out from under."

Captain Davenport debated for a moment, and then McCoy heard the question he had not wanted to hear, but which he knew was surely coming.

"I have no chart of Mangareva. On the general chart it is only a fly speck. I would not know where to look for the entrance into the lagoon. Will you come along and pilot her in for me?"

McCoy's serenity was unbroken.

"Yes, Captain," he said, with the same quiet unconcern with which he would have accepted an invitation to dinner; "I'll go with you to Mangareva."

Again the crew was called aft, and the captain spoke to them from the break of the poop.

"We've tried to work her up, but you see how we've lost ground. She's setting off in a two knot current. This gentleman is the Honorable McCoy, Chief Magistrate and Governor of Pitcairn Island. He will come along with us to Mangareva. So you see the situation is not so dangerous. He would not make such an offer if he thought he was going to lose his life. Besides, whatever risk there is, if he of his own free will come on board and take it, we can do no less. What do you say for Mangareva?"

This time there was no uproar. In McCoy's presence, the surety and calm that seemed to radiate from him, had had its effect. They conferred with one another in low voices. There was little urging. They were virtually unanimous, and they shoved the Cockney out as their spokesman. That worthy was overwhelmed with consciousness of the heroism of himself and his mates, and with flashing eyes he cried:

"By Gawd! If 'e will, we will!"

The crew mumbled its assent and started forward.

"One moment, Captain," McCoy said, as the other was turning to give orders to the mate. "I must go ashore first."

Mr. Konig was thunderstruck, staring at McCoy as if he were a madman.

"Go ashore!" the captain cried. "What for? It will take you three hours to get there in your canoe."

McCoy measured the distance of the land away, and nodded.

"Yes, it is six now. I won't get ashore till nine. The people cannot be assembled earlier than ten. As the breeze freshens up tonight, you can begin to work up against it, and pick me up at daylight tomorrow morning."

"In the name of reason and common sense," the captain burst forth, "what do you want to assemble the people for? Don't you realize that my ship is burning beneath me?"

McCoy was as placid as a summer sea, and the other's anger produced not the slightest ripple upon it.

"Yes, Captain," he cooed in his dove-like voice. "I do realize that your ship is burning. That is why I am going with you to Mangareva. But I must get permission to go with you. It is our custom. It is an important matter when the governor leaves the island. The people's interests are at stake, and so they have the right to vote their permission or refusal. But they will give it, I know that."

"Are you sure?"

"Quite sure."

"Then if you know they will give it, why bother with getting it? Think of the delay—a whole night."

"It is our custom," was the imperturbable reply. "Also, I am the governor, and I must make arrangements for the conduct of the island during my absence."

"But it is only a twenty-four hour run to Mangareva," the captain objected. "Suppose it took you six times that long to return to windward; that would bring you back by the end of a week."

McCoy smiled his large, benevolent smile.

"Very few vessels come to Pitcairn, and when they do, they are usually from San Francisco or from around the Horn. I shall be fortunate if I get back in six months. I may be away a year, and I may have to go to San Francisco in order to find a vessel that will bring me back. My father once left Pitcairn to be gone three months, and two years passed before he could get back. Then, too, you are short of food. If you have to take to the boats, and the weather comes up bad, you may be days in reaching land. I can bring off two canoe loads of food in the morning. Dried bananas will be best. As the breeze freshens, you beat up against it. The nearer you are, the bigger loads I can bring off. Good-by."

He held out his hand. The captain shook it, and was reluctant to let go. He seemed to cling to it as a drowning sailor clings to a life buoy.

"How do I know you will come back in the morning?" he asked.

"Yes, that's it!" cried the mate. "How do we know but what he's skinning out to save his own hide?"

McCoy did not speak. He looked at them sweetly and benignantly, and it seemed to them that they received a message from his tremendous certitude of soul.

The captain released his hand, and, with a last sweeping glance that embraced the crew in its benediction, McCoy went over the rail and descended into his canoe.

The wind freshened, and the *Pyrenees*, despite the foulness of her bottom, won half a dozen miles away from the westerly current. At daylight, with Pitcairn three miles to windward, Captain Davenport made out two canoes coming off to him. Again McCoy clambered up the side and dropped over the rail to the hot deck. He was followed by many packages of dried bananas, each package wrapped in dry leaves.

"Now, Captain," he said, "swing the yards and drive for dear life. You see, I am no navigator," he explained a few minutes later, as he stood by the captain aft, the latter with gaze wandering from aloft to overside as he estimated the *Pyrenees'* speed. "You must fetch her to Mangareva. When you have picked up the land, then I will pilot her in. What do you think she is making?"

"Eleven," Captain Davenport answered, with a final glance at the water rushing past.

"Eleven. Let me see, if she keeps up that gait, we'll sight Mangareva between eight and nine o'clock tomorrow morning. I'll have her on the beach by ten or by eleven at latest. And then your troubles will be all over."

It almost seemed to the captain that the blissful moment had already arrived, such was the persuasive convincingness of McCoy.

Captain Davenport had been under the fearful strain of navigating his burning ship for over two weeks, and he was beginning to feel that he had had enough.

A heavier flaw of wind struck the back of his neck and whistled by his ears. He measured the weight of it, and looked quickly overside.

"The wind is making all the time," he announced. "The old girl's doing nearer twelve than eleven right now. If this keeps up, we'll be shortening down tonight."

All day the *Pyrenees*, carrying her load of living fire, tore across the foaming sea. By nightfall, royals and topgallantsails were in, and she flew on into the darkness, with great, crested seas roaring after her. The auspicious wind had had its effect, and fore and aft a visible brightening was apparent. In the second dog-watch some careless soul started a song, and by eight bells the whole crew was singing.

Captain Davenport had his blankets brought up and spread on top of the house.

"I've forgotten what sleep is," he explained to McCoy. "I'm all in. But give me a call at any time you think necessary."

At three in the morning he was aroused by a gentle tugging at his arm. He sat up quickly, bracing himself against the skylight, stupid yet from his heavy sleep. The wind was thrumming its war song in the rigging, and a wild sea was buffeting the *Pyrenees*. Amidships she was wallowing first one rail under and then the other, flooding the waist more often than not. McCoy was shouting something he could not hear. He reached out, clutched the other by the shoulder, and drew him close so that his own ear was close to the other's lips.

"It's three o'clock," came McCoy's voice, still retaining its dove-like quality, but curiously muffled, as if from a long way off. "We've run two hundred and fifty. Crescent Island is only thirty miles away, somewhere there dead ahead. There's no lights on it. If we keep running, we'll pile up, and lose ourselves as well as the ship."

"What d' ye think—heave to?"

"Yes; heave to till daylight. It will only put us back four hours."

So the *Pyrenees*, with her cargo of fire, was hove to, bitting the teeth of the gale and fighting and smashing the pounding seas. She was a shell, filled with a conflagration, and on the outside of the shell, clinging precariously, the little motes of men, by pull and haul, helped her in the battle.

"It is most unusual, this gale," McCoy told the captain, in the lee of the cabin. "By rights there should be no gale at this time of the year. But everything about the weather has been unusual. There has been a stoppage of the trades, and now it's howling right out of the trade quarter." He waved his hand into the darkness, as if his vision could dimly penetrate for hundreds of miles. "It is off to the westward. There is something big making off there somewhere—a hurricane or something. We're lucky to be so far to the eastward. But this is only a little blow," he added. "It can't last. I can tell you that much."

By daylight the gale had eased down to normal. But daylight revealed a new danger. It had come on thick. The sea was covered by a fog, or rather, by a pearly mist that was fog-like in density, in so far as it obstructed vision, but that was no more than a film on the sea, for the sun shot it through and filled it with a glowing radiance.

The deck of the *Pyrenees* was making more smoke than on the preceding day, and the cheerfulness of officers and crew had vanished. In the lee of the galley the cabin boy could be heard whimpering. It was his first voyage, and the fear of death was at his heart. The captain wandered about like a lost soul, nervously chewing his mustache, scowling, unable to make up his mind what to do.

"What do you think?" he asked, pausing by the side of McCoy, who was making a breakfast off fried bananas and a mug of water.

"Well, Captain, we might as well drive as burn. Your decks are not going to hold out forever. They are hotter this morning. You haven't a pair of shoes I can wear? It is getting uncomfortable for my bare feet."

The *Pyrenees* shipped two heavy seas as she was swung off and put once more before it, and the first mate expressed a desire to have all that water down in the hold, if only it could be introduced without taking off the hatches. McCoy ducked his head into the binnacle and watched the course set.

"I'd hold her up some more, Captain," he said. "She's been making drift when hove to."

"I've set it to a point higher already," was the answer. "Isn't that enough?"

"I'd make it two points, Captain. This bit of a blow kicked that westerly current ahead faster than you imagine."

Captain Davenport compromised on a point and a half, and then went aloft, accompanied by McCoy and the first mate, to keep a lookout for land. Sail had been made, so that the *Pyrenees* was doing ten knots. The following sea was dying down rapidly. There was no break in the pearly fog, and by ten o'clock Captain Davenport was growing nervous. All hands were at their stations, ready, at the first warning of land ahead, to spring like fiends to the task of bringing the *Pyrenees* up on the wind. That land ahead, a surf-washed outer reef, would be perilously close when it revealed itself in such a fog.

Another hour passed. The three watchers aloft stared intently into the pearly radiance. "What if we miss Mangareva?" Captain Davenport asked abruptly.

McCoy, without shifting his gaze, answered softly:

"Why, let her drive, Captain. That is all we can do. All the Paumotus are before us. We can drive for a thousand miles through reefs and atolls. We are bound to fetch up somewhere."

"Then drive it is." Captain Davenport evidenced his intention of descending to the deck.

"We've missed Mangareva. God knows where the next land is. I wish I'd held her up that other half-point," he confessed a moment later. "This cursed current plays the devil with a navigator."

"The old navigators called the Paumotus the Dangerous Archipelago," McCoy said, when they had regained the poop. "This very current was partly responsible for that name."

"I was talking with a sailor chap in Sydney, once," said Mr. Konig. "He'd been trading in the Paumotus. He told me insurance was eighteen per cent. Is that right?"

Mc Coy smiled and nodded.

"Except that they don't insure," he explained. "The owners write off twenty per cent of the cost of their schooners each year."

"My God!" Captain Davenport groaned. "That makes the life of a schooner only five years!" He shook his head sadly, murmuring, "Bad waters! Bad waters!"

Again they went into the cabin to consult the big general chart; but the poisonous vapors drove them coughing and gasping on deck.

"Here is Moerenhout Island," Captain Davenport pointed it out on the chart, which he had spread on the house. "It can't be more than a hundred miles to leeward."

"A hundred and ten." McCoy shook his head doubtfully. "It might be done, but it is very difficult. I might beach her, and then again I might put her on the reef. A bad place, a very bad place."

"We'll take the chance," was Captain Davenport's decision, as he set about working out the course.

Sail was shortened early in the afternoon, to avoid running past in the night, and in the second dog-watch the crew manifested its regained cheerfulness. Land was so very near, and their troubles would be over in the morning.

But morning broke clear, with a blazing tropic sun. The southeast trade had swung around to the eastward, and was driving the *Pyrenees* through the water at an eight-knot clip. Captain Davenport worked up his dead reckoning, allowing generously for drift, and announced Moerenhout Island to be not more than ten miles off. The *Pyrenees* sailed the ten miles; she sailed ten miles more; and the lookouts at the three mast-heads saw naught by the naked, sun-washed sea.

"But the land is there, I tell you," Captain Davenport shouted to them from the poop.

McCoy smiled soothingly, but the captain glared about him like a madman, fetched his sextant, and took a chronometer sight.

"I knew I was right," he almost shouted, when he had worked up the observation. "Twenty-one, fifty-five, south; one-thirty-six, two, west. There you are. We're eight miles to windward yet. What did you make it out, Mr. Konig?"

The first mate glanced at his own figures, and said in a low voice:

"Twenty-one, fifty-five all right; but my longitude's one-thirty-six, forty-eight. That puts us considerably to leeward—"

But Captain Davenport ignored his figures with so contemptuous a silence as to make Mr. Konig grit his teeth and curse savagely under his breath.

"Keep her off," the captain ordered the man at the wheel. "Three points—steady there, as she goes!"

Then he returned to his figures and worked them over. The sweat poured from his face. He chewed his mustache, his lips, and his pencil, staring at the figures as a man might at a ghost. Suddenly, with a fierce, muscular outburst, he crumpled the scribbled paper in his fist and crushed it under foot. Mr. Konig grinned vindictively and turned away, while Captain Davenport leaned against the cabin and for half an hour spoke no word, contenting himself with gazing to leeward with an expression of musing hopelessness on his face.

"Mr. McCoy," he broke silence abruptly. "The chart indicates a group of islands, but not how many, off there to the north'ard, or nor'-nor'westward, about forty miles—the Acteon Islands. What about them?"

"There are four, all low," McCoy answered. "First to the southeast is Matuerui—no people, no entrance to the lagoon. Then comes Tenarunga. There used to be about a dozen people there, but they may be all gone now. Anyway, there is no entrance for a ship—only a boat entrance, with a fathom of water. Vehauga and Teur-raro are the other two. No entrances, no people, very low. There is no bed for the *Pyrenees* in that group. She would be a total wreck."

"Listen to that!" Captain Davenport was frantic. "No people! No entrances! What in the devil are islands good for?

"Well, then," he barked suddenly, like an excited terrier, "the chart gives a whole mess of islands off to the nor-west. What about them? What one has an entrance where I can lay my ship?"

McCoy calmly considered. He did not refer to the chart. All these islands, reefs, shoals, lagoons, entrances, and distances were marked on the chart of his memory. He knew them as the city dweller knows his building, streets, and alleys.

"Papakena and Vanavana are off there to the westward, or west-nor'westward a hundred miles and a bit more," he said. "One is uninhabited, and I heard that the people on the other had gone off to Cadmus Island. Anyway, neither lagoon has an entrance. Ahuuni is another hundred miles on to the nor-west. No entrance, no people."

"Well, forty miles beyond them are two islands?" Captain Davenport queried, raising his head from the chart.

McCoy shook his head.

"Paros and Manuhungi—no entrances, no people. Nengo-Nengo is forty miles beyond them, in turn, and it has no people and no entrance. But there is Hao Island. It is just the place. The lagoon is thirty miles long and five miles wide. There are plenty of people. You can usually find water. And any ship in the world can go through the entrance."

He ceased and gazed solicitously at Captain Davenport, who, bending over the chart with a pair of dividers in hand, had just emitted a low groan.

"Is there any lagoon with an entrance anywhere nearer than Hao Island?" he asked.

"No, Captain; that is the nearest."

"Well, it's three hundred and forty miles." Captain Davenport was speaking very slowly, with decision. "I won't risk the responsibility of all these lives. I'll wreck her on the Acteons. And she's a good ship, too," he added regretfully, after altering the course, this time making more allowance than ever for the westerly current.

An hour later the sky was overcast. The southeast trade still held, but the ocean was a checkerboard of squalls.

"We'll be there by one o'clock," Captain Davenport announced confidently. "By two o'clock at the outside. McCoy, you put her ashore on the one where the people are."

The sun did not appear again, nor, at one o'clock, was any land to be seen. Captain Davenport looked astern at the *Pyrenees'* canting wake.

"Good Lord!" he cried. "An easterly current? Look at that!"

Mr. Konig was incredulous. McCoy was noncommittal, though he said that in the Paumotus there was no reason why it should not be an easterly current. A few minutes later a squall robbed the *Pyrenees* temporarily of all her wind, and she was left rolling heavily in the trough.

"Where's that deep lead? Over with it, you there!" Captain Davenport held the lead line and watched it sag off to the northeast. "There, look at that! Take hold of it for yourself."

McCoy and the mate tried it, and felt the line thrumming and vibrating savagely to the grip of the tidal stream.

"A four-knot current," said Mr. Konig.

"An easterly current instead of a westerly," said Captain Davenport, glaring accusingly at McCoy, as if to cast the blame for it upon him.

"That is one of the reasons, Captain, for insurance being eighteen per cent in these waters," McCoy answered cheerfully. "You can never tell. The currents are always changing. There was a man who wrote books, I forget his name, in the yacht *Casco*. He missed Takaroa by thirty miles and fetched Tikei, all because of the shifting currents. You are up to windward now, and you'd better keep off a few points."

"But how much has this current set me?" the captain demanded irately. "How am I to know how much to keep off?"

"I don't know, Captain," McCoy said with great gentleness. The wind returned, and the *Pyrenees* her deck smoking and shimmering in the bright gray light, ran off dead to leeward. Then she worked back, port tack and starboard tack, crisscrossing her track, combing the sea for the Acteon Islands, which the masthead lookouts failed to sight.

Captain Davenport was beside himself. His rage took the form of sullen silence, and he spent the afternoon in pacing the poop or leaning against the weather shrouds. At nightfall, without even consulting McCoy, he squared away and headed into the northwest. Mr. Konig surreptitiously consulting chart and binnacle, and McCoy, openly and innocently consulting the binnacle, knew that they were running for Hao Island. By midnight the squalls ceased, and the stars came out. Captain Davenport was cheered by the promise of a clear day.

"I'll get an observation in the morning," he told McCoy, "though what my latitude is, is a puzzler. But I'll use the Sumner method, and settle that. Do you know the Sumner line?"

And thereupon he explained it in detail to McCoy.

The day proved clear, the trade blew steadily out of the east, and the *Pyrenees* just as steadily logged her nine knots. Both the captain and mate worked out the position on a Sumner line, and agreed, and at noon agreed again, and verified the morning sights by the noon sights.

"Another twenty-four hours and we'll be there," Captain Davenport assured McCoy. "It's a miracle the way the old girl's decks hold out. But they can't last. They can't last. Look at them smoke, more and more every day. Yet it was a tight deck to begin with, fresh-calked in Frisco. I was surprised when the fire first broke out and we battened down. Look at that!"

He broke off to gaze with dropped jaw at a spiral of smoke that coiled and twisted in the lee of the mizzenmast twenty feet above the deck.

"Now, how did that get there?" he demanded indignantly.

Beneath it there was no smoke. Crawling up from the deck, sheltered from the wind by the mast, by some freak it took form and visibility at the height. It writhed away from the mast, and for a moment overhung the captain like some threatening portent. The next moment the wind whisked it away, and the captain's jaw returned to place.

"As I was saying, when we first battened down, I was surprised. It was a tight deck, yet it leaked smoke like a sieve. And we've calked and calked ever since. There must be tremendous pressure underneath to drive so much smoke through."

That afternoon the sky became overcast again, and squally, drizzly weather set in. The wind shifted back and forth between southeast and northeast, and at midnight the *Pyrenees* was caught aback by a sharp squall from the southwest, from which point the wind continued to blow intermittently.

"We won't make Hao until ten or eleven," Captain Davenport complained at seven in the morning, when the fleeting promise of the sun had been erased by hazy cloud masses in the eastern sky. And the next moment he was plaintively demanding. "And what are the currents doing?"

Lookouts at the mastheads could report no land, and the day passed in drizzling calms and violent squalls. By nightfall a heavy sea began to make from the west. The barometer had fallen to 29.50. There was no wind, and still the ominous sea continued to increase. Soon the *Pyrenees* was rolling madly in the huge waves that marched in an unending procession from out of the darkness of the west. Sail was shortened as fast as both watches could work, and, when the tired crew had finished, its grumbling and complaining voices, peculiarly animal-like and menacing, could be heard in the darkness. Once the starboard watch was called aft to lash down and make secure, and the men openly advertised their sullenness and unwillingness. Every slow movement was a protest and a threat. The atmosphere was moist and sticky like mucilage, and in the absence of wind all hands seemed to pant and gasp for air. The sweat stood out on faces and bare arms, and Captain Davenport for one, his face more gaunt and care-worn than ever, and he eyes troubled and staring, was oppressed by a feeling of impending calamity.

"It's off to the westward," McCoy said encouragingly. "At worst, we'll be only on the edge of it."

But Captain Davenport refused to be comforted, and by the light of a lantern read up the chapter in his *Epitome* that related to the strategy of shipmasters in cyclonic storms. From somewhere amidships the silence was broken by a low whimpering from the cabin boy.

"Oh, shut up!" Captain Davenport yelled suddenly and with such force as to startle every man on board and to frighten the offender into a wild wail of terror.

"Mr. Konig," the captain said in a voice that trembled with rage and nerves, "will you kindly step for'ard and stop that brat's mouth with a deck mop?"

But it was McCoy who went forward, and in a few minutes had the boy comforted and asleep.

Shortly before daybreak the first breath of air began to move from out the southeast increasing swiftly to a stiff and stiffer breeze. All hands were on deck waiting for what might be behind it. "We're all right now, Captain," said McCoy, standing close to his shoulder. "The hurricane is to the west'ard, and we are south of it. This breeze is the insuck. It won't blow any harder. You can begin to put sail on her."

"But what's the good? Where shall I sail? This is the second day without observations, and we should have sighted Hao Island yesterday morning. Which way does it bear, north, south, east, or what? Tell me that, and I'll make sail in a jiffy."

"I am no navigator, Captain," McCoy said in his mild way.

"I used to think I was one," was the retort, "before I got into these Paumotus."

At midday the cry of "Breakers ahead!" was heard from the lookout. The *Pyrenees* was kept off, and sail after sail was loosed and sheeted home. The Pyrenees was sliding through the water and fighting a current that threatened to set her down upon the breakers. Officers and men were working like mad, cook and cabin boy, Captain Davenport himself, and McCoy all lending a hand. It was a close shave. It was a low shoal, a bleak and perilous place over which the seas broke unceasingly, where no man could live, and on which not even sea birds could rest. The *Pyrenees* was swept within a hundred yards of it before the wind carried her clear, and at this moment the panting crew, its work done, burst out in a torrent of curses upon the head of McCoy—of McCoy who had come on board, and proposed the run to Mangareva, and lured them all away from the safety of Pitcairn Island to certain destruction in this baffling and terrible stretch of sea. But McCoy's tranquil soul was undisturbed. He smiled at them with simple and gracious benevolence, and somehow, the exalted goodness of him seemed to penetrate to their dark and somber souls, shaming them, and from very shame stilling the curses vibrating in their throats.

"Bad waters! Bad waters!" Captain Davenport was murmuring as his ship forged clear, but he broke off abruptly to gaze at the shoal which should have been dead astern, but which was already on the *Pyrenees'* weather-quarter and working up rapidly to windward.

He sat down and buried his face in his hands. And the first mate saw, and McCoy saw, and the crew saw, what he had seen. South of the shoal an easterly current had set them down upon it, north of the shoal an equally swift westerly current had clutched the ship and was sweeping her away.

"I've heard of these Paumotus before," the captain groaned, lifting his blanched face from his hands. "Captain Rosendale told me about them after losing his ship on them. And I laughed at him behind his back. God forgive me, I laughed at him. What shoal is that?" he broke off, to ask McCoy.

"I don't know, Captain."

"Why don't you know?"

"Because I never saw it before, and because I have never heard of it. I do know that it is not charted. These waters have never been thoroughly surveyed."

"Then you don't know where we are?"

"No more than you do," McCoy said gently.

At four in the afternoon cocoanut trees were sighted, apparently growing out of the water. A little later the low land of an atoll was raised above the sea.

"I know where we are now, Captain." McCoy lowered the glasses from his eyes. "That's Resolution Island. We are forty miles beyond Hao Island, and the wind is in our teeth."

"Get ready to beach her then. Where's the entrance?"

"There's only a canoe passage. But now that we know where we are, we can run for Barclay de Tolley. It is only one hundred and twenty miles from here, due nor'-nor'west.

With this breeze we can be there by nine o'clock tomorrow morning."

Captain Davenport consulted the chart and debated with himself.

"If we wreck her here," McCoy added, "we'd have to make the run to Barclay de Tolley in the boats just the same."

The captain gave his orders, and once more the *Pyrenees* swung off for another run across the inhospitable sea.

And the middle of the next afternoon saw despair and mutiny on her smoking deck. The current had accelerated, the wind had slackened, and the *Pyrenees* had sagged off to the west. The lookout sighted Barclay de Tolley to the eastward, barely visible from the masthead, and vainly for hours the *Pyrenees* tried to beat up to it. Ever, like a mirage, the cocoanut trees hovered on the horizon, visible only from the masthead. From the deck they were hidden by the bulge of the world.

Again Captain Davenport consulted McCoy and the chart. Makemo lay seventy-five miles to the southwest. Its lagoon was thirty miles long, and its entrance was excellent. When Captain Davenport gave his orders, the crew refused duty. They announced that they had had enough of hell fire under their feet. There was the land. What if the ship could not make it? They could make it in the boats. Let her burn, then. Their lives amounted to something to them. They had served faithfully the ship, now they were going to serve themselves.

They sprang to the boats, brushing the second and third mates out of the way, and proceeded to swing the boats out and to prepare to lower away. Captain Davenport and the first mate, revolvers in hand, were advancing to the break of the poop, when McCoy, who had climbed on the top of the cabin, began to speak.

He spoke to the sailors, and at the first sound of his dove-like, cooing voice they paused to hear. He extended to them his own ineffable serenity and peace. His soft voice and simple thoughts flowed out to them in a magic stream, soothing them against their wills. Long forgotten things came back to them, and some remembered lullaby songs of childhood and the content and rest of the mother's arm at the end of the day. There was no more trouble, no more danger, no more irk, in all the world. Everything was as it should be, and it was only a matter of course that they should turn their backs upon the land and put to sea once more with hell fire hot beneath their feet.

McCoy spoke simply; but it was not what he spoke. It was his personality that spoke more eloquently than any word he could utter. It was an alchemy of soul occultly subtle and profoundly deep—a mysterious emanation of the spirit, seductive, sweetly humble, and terribly imperious. It was illumination in the dark crypts of their souls, a compulsion of purity and gentleness vastly greater than that which resided in the shining, death-spitting revolvers of the officers.

The men wavered reluctantly where they stood, and those who had loosed the turns made them fast again. Then one, and then another, and than all of them, began to sidle awkwardly away.

McCoy's face was beaming with childlike pleasure as he descended from the top of the cabin. There was no trouble. For that matter there had been no trouble averted. There never had been any trouble, for there was no place for such in the blissful world in which he lived.

"You hypnotized 'em," Mr. Konig grinned at him, speaking in a low voice.

"Those boys are good," was the answer. "Their hearts are good. They have had a hard time, and they have worked hard, and they will work hard to the end."

Mr. Konig had no time to reply. His voice was ringing out orders, the sailors were springing to obey, and the *Pyrenees* was paying slowly off from the wind until her bow should point in the direction of Makemo.

The wind was very light, and after sundown almost ceased. It was insufferably warm, and fore and aft men sought vainly to sleep. The deck was too hot to lie upon, and poisonous vapors, oozing through the seams, crept like evil spirits over the ship, stealing into the nostrils and windpipes of the unwary and causing fits of sneezing and coughing. The stars blinked lazily in the dim vault overhead; and the full moon, rising in the east, touched with its light the myriads of wisps and threads and spidery films of smoke that intertwined and writhed and twisted along the deck, over the rails, and up the masts and shrouds.

"Tell me," Captain Davenport said, rubbing his smarting eyes, "what happened with that *Bounty* crowd after they reached Pitcairn? The account I read said they burnt the *Bounty* and that they were not discovered until many years later. But what happened in the meantime? I've always been curious to know. They were men with their necks in the rope. There were some native men, too. And then there were women. That made it look like trouble right from the jump."

"There was trouble," McCoy answered. "They were bad men. They quarreled about the women right away. One of the mutineers, Williams, lost his wife. All the women were Tahitian women. His wife fell from the cliffs when hunting sea birds. Then he took the wife of one of the native men away from him. All the native men were made very angry by this, and they killed off nearly all the mutineers. Then the mutineers that escaped killed off all the native men. The women helped. And the natives killed each other. Everybody killed everybody. They were terrible men.

"Timiti was killed by two other natives while they were combing his hair in friendship. The white men had sent them to do it. Then the white men killed them. The wife of Tul-laloo killed him in a cave because she wanted a white man for husband. They were very wicked. God had hidden His face from them. At the end of two years all the native men were murdered, and all the white men except four. They were Young, John Adams, McCoy, who was my great-grandfather, and Quintal. He was a very bad man, too. Once, just because his wife did not catch enough fish for him, he bit off her ear."

"They were a bad lot!" Mr. Konig exclaimed.

"Yes, they were very bad," McCoy agreed and went on serenely cooing the blood and lust of his iniquitous ancestry. "My great-grandfather escaped murder in order to die by his own hand. He made a still and manufactured alcohol from the roots of the ti-plant. Quintal was his chum, and they got drunk together all the time. At last McCoy got delirium tremens, tied a rock to his neck, and jumped into the sea.

"Quintal's wife, the one whose ear he bit off, also got killed by falling from the cliffs. Then Quintal went to Young and demanded his wife, and went to Adams and demanded his wife. Adams and Young were afraid of Quintal. They knew he would kill them. So they killed him, the two of them together, with a hatchet. Then Young died. And that was about all the trouble they had."

"I should say so," Captain Davenport snorted. "There was nobody left to kill."

"You see, God had hidden His face," McCoy said.

By morning no more that a faint air was blowing from the eastward, and, unable to make appreciable southing by it, Captain Davenport hauled up full-and-by on the port tack. He was afraid of that terrible westerly current which had cheated him out of so many ports of refuge. All day the calm continued, and all night, while the sailors, on a short ration of dried banana, were grumbling. Also, they were growing weak and complaining of stomach pains caused by the straight banana diet. All day the current swept the *Pyrenees* to the westward, while there was no wind to bear her south. In the middle of the first dogwatch, cocoanut trees were sighted due south, their tufted heads rising above the water and marking the low-lying atoll beneath.

"That is Taenga Island," McCoy said. "We need a breeze tonight, or else we'll miss Makemo."

"What's become of the southeast trade?" the captain demanded. "Why don't it blow? What's the matter?"

"It is the evaporation from the big lagoons—there are so many of them," McCoy explained. "The evaporation upsets the whole system of trades. It even causes the wind to back up and blow gales from the southwest. This is the Dangerous Archipelago, Captain."

Captain Davenport faced the old man, opened his mouth, and was about to curse, but paused and refrained. McCoy's presence was a rebuke to the blasphemies that stirred in his brain and trembled in his larynx. McCoy's influence had been growing during the many days they had been together. Captain Davenport was an autocrat of the sea, fearing no man, never bridling his tongue, and now he found himself unable to curse in the presence of this old man with the feminine brown eyes and the voice of a dove. When he realized this, Captain Davenport experienced a distinct shock. This old man was merely the seed of McCoy, of McCoy of the *Bounty,* the mutineer fleeing from the hemp that waited him in England, the McCoy who was a power for evil in the early days of blood and lust and violent death on Pitcairn Island.

Captain Davenport was not religious, yet in that moment he felt a mad impulse to cast himself at the other's feet—and to say he knew not what. It was an emotion that so deeply stirred him, rather than a coherent thought, and he was aware in some vague way of his own unworthiness and smallness in the presence of this other man who possessed the simplicity of a child and the gentleness of a woman.

Of course he could not so humble himself before the eyes of his officers and men. And yet the anger that had prompted the blasphemy still raged in him. He suddenly smote the cabin with his clenched hand and cried:

"Look here, old man, I won't be beaten. These Paumotus have cheated and tricked me and made a fool of me. I refuse to be beaten. I am going to drive this ship, and drive and drive and drive clear through the Paumotus to China but what I find a bed for her. If every man deserts, I'll stay by her. I'll show the Paumotus. They can't fool me. She's a good girl, and I'll stick by her as long as there's a plank to stand on. You hear me?"

"And I'll stay with you, Captain," McCoy said.

During the night, light baffling airs blew out the south, and the frantic captain, with his cargo of fire, watched and measured his westward drift and went off by himself at times to curse softly so that McCoy should not hear.

Daylight showed more palms growing out of the water to the south.

"That's the leeward point of Makemo," McCoy said, "Katiu is only a few miles to the west. We may make that."

But the current, sucking between the two islands, swept them to the northwest, and at one in the afternoon they saw the palms of Katiu rise above the sea and sink back into the sea again.

A few minutes later, just as the captain had discovered that a new current from the northeast had gripped the *Pyrenees*, the masthead lookouts raised cocoanut palms in the northwest.

"It is Raraka," said McCoy. "We won't make it without wind. The current is drawing us down to the southwest. But we must watch out. A few miles farther on a current flows north and turns in a circle to the northwest. This will sweep us away from Fakarava, and Fakarava is the place for the *Pyrenees* to find her bed."

"They can sweep all they da . . . all they well please," Captain Davenport remarked with heat. "We'll find a bed for her somewhere just the same." But the situation on the *Pyrenees* was reaching a culmination. The deck was so hot that it seemed an increase of a few degrees would cause it to burst into flames. In many places even the heavy-soled shoes of the men were no protection, and they were compelled to step lively to avoid scorching their feet. The smoke had increased and grown more acrid. Every man on board was suffering from inflamed eyes, and they coughed and strangled like a crew of tuberculosis patients. In the afternoon the boats were swung out and equipped. The last several packages of dried bananas were stored in them, as well as the instruments of the officers. Captain Davenport even put the chronometer into the long-boat, fearing the blowing up of the deck at any moment.

All night this apprehension weighed heavily on all, and in the first morning light, with hollow eyes and ghastly faces, they stared at one another as if in surprise that the *Pyrenees* still held together and that they still were alive.

Walking rapidly at times, and even occasionally breaking into an undignified hop-skip-and-run, Captain Davenport inspected his ship's deck.

"It is a matter of hours now, if not of minutes," he announced on his return to the poop.

The cry of land came down from the masthead. From the deck the land was invisible, and McCoy went aloft, while the captain took advantage of the opportunity to curse some of the bitterness out of his heart. But the cursing was suddenly stopped by a dark line on the water which he sighted to the northeast. It was not a squall, but a regular breeze—the disrupted trade wind, eight points out of its direction but resuming business once more.

"Hold her up, Captain," McCoy said as soon as he reached the poop. "That's the easterly point of Fakarava, and we'll go in through the passage full-tilt, the wind abeam, and every sail drawing."

At the end of an hour, the cocoanut trees and the low-lying land were visible from the deck. The feeling that the end of the *Pyrenees'* resistance was imminent weighted heavily on everybody. Captain Davenport had the three boats lowered and dropped short astern, a man in each to keep them apart. The *Pyrenees* closely skirted the shore, the surf-whitened atoll a bare two cable lengths away.

And a minute later the land parted, exposing a narrow passage and the lagoon beyond, a great mirror, thirty miles in length and a third as broad.

"Now, Captain."

For the last time the yards of the *Pyrenees* swung around as she obeyed the wheel and headed into the passage. The turns had scarcely been made, and nothing had been coiled down, when the men and mates swept back to the poop in panic terror. Nothing had happened, yet they averred that something was going to happen. They could not tell why. They merely knew that it was about to happen. McCoy started forward to take up his position on the bow in order to con the vessel in; but the captain gripped his arm and whirled him around.

"Do it from here," he said. "That deck's not safe. What's the matter?" he demanded the next instant. "We're standing still."

McCoy smiled.

"You are bucking a seven-knot current, Captain," he said. "That is the way the full ebb runs out of this passage."

At the end of another hour the *Pyrenees* had scarcely gained her length, but the wind freshened and she began to forge ahead.

"Better get into the boats, some of you," Captain Davenport commanded.

His voice was still ringing, and the men were just beginning to move in obedience, when the amidship deck of the *Pyrenees*, in a mass of flame and smoke, was flung upward into the sails and rigging, part of it remaining there and the rest falling into the sea. The wind being abeam was what had saved the men crowded aft. They made a blind rush to gain the boats, but McCoy's voice, carrying its convincing message of vast calm and endless time, stopped them.

"Take it easy," he was saying. "Everything is all right. . . ."

The man at the wheel had forsaken it in a funk, and Captain Davenport had leaped and caught the spokes in time to prevent the ship from yawing in the current and going ashore.

"Better take charge of the boats," he said to Mr. Konig. "Tow one of them short, right under the quarter. . . . When I go over, it'll be on the jump."

Mr. Konig hesitated, then went over the rail and lowered himself into the boat.

"Keep her off half a point, Captain."

Captain Davenport gave a start. He had thought he had the ship to himself.

"Ay, ay; half a point it is," he answered.

Amidships the *Pyrenees* was an open flaming furnace, out of which poured an immense volume of smoke which rose high above the masts and completely hid the forward part of the ship. McCoy, in the shelter of the mizzen-shrouds, continued his difficult task of conning the ship through the intricate channel. The fire was working aft along the deck from the seat of explosion, while the soaring tower of canvas on the mainmast went up and vanished in a sheet of flame. Forward, though they could not see them, they knew that the head-sails were still drawing.

"If only she don't burn all her canvas off before she makes inside," the captain groaned.

"She'll make it," McCoy assured him with supreme confidence. "There is plenty of time. She is bound to make it. And once inside, we'll put her before it, that will keep the smoke away from us and hold back the fire from working aft."

A tongue of flame sprang up the mizzen, reached hungrily for the lowest tier of canvas, missed it, and vanished. From aloft a burning shred of rope stuff fell square on the back of Captain Davenport's neck. He acted with the celerity of one stung by a bee as he reached up and brushed the offending fire from his skin.

"How is she heading, Captain?"

"Nor'west by west."

"Keep her west-nor-west."

Captain Davenport put the wheel up and steadied her.

"West by north, Captain."

"West by north she is."

"And now west."

Slowly, point by point, as she entered the lagoon, the *Pyrenees* described the circle that put her before the wind; and point by point, with all the calm certitude of a thousand years of time to spare, McCoy changed the changing course.

"Another point, Captain."

"A point it is."

Captain Davenport whirled several spokes over, suddenly reversing and come back one to check her.

"Steady."

"Steady she is—right on it."

Despite the fact that the wind was now astern, the heat was so intense that Captain Davenport was compelled to steal sidelong glances into the binnacle, letting go the wheel now with one hand, now with the other, to rub or shield his blistering cheeks.

McCoy's beard was crinkling and shriveling and the smell of it, strong in the other's nostrils, compelled him to look toward McCoy with sudden solicitude. Captain Davenport was letting go the spokes alternately with his hands in order to rub their blistering backs against his trousers. Every sail on the mizzenmast vanished in a rush of flame, compelling the two men to crouch and shield their faces.

"Now," said McCoy, stealing a glance ahead at the low shore, "four points up, Captain, and let her drive."

Shreds and patches of burning rope and canvas were falling about them and upon them. The tarry smoke from a smoldering piece of rope at the captain's feet set him off into a violent coughing fit, during which he still clung to the spokes.

The *Pyrenees* struck, her bow lifted, and she ground ahead gently to a stop. A shower of burning fragments, dislodged by the shock, fell about them. The ship moved ahead again and struck a second time. She crushed the fragile coral under her keel, drove on, and struck a third time.

"Hard over," said McCoy. "Hard over?" he questioned gently, a minute later.

"She won't answer," was the reply.

"All right. She is swinging around." McCoy peered over the side. "Soft, white sand. Couldn't ask better. A beautiful bed."

As the *Pyrenees* swung around her stern away from the wind, a fearful blast of smoke and flame poured aft. Captain Davenport deserted the wheel in blistering agony. He reached the painter of the boat that lay under the quarter, then looked for McCoy, who was standing aside to let him go down.

"You first," the captain cried, gripping him by the shoulder and almost throwing him over the rail. But the flame and smoke were too terrible, and he followed hard after McCoy, both men wriggling on the rope and sliding down into the boat together. A sailor in the bow, without waiting for orders, slashed the painter through with his sheath knife. The oars, poised in readiness, bit into the water, and the boat shot away.

"A beautiful bed, Captain," McCoy murmured, looking back.

"Ay, a beautiful bed, and all thanks to you," was the answer.

The three boats pulled away for the white beach of pounded coral, beyond which, on the edge of a cocoanut grove, could be seen a half dozen grass houses and a score or more of excited natives, gazing wide-eyed at the conflagration that had come to land.

The boats grounded and they stepped out on the white beach.

"And now," said McCoy, "I must see about getting back to Pitcairn."

Sources

A Jack London Checklist

Novels

The Abysmal Brute (1911)
Adventure (1911)
Before Adam (1907)
Burning Daylight (1910)
The Call of the Wild (1903)
The Cruise of the Dazzler (1902)
A Daughter of the Snows (1902)
The Game (1905)
Hearts of Three (1918)
The Iron Heel (1908)
Jerry of the Islands (1917)
The Kempton-Wace Letters (1903) *with Anna Strunsky*
The Little Lady of the Big House (1916)
Martin Eden (1913)

Michael, Brother of Jerry (1917)
The Mutiny of Elsinore (1914)
The Scarlet Plague (1912)
The Sea Wolf (1904)
The Star Rover (1915)
The Valley of the Moon (1913)
White Fang (1906)

Short Stories

Children of the Frost (1902)
Dutch Courage and Other Stories (1922)
The Faith of Men & Other Stories (1922)
The God of His Fathers & Other Stories (1901)
The House of Pride & Other Tales of Hawaii (1912)
Lost Face (1910)
Love of Life & Other Stories (1907)
Moon-Face & Other Stories (1906)
The Night Born (1913)
On the Makaloa Mat (1919)
The Red One (1918)
Smoke Bellew (1912)
A Son of the Sun (1912)
The Son of the Wolf (1900)
South Sea Tales (1911)
The Strength of the Strong (1914)
Tales of the Fish Patrol (1905)
The Turtles of Tasman (1916)
When God Laughs & Other Stories (1911)
Uncollected Stories (date unavailable)

Essays

The Human Drift (1917)
Revolution and Other Essays (1909)

Plays

The Acorn-Planter: A California Forest Play (1916)
Gold (1972) *with Herbert Herron, edited by James Sisson*
Scorn of Women (1906)

Nonfiction works

The Cruise of the Snark (1913)
John Barleycorn (1913)
The People of the Abyss (1903)
Revolution (1909)
The Road (1907)
War of the Classes (1905)

Jack London's Journalism

"The Dignity of Dollars," A piece in the *Overland Monthly*, Volume 36, Issue 211, 1900.

Also published in different form in the collection *Revolution and Other Stories*.

"Editorial Crimes: A Protest," First published in
   Dilettante, February, 1901.

"The Impossibility of War," from *Overland Monthly*, 1900.

"The Story of an Eyewitness," First published in
   Collier's, May 5, 1906.